All That You Want

Michelle Woollacott

*To Rachel
Happy Reading!
Michelle x*

Michelle Woollacott grew up in North Devon before completing a BA Hons in Creative Writing with Film at The University of Gloucestershire. After spending some time travelling, Michelle has returned to Devon where she lives with her husband.

Michelle envisaged the story of ALL THAT YOU WANT in 1999, when the author was eleven years old. After almost seventeen years, she has finally made her dream a reality in publishing her first novel.

You can find out more about Michelle by following her blog, www.michellewoollacottwriter.blogspot.co.uk
Follow her on Twitter: mi_chellew
Like her on Facebook: michellewoollacottwriter

Also by **MICHELLE WOOLLACOTT**

GRANDMA'S ROCKING CHAIR AND OTHER STORIES
STRIKE – short story featured in SEAGLASS AND OTHER POEMS AND STORIES

All That You Want

Michelle Woollacott

All That You Want
MICHELLE WOOLLACOTT

First published in Great Britain in 2016 by
Blurb Publishing
24 Southwark Bridge Rd, London SE1 9HF

michellewoollacottwriter.blogspot.co.uk

Cover design by Claire Woollacott and David Ernsting

This book is a work of fiction.

The right of Michelle Woollacott to be identified as the author of this work has been asserted under the Copyright, Designs and Patents Act 1988.
© 2016 Michelle Woollacott. All rights reserved.

For Jade; my Jodie Parker.
Also for Edward, my soulmate.

ALL THAT YOU WANT

Kiantown, Southwest England, June 2003

I have just finished telling them my secret.

Mum and Dad stare at me across the living room. They picked me up from my last day of college this afternoon and brought me home through the storm. Now it's early evening.

Rain beats ferociously at the windows. An empty wine bottle and three glasses stand on the coffee table. We all feel sober.

I clear my throat. 'Say something….' I urge.

Beth jumps up. 'I tried to tell you!' she yells to our parents. Her sea-blue eyes dance above her freckles.

My father places down his glass. 'Is all this true?'

I nod.

I reach for Mum's hands. She keeps them clasped on her lap. 'I'm sorry I've kept it from you. The fewer people who knew about it the less likely it was to come out. But, I wanted to tell you the truth tonight, before-'

Mum straightens up. 'Are you two girls having us on?'

'Of course not, Mum,' I tell her.

'Wait and see what happens in the next few days,' adds Beth.

Mum nods. A few frizzy hairs stand out from her otherwise composed ponytail. 'Right.' She stands vacantly. 'I'll finish making dinner.' The warm smell of roast-beef wafts from the kitchen.

Dad, Beth and I stand too. 'Come here.' He hugs me. The taste of musty wool tickles my mouth. His arms are tight and safe. He reaches out and brings Beth into the folds.

Finally, I'm in control. I've battled through the uncertainties. I'm breaking through to the predictable; the plan; the happy ending.

MICHELLE WOOLLACOTT

I am an over-seeing eye. I know that right now, Jodie will be sitting at Annie's house, telling her the same truths I have just told my parents. I know I will go up to my room to pack, then I'll have dinner with my family. I know there will be no more secrets and lies.

There's a darkness out there. It's fighting to come in as I stand in the folds of my family, in the safety of my plan, encased in the artificial light of the living room. I look to the window and all I can see is a black wall, but I can hear the rage and disruption just outside. Wind whistles violently through the gas fireplace. It is almost inside.

I push the feeling down, smile at my dad and his unconditional love –and at my sister and her unshakable smugness- and I advance up to my room to pack for my future.

1

Kiantown, July 2000

'All that you want, you can have now.'

It is a grand statement to come from the girls' toilets of a comprehensive school.

I hold my breath inside the cubicle and stare at the graffiti etched into the grey door. I can hear mocking laughter on the other side, above the muffled music from the hall.

'Are you serious?' comes a second voice.

'Yes,' replies the first again, defensively. 'We've left school; the world is our oyster; we can do anything; have anything we want now!'

'Yea, we're adults now,' the other girl giggles.

My stomach churns as I listen.

'We can drink all night and sleep all day, travel round the world,'

'Get a car, a great job, get our own flat –hey, we should get a flat together!'

'Yey!'

I trace my finger over a heart that has been carved with a compass onto the cubicle door and hear clinking and laughter from the other side. Sixteen-year-old girls giddy from bottles they've snuck in.

'Quick, hide it!'

I hear more clinks and scrambles of zips and giggling, then the clomping of high-heels and *Saturday Night* becomes clear. They've opened the door and are leaving. The familiar smell of school toilets is covered by a mist of cheap perfume. The music softens again as the door slams and I'm alone. I run my fingers over the initials carved inside the heart. S.C 4 A.C. Under the

3

heart, in permanent marker, someone has written the word PUKE.

The music becomes clear again as a new girl bursts in. 'Amy, are you in here?'

Clompy heels grow closer. Under the door, toes appear, pointing at me. Pink painted nails poke out of suede sandals.

'Amy?' *Bang, bang, bang.*

I stand up and pull back the lock.

In front of me stands my best friend, Jodie.

'Oh, Ames.' She puts her arm round me and leads me to the sink. 'Come on, Hun, let's sort you out.' From her bag she conjures mascara and lipstick and lies them on the sink.

I peer into the mirror and am greeted with the sight of black streaks running down my cheeks. I turn on the tap and wash my face.

'You're missing out on all the dancing!' Jodie beams.

I meet her gaze in the mirror. Gorgeous dark hair flows down to her chest, framing her exotic face. She is blessed with flawless skin and deep eyes. She wears a bright red boob-tube over her denim mini-skirt. Her stick-on nails look so elegant – she had tried to stick a set on me, but they didn't have much to cling to with my bitten stumps.

I still taste salt-water as I look to my own face. The mascara now washed away, stains still cling to my cheeks. My own skin is pasty and blotchy; my hair, usually in a ponytail, feels wayward as it hangs shoulder length and mousey; neither dark blonde nor light brown. Unremarkable. My gaze drifts down over my reflection to my ultimate mistake; I'm wearing a black dress.

'I can't go out there like this,' I tell Jodie.

'It'll be alright; nothing a bit of make-up won't fix.' She hands me the powder.

'That's not what I meant,' but I apply it anyway.

'You look gorgeous, Ames.'

'What's Matt going to think?'

'Oh, forget him, Ames. If he hasn't seen, in the last four years, what a catch you are, then he's not worth the tears.'

'Tonight's my last chance, Jo. I've ruined it. Now he's moving to *Newcastle.*'

'Well, let him.'

ALL THAT YOU WANT

'It's the opposite side of the bloody country.' My hand is wobbling so much I can't hold the eye liner steady.

'Here, let me.' She takes it from me and leans her face close to mine in concentration. 'Do you know what, one of these days you're gonna meet a bloke who worships you, and you'll wonder why you ever wasted so much time on Matt Scotts.'

Behind Jodie, the door swings open. In marches a sharp-nosed year-eleven, with a straight midnight bob and a black mini-dress, supported by spindly legs and spiky shoes. Kay Summers.

She rips a flyer off the wall and strides straight for me.

'Did you read this?' She shoves the poster in my face. '*Kian Hill Year 10 and 11 End of Year School Disco. Dress Code: Year-elevens – black formal evening wear. Year-tens – colourful disco attire.*'

'I misread it, that's all.'

Jodie jumps to my defence. 'It was an easy mistake to make, Kay.'

Kay stares at me. 'This night is about the year-elevens. We don't even want you year-tens here.' Her bag clinks, drawing our eyes to it. She yanks it back under her arm but it's too late. We've spotted a vodka bottle. 'It's our night,' she carries on. 'It's not about a little attention seeker like you.'

'I'm not trying to draw attention to myself–'

'Whatever stunt you're trying to pull, Matt Scotts is **never** going to be interested in you. He never has. He's leaving and he's not going to give you a second thought.'

I feel the tears behind my eyes again but fight them back.

The door opens once more. In walks another Little Black Dress, her soft light-brown hair bouncing on her shoulders as she approaches. Sarah Chine, ever the referee, shoots me a concerned smile, blatantly seeing through the mask of blusher.

'You ok, Amy?'

I nod.

Jodie stands closer to me. 'Oh yes, Kay's just having a dig about her dress.'

The new comer's face softens. 'Oh, you dozy thing. Trust you.' She shrugs, 'it's nothing to go hiding in the toilets over. You look lovely. Doesn't she, Kay?'

Kay's face hardens further and she grits her teeth. 'Yes. Lovely.'

Sarah leads Kay away. At the door, the witch turns back and locks eyes with me. 'Hopeless case.'

The only downside to Sarah Chine, my next-door-neighbour and surrogate big sister, is her best friend, Kay Summers. Sarah has looked out for me all my life; we played together in our back gardens and she showed me the ropes at school. Kay hadn't liked it when I started Kian Hill, a year after them, and taken up so much of our mutual friend's time. Kay is like a waxing strip; if you want smooth legs you have to put up with the pain. Kay is the pain I have to endure if I want to be friends with Sarah.

'Come on, Ames.' Jodie throws the last of her make-up back in her bag. 'We can't leave Annie holding the coats all night.'

Annie, the owl; the studious one.

Sarah, the hen; the motherly one.

Kay, the snake; the bitchy one.

Jodie, the fox; the sexy one.

So what am I? Amy the mouse? The unnoticed one?

I peek out of the loo door. As I'm about to walk across the floor, I don't know what I'm more scared of; that everybody might laugh at my wardrobe mistake, or the thought that no one might even notice me.

Jodie prowls across the floor and I teeter behind. We return to Annie at our table, in her sparkly blue top, peeking out through her owl lenses from the bundle of coats on her lap, her wispy blonde curls on end, as though on guard over our cans of coke.

'You *can* put the coats down beside you, you know,' Jodie smiles at her. Then she turns to me. 'Don't listen to the old witch.' She laughs; 'look at her up there.'

Most of the year-elevens have congregated on the stage. The drama hall is set up with tables and chairs around the edge and on the platform, while the middle of the room is left open as a dance-floor. In one corner stands the DJ, and coloured disco lights flash onto the floor. Above the stage is a large banner that reads, '*Kian Hill Year 10 and 11 End of Year School Disco*'.

ALL THAT YOU WANT

Girls and boys in bright tops and blue denim bottoms dot the lower part of the hall, while a sea of black ties and LBDs fills the stage.

The stage is where we are looking now. We can see Kay, trying not to fall over, drapsing herself all over Thomas, who is clumsily holding her up. He flicks his floppy hair out of his eyes and spots Jodie and I laughing across the room. He chuckles back to us.

Kay spots our exchange and shouts at him. Sarah is quick to the rescue and begins dancing with Kay as a new song comes on. The witch smiles and loosens up, drunk and easily distracted.

'Oh dear,' smirks Jodie from our view point. 'Why does he put up with her?'

I shrug. 'He loves her, I suppose.'

Jodie scans the room and nudges me with her elbow. 'Target identified.'

I follow her gaze.

There, sitting at a table by the drinks stand, with a group of friends, his floppy brown hair framing his beautiful face, his suit jacket slung over the back of his chair and his white sleeves rolled up revealing his gorgeous brown forearms, is Matt Scotts. Prickles run over my scalp.

I know I'm staring but I have to drink him in. This is the last time I'll see him. Newcastle might as well be on the moon, as likely as I am to see him again. He'll be up there... doing what..? Working.... making new friends... dating... living his life. He might as well be wiped off the face of the earth. In a parallel universe. Not giving me a thought.

It was about a month ago Kay let it slip he was going. I'd met Sarah at the buses to walk home, and she was waving Kay onto her bus. Matt had already stepped on and I was scanning the windows to see where he would sit.

'Oh, she's so desperate.' Kay broke my daze as she hopped onto the bus. 'He's moving away, you sad-act. Get over it.'

My ears began to ring. My vision went blurry. It was as much as I could do to stand up.

MICHELLE WOOLLACOTT

All the way home, I badgered the rest of the information out of Sarah. She had known, of course. She told me he would leave the day after the disco; he was going to Newcastle for his parents' work. I pestered and pleaded her but she didn't know any more than that. I tore down my front path and slammed the front-door without saying goodbye.

After spending the first part of the evening crying into my pillow, I'd resolved to make a plan. At the disco, I would tell him how I felt. I would not let him go without taking my chance.

I jump as Jodie shoves some coins into my hand. 'Go and get us a drink, Ames.'

'No way.'

'And ask him if he wants to dance too.'

'I don't think so.'

'Annie, do you want one?'

Annie pushes her glasses up her nose and shakes her head, still clutching the coats.

'Go on, Amy. I'm thirsty.' Jodie tips her can upside down to prove it's empty.

I sit firmly.

'He's moving away tomorrow.'

My heartbeat quickens. I looked at my wrist. But I've left my watch at home; it doesn't go with this outfit. 'Ok, I'll get you a drink.' I stand up. 'But I'm not asking him to dance.'

I shuffle across the hall, sure everyone's eyes are bearing into me. *Look at that hopeless case.*

I can't look at his table as I order Jodie's coke from the dinner-lady. I pay and turned around.

I bump right into someone queuing behind me. 'Sorry.' I look up.

'Don't worry.' It's him.

The slight touch from the collision goes right through to my insides.

His floppy hair nearly covers those yellow-green eyes. He smells like he's probably wearing his dad's aftershave.

ALL THAT YOU WANT

'Sorry...' I stutter again as he steps past me. 'You... getting a drink then?'

He looks at me. 'Yeah.'

'I... heard you're off to Newcastle.' I stand with him as he orders his drink.

'Yeah, Dad's job. Leaving tomorrow.' He is leaning on the drinks table with both arms. His black tie dangles onto his clasped hands.

'Oh right.' I pull my black skirt down, suddenly feeling it is too short. The can is cold in my palm and I twist my hand in to hide my ugly nails. 'You gotta have a dance then, before you go..?'

'Yeah, maybe.' The dinner lady hands him his can.

'Right.' I step back. 'Ok. Good luck with it all, then.'

I step away and bump into the next person in the queue. It's Sarah.

'Hey!' she beams. 'I've gotta come and have a dance with you in a minute!' She nudges my arm and steps forward to the drinks table. Matt glides back to sit with his friends, nodding at Sarah and me.

I shuffle back across the room, sure everyone is thinking what a sad-case I am, with the wrong colour dress, that's far too short. What kind of desperate idiot would ask him to dance? I had planned to declare my feelings and so far all I've managed is a stuttering, mumbling proposition.

I reach our table as *Cotton Eye Joe* begins.

'Come on!' Jodie yells, jumping up and grabbing my arm. 'Come on, Annie!'

'No, I'll stay here and watch the drinks.' She looks at the single can I've placed on the table and corrects herself. 'Drink.'

'It'll be fine, Annie. It's not even open.'

'I'm fine here for now. I might come in a bit.'

Jodie sighs at her. 'Alright. We'll just be here.'

Jodie grabs my opposite arm and swings me round on the dance-floor. Soon I am dizzy and laughing. She swaps arms and swings me round the other way. Everyone on the dance-floor is doing the same. Suddenly, someone else grabs my arm. I looked up. It is Sarah. We swing round while Jodie happily swings from boy to boy –even grabbing one of the teachers to join in. Everyone on the dance-floor is swinging round, swapping partners, as I, too, swing from arm to arm.

Matt, I just want to wish you luck before you go. That's what I'll say. *I just want to let you know, I've always...* I've always what? I swing to the next person's arm, unseeing. *I've always... thought a lot of you... I've always liked you.* Too much... I've never been able to say more than a few sentences at a time to him. He must know. Everyone must know. Kay says it's written all over my stupid face.

I look around for Jodie and she is no longer nearby. Then I spot her, ascending the stage steps to year-eleven territory. If she is trying to be inconspicuous, she will struggle in that red boob-tube.

I see Kay, sitting, drunk on the stage-floor, whispering sweet-nothings to Thomas. He is trying to force water down her throat.

Then I understand Jodie's mission.

Kay's bag lies unattended on a nearby table. My best friend slides the vodka bottle from the witch's bag into her own and begins to descend the stage steps. The drunkard jumps to her feet and grabs my best friend by the shoulder.

Kay has apparently sobered up surprisingly quickly and is now staring down at Jodie from the platform.

From my viewpoint, I can't make out what is being said between them, but I guess it is something along the lines of the younger girl threatening to tell the teachers where she found the drink, because Kay sits down on the top step, defeated, permitting Jodie to continue down the steps with her bottle.

Most of the teachers have joined in the dancing. Even Annie is laughing from her pile of coats. But my eyes still follow Jodie.

She is approaching Matt's table. I freeze.

Matt and his mate have turned from their table to watch -and laugh at- the scene on the dance-floor.

I cannot believe what I'm seeing. Jodie is slipping a drop of vodka into his drink.

He turns just as she is stuffing the bottle back into her bag.

She smiles, and I lip-read; 'Hi...' She leans forward towards Matt's friend, her low top in his eye-line.

ALL THAT YOU WANT

Now the three of them are talking. I wish I could hear what they are saying. Whatever it is, she must have got away with it, because now she is stalking back onto the dance floor. He does not once glance at his can.

Jodie reaches me with a cheeky grin on her face.

'What are you doing?' I hiss. 'Spiking Matt's drink?'

'I'm only trying to loosen him up a bit so he'll stop thinking he's too cool to dance.'

'Jodie, you can't put vodka in people's drinks without them knowing!'

'Oh, it was only a tiny bit. I was doing Kay a favour; she's had enough.

Before I can argue anymore, it happens. All the swinging on arms, the dizziness, and the alcohol cause a domino effect. First, a year-ten boy falls onto the dance-floor on front of us, pulling his partner down. Then, another pair of dancers trips over them. Jodie pulls me back to our seats and it isn't long before a mass pile-up can be seen in the middle of the dance-floor.

One of the boys near the bottom of the heap hits someone to get them off him. That someone hits him back. Now, it's all broken out of control.

Mr Banton, Head of English, and one of the few teachers not to have joined in with dancing, has found Kay sitting on the stage steps. He turns from her to see the chaos on the dance-floor.

Banton signals to the DJ to stop the music.

The lights come up.

'Right!' yells Banton above everyone.

The room falls into silence.

'Good grief!' shouts the teacher from the stage. 'This is your end-of-year disco! Is this the memory you want to leave?'

Silence.

'I have reason to believe that some of you have been drinking.' Behind him, Kay heaves. Old Banton continues to address everyone. 'Some party you have made this.'

'Some party, sharing with the year-tens,' a year-eleven calls out.

'I beg your pardon?' Banton yells.

Silence greets him.

11

MICHELLE WOOLLACOTT

'I understand a lot of you wanted segregated parties. But that is not the way Kian Hill works. We are an *inclusive* school.'

It is clear Old Banton has missed the point completely.

'Goodness me, what Mr Millows must think, I don't know.' Next to him, on the stage, stands a man with a camera. 'Boys and girls, this is Bert Millows; he's a photographer.'

Bert Millows waves.

'Now,' continues Banton, pulling at his collar. 'I want everyone in rows facing Mr Millows for the leaving photograph. *Everyone;* that's year-tens too. In fact, you're going to stand one year-eleven, one year-ten, alternating. You've got to have someone who's *not* in your year either side of you.'

Huge groans arise.

'Now!' yells Banton.

Everyone begins to move, directed by Banton and the photographer, while Miss Arnold, a P.E. teacher, takes Kay outside to get some air and probably to call her parents, with Thomas puppy-dogging behind them.

It is surprising how quickly ordered lines are forming in the school hall from the chaos of a few moments before.

On either side of me, my arms are grabbed. Sarah and Jodie lead me behind Matt. They push me forward into line and before I know it I am standing between Sarah and him.

Matt looks at me and smiles indifferently.

The camera man stands in front of us with his tripod. 'Say cheese!'

2

Kiantown, September 2000

'Alright, I'm up,' I mutter.

It take me a few seconds to realise the chirpy, cocky voice pulling me awake is not that of someone in the room. It isn't talking directly to me when it introduces, 'from their new album, Westlife's *Loneliness Knows Me by Name.*'

I groan and crawl deeper into the covers, not allowing this morning to come in.

I had to change my shrill *ringing* alarm clock for a *radio* alarm at the beginning of the summer, after the vibration had knocked the photo of the disco off the bedside table. I'd also had to replace the cracked frame. I can't get used to the change.

The summer hasn't been long enough. The autumn term is here too soon, like an unexpected guest before the house has been prepared. Like an enemy army creeping up before shields can be found. This day has been thrust upon me.

I am *not* going. I'm going to stay under the duvet all day, and all of tomorrow, and go back to the blissful, unthinking depths of sleep.

I turn off *Loneliness Knows Me by Name* and close my eyes.

I have forgotten two things: Beth and Mum. They are bounding through my door, tweeting in chorus, Beth shaking my arm and Mum ripping back the curtains, forcing the day into the room.

'Amy!' Beth sings, already dressed in her crisp secondary-school uniform. Those sea-blue eyes stare at me out of her freckled face. 'My first day at big school! What time are we leaving? Eight o'clock?'

I shove her off me. 'I'm not going. I'm ill. Leave me alone.'

Lenny Hunter smiles down at me from one of the many posters adorning my walls. My finger-nails throb from where I bit them until I fell asleep.

Mum is at my side. 'What's wrong, Honey?' Her Florida twang still clings to her accent after all these years. Mum was born in Miami, where our eccentric maternal grandmother still lives. Mum fell in love with our Cockney fair-haired dad and moved across the Atlantic, and here they settled, in the southwest of England. The three of us females are cursed with mousey in-between hair. Today Mum wears hers in a messy pony tail. Beth's is neater than usual this morning.

'My head. Stomach. I feel sick.' My eyes are still closed.

'You were fine last night.' Mum flicks the end of *Loneliness Knows Me by Name* back on. 'It's your first day of year-eleven.'

'Don't forget to tune in to *Drive Time* tonight, where we'll be joined by Bliss Magazine's editor to reveal their competition winner —massive prize-' the DJ is warbling now.

'You've got to walk me, Amy,' chirps my little sister. 'You're not making me go on my own?'

I can't keep my eyes closed as Beth's dart across my face, trying to read it. Those innocent frightened eyes. What would I have done if Sarah hadn't walked me in on my first day? If she hadn't looked after me at break times and lunch times until I'd made friends in my own year? I sigh. 'Eight-fifteen.'

Closing our own front door, I stare at the door on the other side of the separating wall and will it to open... for Sarah to appear and walk to school with us.

It opens. Sarah's mum smiles. 'Morning, girls! Amy, look out for the post tonight; Sarah's sent you a letter with photos of her new flat —it's really big! You'll like it. Good luck today, Bethany!'

We smile at Mrs Chine and leave through our gate.

Just as Sarah had taken me, I walk Beth over the patch of un-growing grass, trodden into submission by thousands of children. Beth has never stepped there before. I take her to the buses, where I first saw Matt, four years ago.

We meet Jodie and Annie off the bus and I shiver. Only Jodie would wear a mini-skirt in September. She works it though, completely aware of the boys ogling her legs. Annie, like Beth and I, wears sensible black trousers. Annie's untameable blonde hair is forced back into a plait but frizzes still escape.

We show Beth to reception, just as Sarah showed me, four years ago.

As the morning unfolds, school is buzzing. The year-sevens are gob-smacked at how much bigger it is than their primary schools. The little explorers hold their maps tightly, trusting the year-eights who send them the wrong way. The year-elevens embrace the power of the prefect badge, and make the most of telling everybody to *walk* in the corridors and tuck in their shirts.

I am surrounded by more people than I have been all summer, but I feel as though I'm in a derelict building.

School has always been the place where he was. I'd only focused on my year and the year above me. I'd never noticed anyone younger than me. Did that mean he'd never noticed anyone in the year below him?

Now, *I* am year-eleven. There is no-one above my year. I'll never get back what was here. I don't want to be in this place.

In English after lunch, I say I'm ill and need to see the nurse. Old Banton believes me; I'm never ill. I always want to be here; to be in the same building as *him*.

I leave the classroom and make it straight out of the school gates.

I wander to the Riverfront Café, and sit with a cappuccino, keeping my coat on to hide my school-uniform.

The froth lies on top of the mug in a perfect swirl, flawless and undisturbed. I cup my hands around it and let the warmth run through me. The steam flows through my nostrils, filling my head and my throat, almost covering the damp smell that hangs in the air.

I am sitting by the window with the river beneath me. Out of the opposite window, I can see a window-cleaner climbing a ladder. From where I am, I can't see the top. The man's feet disappear above my view.

I am a September baby. If I had been born twenty-one days earlier, I would be in Matt's year. If I was in his year, would he have noticed me? Would he still have gone hundreds of miles away, to Newcastle?

No-one else can have ever felt this way, surely, otherwise how could they go about their drab lives? How can people do things that don't matter, like going to school? If Kay loves Thomas - if Kay feels *this* for Thomas, how can she treat him the way she does? If Mr Banton loves Mrs Banton – assuming there is a Mrs Banton, -how can he worry about grammar and punctuation? If I had Matt, I'd never shout at him or put him down. I wouldn't ever go to school or work. I'd just shut myself up in our little place together, and never want to be away from him. We'd have a special place. Maybe in the orchard. Or maybe we'd have our own little flat. We wouldn't need anyone else because I'd just take in every bit of him. I'd be able to touch his hands whenever I wanted. Study his face. Get lost in him. I wouldn't need anything else in my life. I wouldn't be able to concentrate on any task. I wouldn't be able to function anywhere, doing anything without him, because I wouldn't be able to think about anything else. I'd probably get run over walking down the road, or if I worked in a shop, I'd give the wrong change. Or if I got my dream job of being a journalist, I wouldn't be able to think of anything to write about but him. I couldn't write about trivials like village fetes, or business affairs, or lost cats. Matt would consume every part of me.

Maybe I'm nuts. Maybe nobody else really does ever feel this sick. If that's true, I'm the luckiest person there is. And I don't care if that makes me crazy, they can lock me up. I'm going to be mad about him for the rest of my life anyway; I might as well lie in a padded cell than rotting in my room, getting in my parents' way until I'm an old woman.

Four years of missed opportunities; when he and I got blamed for the graffiti and spent a whole lunchtime alone together scrubbing it off; when I snuck back after school to find my confiscated key-ring and he helped me hide from Banton; when I was sitting in the Orchard and the football came over the hedge and he came to get it. I'd thought I had all the time there is. I never thought school would end.

Out of the window near my seat, fallen leaves float on the river. The froth on my mug has spilled over the edge and my fingertips are cold again. Out of the opposite window, the man climbs back to the bottom of the ladder. If only I could climb back down to the beginning.

I jump up, resolute, the sudden scraping of my chair turning the other customers' heads. I grab my school bag and am out of there.

This is my last chance to do something about it. I stride faster, as if I can make up for all the wasted years of hesitation. I am going to the train-station to buy my ticket. In the morning, I'll say bye to Mum and set off for school as usual, and school would assume I'm ill. By the time Mum realises, I'll be in Newcastle.

I'll phone Sarah at college and get his address. He isn't out of reach; he's just *up north*.

My stomach flips as I edge into the draughty station. The queue is short. My chest tightens.

'Next please.'

I'm shivering in the concrete building.

The old lady behind me taps my shoulder. 'It's you, dear.'

I shuffle out of the way and murmur, 'After you.' I almost run out of the station.

I can't do it for the same reason I couldn't do it at school. I can't hear him say it. I don't need to hear it; I *know*. If he feels anything, he'd have acted on it at school. He wouldn't have moved hundreds of miles away and left me here.

My dawdling takes me back to school. I am *not* going to class. I make my way to the bottom of the field and clamber through the hedge. I fitted through that gap much easier when Jodie and Nicole and I first discovered it on one of our year-seven expeditions.

The cherries lie on the ground beneath the tree. They are bright and vibrant against the dull grass. I turn to the hedge I've just climbed through, and notice, for the first time, newly sprouted blackberries.

MICHELLE WOOLLACOTT

Soon the blackberries will be ripe, and in the spring the fallen cherries might be baby trees. Next summer their parents will hold new fruit.

In the distance the bell rings. School is over already.

I meet Beth at the gate. She bounds up to me and pours out the tales of the first day of her new adventure. I amble home and she skips beside me.

After the hugs and enthusiasm at Beth's stories, Mum turns to me. 'Oh, a letter came for you this morning.'

I smile as she hands me the white envelope.

3

It begins to rain at midnight, and I take the letter from under my pillow. I walk to the window. The torrent is falling fast and dense. The envelope is creased, although it only arrived today. The words are printed onto my brain, but the reality of what they mean is still whirring in the air. Not photos of Sarah's college flat.

'Congratulations! You've won *Babe Magazine*'s *'Win A Star Date with Lenny Hunter' Competition*!'

The words flow off the page as the wind picks them up and carries them around with the rain. It is really strong now. The wind hammers at the window.

I think back to that insignificant day, months ago, when I decided to fill in the shiny slip from the magazine for a chance to meet the new Hollywood star. What the hell, it was only a bit of fun. Somebody had to win. Of all the hopeful applicants, what were the chances it would be me?

I am going to Hollywood. I am going to meet Lenny Hunter; the new teen pin-up who recently shot to fame through his role in a gangster blockbuster called *Blood*. In the half-light, I stare at the poster beside my bed. Lenny Hunter; with his golden hair and bronzed skin and green eyes, who'd broken free from his corrupt gang-lord father as a small side story, but had inadvertently stolen the hearts of young girls on both sides of the Atlantic.

The storm picks up all through the night and all the next day, blowing me to the weekend.

On Saturday the train takes Jodie and I forty miles out of our small town to the city. Jodie revels in the buzzing high-street, prowling the shops, whisking me through all the stores we don't have at home. She picks out skirts and jeans and boots and jackets and crop-tops and long-tops and strapped-tops and sleeved-tops. She dresses me up and twirls me round and bustles me to the next shop.

The gale continues, scooping up leaves and crisp packets and broken umbrellas.

We come to the dresses. 'Not the one with the sequins.' Jodie is adamant. 'It's too young-looking.'

We decide on a black, strappy cocktail dress with black, strappy shoes to match. Jodie flirts outrageously with the shop assistant and we get student discount, even though we don't have a student card.

The dress is short. I'm not sure Lenny will want to see that much of my legs. 'Doesn't it look a bit... Posh Spice?'

'What's wrong with Posh Spice?' Jodie asks.

'She doesn't seem much fun.'

'Posh Spice is sexy.'

Before catching the train home, we stop at Sarah and Kay's shared college-pad to show them my new outfits. We ignore Kay's smirks from the bedroom doorway as gentle Sarah and glamorous Jodie practice my make-up and my hair. I beg Sarah to come home to do it for me on the day.

'Oh, Ames, I wish I could. Anyway, you've got Jodie to do it.'

'Yea, what's wrong with me?'

I look at the hurt expression on Jodie's beautiful chocolate skin. 'Do you think I should have some sun-sessions before I go?'

'No!' The duo cry in unison.

October 2000

The storm has blown a month of school away, my sixteenth birthday barely mattering. Now I am on a private jet.

Babe Magazine's press people share the cabin with me and shoot advice that skims the bubble that encases me. Mum sits beside me, chirping away, but I don't hear her.

ALL THAT YOU WANT

Jodie has fixed my make-up expertly but she insisted I leave my hair down; 'You can't wear a ponytail to meet Lenny Hunter!' I wear my big jacket over my tiny dress and wish I'd had those sun-beds.

Jodie managed to stick false nails on so I can't bite them. I run the tassel of my coat over my teeth, the fabric becoming softer as it grows moister. The end begins to part and I can run my tongue between the fibres. I wish Jodie was here. 'Give him a kiss from me!' she said when she had waved Mum and me off. *Kiss* him! I don't even know how I'm going to *speak* to him.

'Helloooo!' The door at the end of the gangway flings open out skips a happy young flight attendant in a red uniform with a skewwhiff hat. 'You must be Amy! I'm Barry, your humble and oh-so-jealous steward!'

I smile as best as I can with the tassel still tight between my teeth. His are the only words I've heard since boarding the plane.

'I've come to see what you want for lunch.' He looks at me. 'Jacket tassel, I see. Do you want that roasted or fried?' he winks at Mum. He looks at me. 'Honey, you look as if you're going to the electric chair, not to meet Lenny Hunter.'

He's right. My whole body is tense, and my face is screwed up. I'm pulling my coat around me like my life depends on it.

'Stop hiding behind that jacket, Sweetie, and let me look at you. Come on, you can't meet Lenny in that soggy number.'

Grudgingly, I relent and take the chewed-up thing off.

'Stand up; let me look at you.'

I sigh. Up I stand.

Barry looks over my spaghetti-strap dress. 'Turn around.'

I oblige.

'Honey,' he says decidedly, hands on hips, 'if I looked like that, I'd have Lenny myself. I've just split with my girlfriend; maybe I ought to try the other team. Everyone always assumes that about me anyway.'

I quickly sit back down beside Mum.

'Do you play cards?' Barry asks.

I shake my head. 'Not really. I mean, sort of..'

21

'Ok, well it's about time you learnt.' He slides into the seat opposite me, pulls out a deck of cards and fans them in his hands. 'Pick a card, any card, and don't look at it.'

Mum folds her arms across the table and leans towards him.

'You mean, don't show you,' I correct him.

'No, I mean don't look at it!'

So I pluck a card, clumsily, not used to my stick-on nails, and hold it, face down on the table.

Barry moves the pack away and holds out his hand. 'Now give it to me, still without seeing it.'

I frown but hand it to him

Barry looks at the card, without showing me.

'Ok, now through the power of telepathy, you're going to tell me what the card is. Ok, choose two suits; hearts, diamonds, clubs or spades. Choose two.'

'Ok... hearts and diamonds.'

'Ok, so that leaves clubs and spades. Now choose clubs or spades.'

'Er, spades.'

'Ok, spades. Now choose; the six, seven or eight of spades?'

'Um, seven.'

'Ok, that leaves the six or the eight. Which is it?'

'The eight?'

He turns the card over, revealing the eight of spades. 'That's magic, that is.'

'Hang on, you were inconsistent. You sometimes discarded what I said and left in what I didn't, or sometimes you left in what I said and discarded what I didn't say, depending on what suited you.'

'No, no, it's magic, Amy.' His eyes twinkle.

'When I said hearts and diamonds, you left in clubs and spades. But if I'd have said spades and clubs you'd have said ok, spades or clubs?'

'Not at all, it's magic!' He smiles cheekily.

'Ok,' I smile. 'It's magic.'

This flight attended might be treating me like a child, but right now, to be cocooned is just what I need. Barry immediately saw it. I am grateful for that, even if I can't work out which team he bats for.

'Amy, we're in California.' The flight attendant's gentle but excited voice wakes me. I jump at the intrusive poke on my lips and smell the pink waxy smell as the steward touches up my lipstick.

I jump again as I realise what he has just said, and smudge the lipstick. The plane has landed.

'Hey, hey, stop shaking.' Barry hands me a compact mirror.

I frantically touch up my make-up and smooth down my hair. The windows are black so I can't see if the storm has followed us here.

Barry winks. 'Knock him dead.'

Mum has risen from her seat, and is pulling on her coat and touching up her own make-up.

The magazine people surround me, straightening my clothes and hair and talking at me at once. They bustle me to the door and I stand as tall as I can.

'Give him a kiss from me!' I hear Barry call.

I grin, thinking how much he reminds me of a friend of mine.

The door opens, like a porthole to another world. I smile one last time at Barry through the press people's heads, and descend the stairs.

4

Hollywood, October 2000

A sheet of noise hits me from the swarming airport.

Crowds of fans cheer behind a barrier of camera flashes. The *Babe Magazine* people position me for photos, elbowing Mum to the side, while bodyguards surround us.

Before I can kid myself the fans and press are for me, I see what the commotion is about. A stretch-limousine is parked on a red carpet in front of the barriers. An army of bodyguards surround one of the rear doors as it opens.

I shoot a quick look to Mum to make sure she's still there, feeling like a toddler on the first day of nursery.

The crowd goes mad.

And he emerges.

Golden hair, bronzed skin, dark sunglasses. Sparkling through flashes, is Lenny Hunter.

He wears a smart suit with a black tie and is far from where I stand at the foot of the aeroplane. From my position, it is as though I am seeing him in concert. He doesn't even look my way, but instead waves at the crowds. He approaches the barriers and the cheers grow louder. He obliges them with smiles and autographs and a few words for some of the paps.

And then he turns to me.

My chest is sharp. My lips feel dry, although I've just applied lipstick. A breeze blows through my skirt my hands spring to it. My legs are shaking. I try to smile and keep my face cool. He is striding this way.

All around me is noise; the crowd is roaring; the magazine crew is giving orders. But I can't hear a thing.

ALL THAT YOU WANT

I can't help but gulp. Each bodyguard around him holds a neutral face, but he is smiling. At me.

My stomach flutters and I can barely catch my breath. I've never felt this before. The most similar feeling I've experienced to this was the stomach-soaring when I looked at Matt. But Matt Scotts has never walked towards me with this purpose.

He lifts his sunglasses. Those green eyes from the big screen, from the magazine covers, from the posters in my room, are looking at me.

And then he is right in front of me, holding out his hand. His skin is tanned and his fingernails are perfectly cut to the top his fingers.

'Hello, you must be Amy.'

Trembling, I raise my own hand to him, trying to hide my stick-on nails.

'I'm Lenny. Pleased to meet you.'

From the ceiling, elegant chandeliers dazzle in the dim light. Candles hold every table aglow, each its own small island. Shadows skip and dance about the restaurant.

On the table next to Lenny and I, a couple are leaning in and feeding each other. They kiss.

On another table close by sit the bodyguards, and on another, Mum with the *Babe Magazine* team, sneaking me the occasion thumbs up while they point the camera.

'So...' Lenny asks, 'where in England are you from?'

'Erm... the southwest...'

He looks blankly. 'Is that near London?'

'Um, well, the other bottom corner... near the coast.'

'Oh – it must be nice living near the ocean. I grew up in Chicago.'

'Oh... I suppose you have a nice house there..?'

'Well, I er, bought a place for my mom, and I go back there when I go home. I seem to spend more time in Hollywood these days.'

I see a change in his face. It can't be... embarrassment..?

Our little booth is suddenly closing in on us. I shuffle back and take a mouthful of salad, carefully manoeuvring the cutlery with my alien claws. I chew and chew but can't swallow. The leaves refuse to bend or tear in my mouth.

One of the *Babe* team approaches us and bends down to me. My cheeks are full of food. 'Try to look a little more relaxed, darling. Smile a little, ok?'

I can't answer.

She nods to herself and returns to her seat.

Lenny's face is soft as he smiles at me.

I concentrate on the plate as I saw ferociously at the lobster. The fishy smell turns my nose, and my throat refuses to allow the lettuce to pass. A piece of the stubborn crustacean escapes, shooting into the candle.

I sink into my seat, wishing the extinguished candle could have left us in darkness.

Two emeralds glimmer at me.

I sink further into the seat, willing it to swallow me.

'I guess that's what you think of the lobster.' The jewels are smiling.

I have to turn from them. My eyes fall again on the smooching couple's table, then to the frowning magazine people.

A waiter is here, bringing our table back into light. 'How's your meal, Madam?'

Lenny looks at me. 'Actually, we've finished. Thank you very much.' He pushes the full plates towards the waiter and leans in to me. 'Let's get out of here.'

The ocean creeps at our bare feet, surprisingly still warm although the sun has gone down. The sand feels cold beneath my toes. The breeze tugs gently at my black dress.

Further up the beach, out of ear shot, the bodyguards and the *Babe* team have caught us up and now they hover, somewhat disgruntled at our last minute change of venue. Mum sits with them, happy to go with the flow.

Between us on the rock where we sit is a pizza. I have lost a nail so bend my finger casually to hide the flaw. I hope the acrylic is not in the pizza.

ALL THAT YOU WANT

'I didn't always have a big house in Chicago, ya know. I grew up in a run-down two-bedroom apartment,' he confesses. 'And when I'm shooting, I stay in a trailer...'

'A trailer? Oh, a caravan?'

He nods.

The Pacific, potentially so frightening and mighty, is singing with gentle breath.

'I wanted to impress you I guess... dumb, huh?'

I don't know where to look. But he is looking away too.

'Those restaurants scare me,' he confesses. 'You've always gotta be on your best behaviour.'

I spy the top button on Lenny's shirt is now undone. The smooth dip at the top of his chest makes me feel funny. 'I wouldn't think anything could scare you.'

Those eyes dance again. 'D'you know, this time last year I was working as a pizza delivery boy? No kidding. Now I've starred in a *movie*... *every*body knows who I am.'

He's twenty, but at this moment he looks like a little boy. I have to stop myself putting my arms around him. 'I do have some idea what it's like... to have no control over, well, changes in your life. For me, I'm in my last year of school... And then what..?' As I say it I feel silly. 'I know it's not the same thing-'

'But it's scary.'

I nod. 'But you know what, I don't really want to be at school for the rest of my life. How fun would life be if you knew what was going to happen next year?' The ocean stretches out before us, vast and endless; a sheet covering whatever secrets are hidden beneath. It breathes quietly in and out.

'I might have a chance to be in a movie after Christmas, in England. This job could take me anywhere in the world.' The stars twinkle on the water. He snatches another slice of pizza.

'My next door neighbour, Sarah, she's moved up to college already. And my friends in my year... what happens when we leave school and we don't see each other every day?'

'If they're real friendships, you won't lose them.' He munches his pepperoni.

We sit silently for a few moments. His cheeks dimple as he chomps. I think of the scene from *Blood*, where he lies the dancer down on the sofa-bed and kisses her collar bone. The lights are low and the music is soft. His chest is bare as he leans over her, and tonight I can't help looking at his white shirt and wondering if it was his real chest or a body-double.

'You're right; not knowing what to expect is probably not a bad thing.' He glances behind us. 'Hey,' he whispers, 'shall we give these guys something they won't expect?'

'What do you mean?' I whisper back.

'How fast do you think they can run?'

I look to the bodyguards -carrying a little excess weight- and then to the magazine group, loaded down with cameras and equipment.

He grins mischievously and holds my hand. His hand is soft but strong. 'Go!'

Before I know it we are racing along the sand in bare-feet, our shoes, along with the motley crew, strewn behind.

I don't look back, and let him take me further along the beach, jumping over rocks and dodging pits, not knowing where we are going but laughing all the way, until finally he leads me over a stone wall and we crouch.

'Why are we doing this? They'll have seen us!' I laugh.

'But they weren't expecting it!' He laughs, too.

'Neither was I!' I catch my breath. Our faces are close together and I'm sure he is staring at me with those emerald-green eyes.

He quickly looks down. Something on the ground catches his eye. 'Look at this.'

I follow his gaze to the rock-pool just in time to see a hermit crab climb out from its borrowed seashell.

The breeze flutters under my dress and I shiver.

'It's getting cold. Let's go.' He helps me back over the wall and we ambled back, hand-in-hand, towards our shoes and to the vague blurs of figures in the distance, who are still scrambling to catch us up.

5

Back at the hotel, we say goodnight to the magazine people and to Mum, who return their respective rooms for the night. It is now just the bodyguards, Lenny and me.

'So...' Lenny shuffles, 'what do you say to a drink before we go to bed?'

The last thing I want to do is go to bed. 'Yea, sure.'

So we sit in the hotel lobby and Lenny introduces me to ginger beer, a taste I can't immediately warm to, but I sip it nonetheless.

'So, tell me about you,' he asks.

'What do you want to know?'

'I don't know. Something... important to you, or... some*one* important to you.'

'What do you mean?'

'Like... who are you close to at home?'

'My best friend Jodie Parker. I love her. She looks out for me. She took me clothes shopping for this trip; she did my make-up. She sticks up for me. Phones me about everything.'

'You're lucky to have someone like that in your life.'

'What about you? Do you have a best friend?'

'No. Well, there's my agent, Clive. He looks out for my interests, I guess. I can call him about things. But it's just business, really. We don't have that closeness. So what's Jodie like?'

'Well she's... she's always the life and soul of the party. But, I don't know if she's really happy.'

'What do you mean?'

'She's always been bolshie. But it's a front. Like... this new boy came to our school when we were twelve. They were a right pair together. But then… there was this accident. She was devastated. I know she never got over it. It's been three years. I don't know, I hope she'll let someone get close to her again. She dates a different guy each week. She's the…. habitual flirt who avoids relationships.'

'I suppose you look after her.'

'I try. She looks after me most of the time. I don't know how she does it every day.'

'No, you care about your friend. She must appreciate you being there.' His eyes twinkle. His shirt is loose and I can see more of his chest and I shiver.

We sit in our cocooned booth, sipping the alien concoction. A lone bodyguard is parked on a table near the door. His head is drooping and he is struggling to keep his eyes open. Lenny and I laugh at his bobbing head. We are the only dwellers of the lobby-bar. The barman is nonchalantly wiping glasses, nodding to the soft music.

'Do you think he's waiting for us to go?' I smile.

'I guess so. I guess we should go up now. It's getting cold.'

My bare knees and shoulders are prickling with goose-bumps.

Lenny stirs the bodyguard and tells him he is off duty. The three of us travel up in the elevator together in silence. At my floor, Lenny bids goodnight to the bodyguard.

He clears his throat. 'I'll see Miss Minor to her door.'

So, at my hotel-room door, the actor kisses my cheek.

I close my eyes and my chest sinks at the thought that this evening is ending.

Then he whispers, 'Wait for me.'

My chest thuds.

I watch him disappear back into the lift. I hover in my doorway, unsure of his meaning, shivering even more now.

Before long, the elevator doors re-open and Lenny appears, holding a blanket. At last we are un-chaperoned and I have to remind myself to breathe.

'I thought we could… talk a little longer. But you're getting cold, so,' he gestures to the blanket. He motions to a bay in the window.

ALL THAT YOU WANT

We sit and Lenny throws the blanket over our knees. Behind us lie the lights of the city. The star lays his jacket over my shoulders to protect my back from the cold window. We lean in, shoulder to shoulder. I am instantly warm, but I'm still shaking.

'So...' I stutter, 'I've told you about my best friend. Now it's your turn.'

'I told you, I don't really have a best friend like that.'

'So... tell me something else about you. Like, how you grew up.'

He shifts. 'I could tell you about my mom...'

So Lenny tells me the story of the day he came home from school, at fourteen, to the stench of smoke.

He pushed open the apartment door to thick, dirty smoke, which had already begun to fill the room. His mother lay motionless, drunk, in the armchair of their poky apartment, a cigarette having fallen from her fingers into the waste-paper basket at her side. Sparks glared from discarded tissues and papers. His shouts didn't wake her.

The boy darted forward, his eyes stinging, his nose curling, and grabbed the basket. He screamed at the burning metal. Pulling down the sleeves of his jacket and bracing himself, he picked up the 'trash-can' once more and raced for the kitchen. As he held the basket under the 'faucet' in the sink, a singeing sound took over the kitchen. Then, after a while, there remained just a dampened trickling noise. The fire was extinguished. Lenny rushed around the apartment, opening all the windows with one hand and pulling his jumper around his mouth and nose with the other. Next, he ran back to shake his mother. Still she would not be roused. He yelled and pulled at the lifeless figure.

The smoke was clearing and finally, the woman seemed to rasp, a rattling, desperate intake of air. Lenny held his own breath. Then, she let it out in a whistling smoker's snore.

'Come on, Mom.' With his almost-grown fourteen-year-old body, he managed to support her frail physique - which, to him, appeared to be shrinking by the day - and help her to bed.

Her breathing now seemed regular, her chest rising and falling as he covered her weak body with the blanket. After placing a glass of water by her bed, he hunted the cupboards for something to eat, suddenly starving. With the dregs of a packet of rice, half a tin of beans and some scrapings of butter, he managed to make himself meal. He gulped down a glass of water and realised what had been wrong. There had been no blaring warning sound as he had entered the building.

He took the stool and removed the old battery from the smoke detector. He searched drawers in vain for spares. He managed to find a few coins and wondered if they would be enough to buy batteries on his way to school in the morning.

'Didn't you call the fire-brigade? I think they run free smoke-alarm checks at home. Do they over here?'

'No…. I don't know. I didn't call anyone; I didn't… take her to the emergency room. I was so worried about her, but more than that I was scared they'd… take me away. She's my mom, you know?'

I realise Lenny is holding my hand under the blanket. Or am I holding his? His palm is warm and his fingers press into the back of my hand. Our legs are pressed together. Involuntarily, I squeeze his hand.

We sit in silence for a few minutes and I don't know what to say to his story.

Suddenly, I have a thought. 'Lenny… isn't there a swimming-pool in the hotel?' I instantly regret it, knowing I must sound shallow. But I am pitifully attempting to… I don't know, lighten the mood.

'Yeah, but it's closed.'

I raise an eyebrow. 'But you're Lenny Hunter.'

Before I know it, Lenny has charmed a night-guard to slip us the pool key. We have changed into our swim-suits and enjoy the whole pool area to ourselves.

Sitting in the bubbly tub, tingles prickle over my legs. I've lost three nails by now. The bubbles lift me out of my seat and I am floating up, so I grab Lenny's arm, laughing, and force myself back down. His upper arm flexes at my grip. I've never been this close to man's bare chest. I watch the water trickle down his torso and I know now it was his real body in *Blood*. He is right beside me. I put my hands across my belly and flatten my bikini. I can't tell if the bubbles are outside or inside my body. Jodie would probably sit on his lap and throw her arms around his neck. I wouldn't dare.

ALL THAT YOU WANT

He splashes warm water in my face. I splash him back. A droplet falls down his temple and he smiles a glistening smile.

The light is low and blue.

'Do you fancy a swim?' he asks.

So we emerge from the hot bubbles. I'm sure he looks at me as he reaches the edge of the pool. I look up at him and he quickly looks away. He dives into the pool but I am not so brave. I watch him swim a length with ease, his shoulder blades flexing in a perfect rhythm.

I edge into the cold water, shocking after the heat of the Jacuzzi. Every pore in my body pricks up, alert.

I'm in to my waist, and decide I need to plunge the rest of the way. Icy water engulfs me. I kick off from the wall and swim towards the middle of the pool. As I come up for air Lenny is already swimming back towards me. He stops in front of me and we tread water. The lower half his body is distorted. His face is sparkling wet. I struggle to meet his eyes.

He swims a little closer and I kick frantically to stay afloat. I wonder what would happen if I held his shoulders to keep me up.

'Shall we...' he begins. 'I guess we should go to bed. It's getting late.'

Lenny has returned the key to the night-guard and we ascend the stairs, wrapped in our towels. As we approach my floor we hear a night-porter. We duck into a crevice as he passes, both of us trying not to giggle, clinging to our towels, water dripping from our hair.

We reach my door and it's really time to say goodbye.

'Well, goodnight, Amy. I'll see you in the morning.' As we are standing here, alone and almost naked, he leans in and kisses my cheek. His breath passes over my wet skin as he moves back.

I watch him as he waits for the elevator, his towel around his waist, his exposed back dripping. He looks back at me. I open my bedroom door as the lift doors part for him. Throwing me a little wave, he steps in, leaving a dripping pool where he was standing.

I imitate his gesture as the doors close. Then, pulling my towel tighter around me I step into my room.

Upstairs is the man I will spend tomorrow with.

Once dry and in my pyjamas, I sink into the crisp hotel quilt. I close my eyes and think of Lenny in the movie kissing that dancer's neck. And I know that, for now, I don't mind being between shells.

6

Screams shoot down from above our heads, forcing us to look up at the specks that are the passengers dangling upside-down. Back the right way up, the ride plunges to earth with unrelenting speed.

I look at Lenny. 'You want to *go* on that..?'
'Maybe later.' He steps away.
'You can go on your own then,' I mumble.
He turns back. 'Pardon me?'
'Um, shall we get a drink?'
He grins. 'That's a better idea.'

The bodyguards and *Babe Magazine* crew have been shadowing us all day. The theme-park smells of sweet candy floss and sticky cola. Mum hovered at the beginning, but now has wandered off to find the café.

Lenny moves around the park with an assured stride, and oozes that sparkle only true celebrities have a way of doing.

As we sit with our ginger-ales, a bodyguard stands in each of the four corners of the table. The tourists can look, but can't get too close. The burly blokes have positioned themselves at about a two meter radius, and, with the noisiness of the theme-park, we are safe that if we speak quietly enough we won't be heard. I tell myself to be cool.

'So then, what's this film about? The one after Christmas, in England?'
'It's a rom-com.'
'Oh yea? Are you going to play the hero- no what do they call it? The protagonist? The main guy.'
'No, I'm up for his best pal.'

'So you're not the one that gets the girl?'

'No. It would be good if they made a film where the main guy didn't always get the girl. It's, it's quite formulaic, but it's gonna be fun.'

'Yea. I love those films.'

'Even though they're all the same. I dunno, I might get to be the one that gets the girl. One day.'

I stir my bitter drink with my straw. 'Well, look how far you've come already. In a year.'

'I know; it's like… if I hadn't auditioned for that role last year –if I hadn't gone to acting school in the first place… it goes to show. You've got to take risks for what you want, even if the odds are against you.'

I nod. 'If I hadn't entered that competition, I wouldn't even be here now. You've got to go for things in life. Take your chances.'

He laughs. 'Well, we *are* being all philosophical aren't we?'

I put my drink down. 'Let's do it. Let's ride it.'

He moves back in his seat. 'I didn't mean… I wasn't talking about *that* kind of risk-taking.'

I stand up. 'Come on, we're doing it.' I grab his hand and pull him up.

The world has become a blur. The tiny people below whoosh past and we both scream.

'Don't look down!' Lenny yells beside me.

My stomach flips as we are spun upside down. I keep my eyes clamped shut. Gripping the bars as hard as I can, I'm sure it feels rickety. Two more nails ping away - I daren't look where. A scream erupts from the bottom of my lungs, but is drowned by everyone else's.

Not a minute too soon, we were back up the right way. My stomach remains at the top as we are plunged to the earth. My head is forced back in my seat as the ground whooshes up to meet us. My eyes are tight again.

The world is spinning as we step off the ride to meet the bodyguards. I can hear Lenny laughing beside me, but can't see clearly. I stumble forward, dizzy. My legs are quickly lost, and I fall.

'Whoa!' Lenny catches me, still laughing.

I can't help laugh too. I look at him until his three heads become one. We stop giggling and stare at each other a second longer.

'Was it worth taking the risk?' he asks, almost seriously.

I catch my breath as he holds me, and the world is finally still. 'Definitely.'

He pulls me to an upright position. 'Come on.' He takes my hand and we stroll on, looking for the next adventure.

The Limo pulls up outside the hotel and we climb out, both tired after a long day's thrill seeking. Mum reluctantly leaves her complimentary champagne glass in the car and the bodyguards escort us to our floor.

'Night, Darling.' Mum kisses my cheek. 'I'll leave you two to say your goodnights. Night, Lenny.'

'Goodnight, Mrs Minor,' Lenny smiles.

Mum disappears to her hotel-room, adjoined to mine.

'I guess I'll see you in the morning, then,' Lenny says, outside my room.

'To see me off.'

'Thanks for a great weekend, Amy. It's... it's sad it has to end.' He moves towards me, slowly at first... then he hugs me hard. I embrace his hold. His words and his actions feel genuine. But he is an actor.

'Well... night...' I open my bedroom door.

'It's been... fun. I hope you thought so too.'

I nod and smile.

'Night, Amy.' He turns away as I close the door.

I lie on the bed, wide awake, listening to my heart beating.

I hear the presence of the bodyguards outside the door. The light glows beneath it.

I think back to that night in July; the school disco, the missed opportunity I wallowed over for months. I hadn't told Matt how I felt.

I remember all the times Kay Summers told me Matt Scotts wouldn't touch me with a bargepole. I reflect on all the moments Matt looked past me. I was nothing.

Then, I think of how Lenny has treated me; the tender attention he has given me; how he opened up to me. Could he really think anything of me?

I am, finally, something.

I picture the hermit crab leaving his shell and searching for the next one. Did he have a choice about what it would be?

My mind turns to today at the theme park… taking a risk. Doing something that scares me.

I don't know what the next chapter of my life will be, after the safe haven of secondary school, but I have to take a leap.

All that you want, you can have. I know what I want. And I am going to do something about it.

The light under the door beckons me. Before I know it, I'm off the bed and stepping into the corridor.

I approach the lift to Lenny's private floor. The elevator is guarded by two bodyguards. 'Can we help you, Miss Minor?' asks the biggest man I've ever seen.

'I want to talk to Lenny. Just for a minute.'

'Miss Minor, I must suggest that you return to your room,' the giant ushers.

'Please, just ask him if I can talk to him for one minute. Just ask him. If he says no, I'll go to bed. Please just ask him.'

'Miss Minor–'

'Please. Just ask him.'

So I wait with bouncer-number-two while the first travels up in the lift to Lenny's rooms.

I smile at the big bloke. He keeps his face straight.

He won't talk to me. I'll just go back to bed, I think.

A few minutes later, the lights above the elevator stair-case back down. The doors open and the bouncer appears. 'He said for you to come up.'

I blink.

The doors begin to close but the giant holds them ajar. 'Are you coming?'

Am I?

ALL THAT YOU WANT

I hold my breath and dart into the lift with the bouncer. My stomach flips as we rise. In no time, the metal doors expose me. Lenny is looking at me. I can't meet his gaze.

I stare, unable to speak. Both Lenny, opposite me in the small private hallway, and the bouncer next to me in the elevator, are regarding me expectantly. The elevator doors begin to close again and the three of us dash to hold it open. I jump out. The bouncer steps out after me and the doors gently close.

'Lenny, I, just... wanted to talk to you...'

'What is it, Amy?'

The bouncer stands right over us.

'Look, come in for a minute.' Lenny takes my arm.

I look at the bouncer.

'Mr Hunter, I must advise you not to put yourself in a compromising position.'

My cheeks burn.

'I'll leave the door ajar. Thank you. Just give us a couple minutes.' Lenny steps into his room and I follow.

Light streams in from the gap in the door and we walk to the far side of the boudoir. He flicks on a light. The giant bed eclipses the room.

'Lenny, I don't want... what he was suggesting.' I am burning red. 'I definitely don't, I just want to talk. I don't want to get you into trouble-'

'Amy, just tell me what it is.'

I flick my hair out of my face. He is beautiful and I just have to try. 'It's... I...' I am shaking. I take a breath, aware of the bodyguard outside, knowing we can't be long. 'I just wanted to say... I've had a great time, and I like you, and I just want to... stay in touch... I mean, only if you want to, you probably don't want to. But I just.... had to take the risk... to take control of my next... shell... jump off the top rung of the ladder... I just really like you. I'm putting it out there. There. I've made an idiot myself. I'm going to bed now.' I turn to the door.

He grabs my arm and jerks me back to face to him. Before I know what's happening, his soft lips are pressing against mine.

Suddenly I am not shaking as the kiss prickles right through my body.

As he gently pulls away, I dare to open my eyes, and see his, wildly close. 'Does that answer your question?'

7

The crowds roar as Mum, Lenny and I emerge from the limousine at the airport. We wave and the *Babe Mag* team usher Mum and me to step back as Lenny once again obliges the onlookers.

With the autographs signed and a few questions answered for the paps, Lenny returns to us. I hide the taste of last night's kiss in my mouth.

The *Babe Magazine* people photograph Lenny and I saying goodbye, positioning us for the farewell hug. Lenny leans in and I hold my breath. He plants a soft kiss on my cheek. I resist the urge to bring my hand to my face.

'Ok, it's a wrap,' says someone at my side, but my eyes remain on Lenny. Our hands are joined in the last position we were staged in.

The doors open on the private jet and the stairs are wheeled over.

Those emerald eyes bear into mine. 'I've had a really great weekend,' he tells me.

'Ok, Miss Minor, the plane is ready,' says the voice at my side.

'Me too,' I tell him. 'It was great meeting you.'

The magazine team have begun boarding the plane.

'Well... bye Lenny.'

The woman at my side leads me away.

'Bye, Amy,' he calls. 'Have a safe trip.'

'So how's the luckiest girl in world?' Barry bounds towards us as we take our seats. 'Details, I want details!'

MICHELLE WOOLLACOTT

My face glows as brightly as his red suit. 'Feeling lucky,' I say. 'Very lucky.'

Kiantown, October 2000

Beth and I wait at the school-bus drop-off point for Jodie and Annie. My little sister's sea-blue eyes are almost transparent. She has a nice group of friends in her own year who she'd usually have ditched me for by now, but today she wants to hang by me. So, apparently, does everyone else. Girls and boys from all years, who have never given me the time of day before, this morning flock around the buses to glimpse the girl who met Lenny Hunter. I wish Kay Summers was still at school to witness this. I picture her, swaggering about the school as if she owns the place. I hear her spit, *Matt Scotts wouldn't touch you with a bargepole.* I try to think of Matt, but Lenny takes over my whole being. I smile to myself. *Matt who?*

'What's he like, Amy?'

'What did you do together?'

'Is he funny?'

'Is he really short? I heard he's really short.'

The questions fly from all directions as Beth squashes herself against my leg. I grip my shoulder-strap to hide my nails – I ripped off the remaining two falsies last night, and I'm once again left with stubs.

'He was… really down to earth,' I shrug, aware that my face is beaming despite my casual words. 'Really… just… friendly. Normal.'

I spot Jodie and Annie's bus pull in beyond the swarms, bringing the promising whiff of exhaust fumes.

'What did you say to him?' Their hunger for gossip is like seagulls' to dropped pastry. Only this time it's more than crumbs that have fallen, it is the rarity of a whole pasty.

'Are you gonna be on TV?' someone pecks.

'We just talked about, life and stuff, I dunno, we had dinner, went to the beach, went to a theme park. It's gonna be in *Babe Magazine* next month.'

Through the crowd I make eye contact with Jodie as she and Annie step off the bus and fight their way towards me. Annie

ALL THAT YOU WANT

pushes her glasses up her nose. Jodie totters in her little skirt, and I pull down my knee-length one.

'Is he just as fit in real life?'

'Did you get a kiss?'

'Did you tell him about us? Like, where you come from and your school and that?' They peck away for something meaty.

I throw them a few more crumbs as Jodie nears. 'Yeah, I told him I was in my last year of school, and told him about my friends and family and stuff.'

As Jodie and Annie reach my side, the shrill ring of the bell emanates from inside the building.

'Better get to registration,' Jodie calls, taking my arm.

Jodie, Annie, Beth and I turn from the flapping flock.

'Catch you later, Amy!' calls someone who has never spoken to me before.

In the registration room I rip a sheet from my record book and pass a note to Jodie. 'The Orchard. Break time.'

So it is here, through the gap in the hedge at the bottom of the school field, in the over-grown garden of an abandoned house, that we'd once fondly referred to as *The Secret Garden*, that I tell Jodie; 'He kissed me.'

As the words leave my mouth, they sound so far-fetched. But I think of his hard grip as he pulled me back, his warm breath, the feel of his soft, hard lips. My heart quickens. It happened.

She stares at me, open-mouthed. 'Tell me everything.' She grabs my hand and sits on the ground.

I sit beside her beneath the ancient cherry tree and oblige.

Kiantown, November 2000

'One day, God called Adam to him and said, "Adam, there's good news and bad news. The good news is I gave you a brain and a penis. The bad news is you've only got enough blood to operate one at a time!"' Jodie chortles down the phone.

I can't help but laugh. It's been three long weeks since my competition-win to Hollywood and, of course, I haven't heard a word from the actor. Now, I sit on the bottom stair after school, while Mum washes up the dinner things in the kitchen, gripping the telephone to my ear.

'Why do men like sexy women? Opposites attract!' Jodie is off. 'What did God say after creating man? I can do better. There are loads more, Ames: Why do men name their penises? Because they want to be on first-name terms with the person who makes all their decisions.'

'Jo, you know I didn't...' I lower my voice in case Mum and Dad are listening, '*sleep with him.*'

'I know; that's why you haven't heard from him.'

What did I actually expect? That the kiss would be the beginning of some great romance? What an idiot.

'Men are like mini-skirts; if you're not careful, they'll creep up your legs.'

Thank bloody God I didn't sleep with him.

'What's a man's definition of a romantic evening? Sex... What do you call a man who expects to have sex on the second date? Slow.'

I laugh, realising how much effort my best friend must have gone to. 'Where did you find all these?'

'A book from the library; *Why Women Don't Need Men.* Why do men have a hole in their penises? So oxygen can get to their brains... If they put a man on the moon, why can't they put them all there?'

I laugh. 'Too right. And Lenny Hunter and Matt Scotts can be the first on the rocket.'

'Men are all the same, they just have different faces so you can tell them apart... The definition of a bachelor is a man who has missed his chance to make a woman miserable.'

'Yeah,' I concur. 'His loss.'

'Exactly. Why do doctors slap babies' butts after they're born? To knock the penises off the smart ones! What's the difference between a man and E.T? E.T phoned home.'

I stop her. 'But this isn't home. I only spent one weekend with him; he doesn't have to ring me. Maybe he just didn't want to hurt my feelings. It wasn't a real date; I won a competition. I shouldn't have expected anything-'

'Amy! *You told me* what he said to you. He led you on. He made you feel like a- made you feel silly.'

ALL THAT YOU WANT

I squeeze the phone cord. 'At least I've learnt from this. I've learnt it's *never* a good idea to tell a guy how you...'

'Look, who needs men?'

'Not us!'

'Good girl. Listen, I've got to go and do coursework.'

'Me too.'

'See you tomorrow. Oh- one more; what's the difference between a BMW and a porcupine? Porcupines have pricks on the outside.'

The robbers tear out of the room, knocking the cot sideways.

The action on the screen isn't easy to ignore. 'Turn it down, Beth, or you can go back to your own room.' It is nearly impossible to concentrate on GCSE geography with a little sister perched on the end of your bed watching the very film you don't want to see. That's the way it is in our house. We have to wash up after dinner, do our homework, go to bed on time. There's not much room for negotiation with our dad. The only person he'll back down to is Grandma.

'It's the scene! It's the scene!' cries my helpful sister.

I stare at the emerald eyes on the TV. I am glad, now, that Jodie was the only person I told. I'd been dying to tell everyone. I can hear Kay Summers laughing at me.

Beth laughs, screwing up her nose, her freckles dancing. 'You're dumb-struck by him.' Her piggy eyes have that look about them that she gets when she is in the mood for winding me up.

I scowl at her. 'Are there any films you actually like for the story, and not because there's a guy you can drool over?'

Beth laughs again, gesturing toward my video collection, which comprises mainly of Johnny Depp and Leonardo DiCaprio films. 'Says you.'

'Johnny Depp is a talented and diverse actor.'

'Right. And Leonardo DiCaprio?' She picks up Baz Lurman's *Romeo and Juliet*. 'I bet you don't even understand this.'

I cross the room and snatch it from her. 'Just because Shakespeare is beyond you. Some of us can appreciate the beauty of the language.' I shove it back with the others and

45

slump back at my desk. '*Some of us* have got coursework to do. Watch the film or go to bed.'

'Don't tell me you bought this because you *like* fighting films?'

'*Blood* has very poignant themes and messages, actually.'

'Really? And what would they be?'

'Watch it and you'll find out. Stop talking or you can go back in your own room. You're meant to be in bed. Mum'll hear you if you don't shut up.'

Beth gazes blankly at the TV, pretending to watch it. On the screen, the baby lies motionless in an incubator, with tubes and bruises covering her body, her distraught mother at her side.

How I drooled over *Blood* five months ago. Although I'd never admit it, Beth was right; I had no interest in the film. I wouldn't even have gone to see it but that it was Dad's Fathers' Day treat; a family trip to the cinema. But when I got there, he captured me. Me and every other girl in the Western world, it seemed, because after this film, it was the club landlord's son; a minor character, that everyone remembered. Suddenly his posters were in all the magazines; he was on billboards; in TV interviews. And then, there was the competition in *Babe* magazine. Someone had to win it. Only an idiot would believe it meant she was someone.

I'm quickly going off this film. Now that I know the real Lenny Hunter is a user who tricks girls into falling for him, when he has no intention of seeing them again.

I try to concentrate on the volcanoes and earthquakes and tectonic plates that swim in my textbooks.

Beth's silence is short lived. 'Imagine if you two had got together.'

'Grow up. Like he'd be interested in me. The only reason he'd be nice to me, and give me the time of day -and even *run* that competition in the first place- is for publicity. I'm no-one, Beth.'

'He's only had a *small part* in *one* film. He doesn't know how to be fake yet. You probably met him at the stage in his career when he's still most down to earth.'

I scribble out the last sentence I have written, and make a hole in the paper as I do, not able to erase the image of our

ALL THAT YOU WANT

pizza on the beach, nor the big, stabbing hole in my stomach. I stand up. 'I'm too old for posters. You can have them if you like, for your room.' I begin tearing down my Lenny Hunter pictures.

Beth gasps. 'What was that?'

'What?'

'That, scrape... tap, on the window... There it was again!'

'A bird?'

'What, pecking the window or flying into it?' She looks at me. Cautiously, she makes her way to the window and pulls the curtains back. She freezes. 'There's a man down there... he's throwing stones, or maybe sticks...'

I run over.

Beth stiffens. 'Is this gonna be like in *Scream*? Should we call the police?'

A figure is walking towards us across the garden.

'A secret lover, Amy?' My sister opens the window. 'Hey, Romeo!'

He stands directly below the window.

'Is he going to try and climb up? Have some originality.'

The man peers up.

Beth jumps back from the window. All her breath is gone. She looks at me, then at the TV.

I blink, and look at him again. On the screen, the baby cries. Music to the mother's ears. The tubes are removed. Her child can breathe on her own.

Beth creeps back over to me, holding my arm and peering down from behind me. Even in the half light, as Beth and I strain our eyes, there is no doubt. The face looking up at us is the face on the posters on my wall; the face on the TV screen. My stomach jumps.

Lenny grins. 'Wherefore art thou Amy?'

8

'I thought we'd have a… romantic meal…'

I take in the camping stove and the tinned beans and hotdogs. I don't like to say that it is eleven p.m. and I had tea a few hours ago. I am wearing joggers and no make-up; a bit different to how he last saw me in my strappy dress and high-heels in Hollywood.

We are behind the hedge on the far side of the river at the back of my house. When he'd led me from the back garden down the bank, across the bridge, and into the field, I saw not only that he had brought with him, but had already pitched, the two-man.

I'd stopped. Girls our age have it drummed into us what lads are after.

'What's wrong?'

What's a man's definition of a romantic evening? Did he think he could just turn up here, after not speaking to me for a month, and expect to me to jump in the tent with him?

Evidently, he'd read my face. 'No… it's just for *me* to sleep in… I got the train from London, I didn't want to book into a hotel; that can be traced; so I brought this… I thought, we could just, sit for an hour or so, talk… then you can go home, and I'll leave in the morning…'

I'd sighed. 'I've got school in the morning. I can't stay long.'

He'd smiled and unzipped the tent.

Now he is cooking our midnight feast, flicking his golden hair out of his face. I am zipped in his sleeping bag, poking my head out of the tent. 'So… you've been in London? Why…?'

'I'm… doing that rom-com.'

ALL THAT YOU WANT

'You are? Well done.' But I stay where I am.

'Yea... I thought I'd come see you before things really get started.'

What do you call a man who expects sex on the second date?

'It seems like ages.' Those emerald eyes sparkle.

Yes, it bloody seems likes ages. I look away. *Men are like mini-skirts...*

He moves towards me with two plates of cooked food. I slide back. He follows me in, hands me the plates and pulls the zip closed. We are encased in the green-grassy smell of the tent. I wonder how loudly I can scream. My house is close on the other side of the narrow river; Mum and Dad can be alerted easily enough. I am glad now that Beth caught him. My sister had to be bribed to keep schtum with a kiss on the cheek and an autograph from Lenny, and a promise from me to do her share of the washing-up for a month. The autograph can easily be explained; I'd brought it back from Hollywood last month. The lie is far more plausible than that the actor had come to find me.

I bring the rubbery hot-dog to my lips. The beans taste metallic.

'Sorry... it's not very spectacular... I'm sorry I haven't been in contact... I had to wait until I came to England to see you in person... I brought you a gift.'

'What..?'

He fumbles in his rucksack and pulls out a small cardboard box. 'It's a cell.. or, a mobile phone.'

'What..? You can't... Why..?'

'I couldn't call your house-phone. Who would I say I was?'

'But-'

'You have to charge it for sixteen hours before you can use it. So, if you plug it in tonight, I can call you tomorrow night... if that's ok?'

I feel my face soften.

'When's a good time to call, when you'll be on your own?'

'Um... after dinner,' I shrug. 'I'll go up to my room. About seven?'

'Seven.' He picks up the plates. 'I'll get rid of these.' He scrapes the tinny food outside.

I bite my lip, watching his hunched body throw away his efforts. 'Sorry...'

'Hey, you've probably eaten anyway.' The wind sneaks in as he holds the zip open. I pull the sleeping bag up. He closes the tent and turns to me. 'I've been going mad not being able to talk to you. I didn't know what to do. So I figured this was the best way, to find you when I came to England. But now, now you've got the cell, we can speak every day. If you want to..? I know *I* do...'

The ice in my chest begins to thaw.

'I want to talk to you every day... I can't stop thinking about you, Amy.' He holds out his hand to me, and I notice again his perfect fingernails, cut to the top of his fingers like a netball player.

I force my gaze up to his face. Slowly, I unzip the sleeping bag and, trying to hide my chewed nails, reach out my hand.

He takes it and stares into my eyes.

I am aware of my body leaning towards him. My lips brush his and we are kissing. All the stiffness in me has melted. He is here.

Finally, I pull back and smile at him.

He smiles a smile that looks like relief. He stares at me a moment longer.

Suddenly, I see the tent anew. It is no longer a cold, uncomfortable unknown, but a cosy hideaway.

'You know, "wherefore" means "why",' I grin.

He frowns, not following.

'When you came to my window, you said, "wherefore art thou Amy?"; *why are you Amy?*'

'It means "where", doesn't it? *Where is Amy?; Where are you, Amy?*'

I laugh. 'No, it's: *What is in a name;* why are you Romeo Montague? Juliet has just discovered Romeo is a Montague.'

'Oh. Well, I meant, *where are you, Amy?* Because your sister had called me Romeo, I thought I'd... play along... I don't know... I was trying to be... funny... I don't know... I got it wrong...'

I laugh. 'It was... sweet... Anyway... what's it like in London?'

ALL THAT YOU WANT

'It's... well, a dream, but... I'm fine as long as Clive tells me what to do. At school, at home, no-one really took notice. Now I'm... I don't know. People can't do enough for me.'

I smile at him.

'It's, "Is your dressing room satisfactory, Mr Hunter? Do you have enough fruit? Would you like more towels?"' he grins. 'I'm telling you, I could have built a fort with my mound of towels, so I joked, "I might need more towels in here," and the runner ran off, shouting, "who forgot the extra towels in Lenny Hunter's dressing-room?" I could have died.'

I laugh.

'I forget I'm not at home; I'm not a pizza-boy anymore. People offer me coffee, and I say, "It must be my turn."'

'So it's the life of luxury then?'

'Except I sleep in a trailer...' He reaches for his bag. He pulls out a deck of cards. It must be an American thing. 'Wanna play?'

I smile and nod.

He splits the marshmallows he's brought for toasting between us. 'To use as tokens to bet with'.

He teaches me how to play *Twenty-One* and I show him how to play *Rummy*. The tent warms up further. We hear the first taps of rain on the tarp and huddle closer.

'Your Dad teach you card games too?' I ask. 'Rainy-day-family-time? Instead of *too much T.V.*, it was cards or scrabble for us.'

Lenny smiles. 'No, I played cards at acting school. Mom let me sit in front of the T.V. God forbid she would have to *do* anything with me.'

I shuffle. 'Yeah well, I'd rather have been allowed to watch T.V. Dad would say we could either play board-games or put the hoover round.'

Lenny laughs. 'My dad wasn't around when I was growing up.'

'Working?'

'No... he... left my mom when she was pregnant with me.'

'I'm the oddball in this day and age; to actually have my parents still together.' I don't know why I say that.

51

'You're lucky. My... my mom and dad were both actors. They toured in a travelling theatre group. They had dreams. They were gonna make it big.'

'What happened?'

'I came along. By the time Mom realised she was pregnant, it was too late for a termination. She had to leave the group. My dad decided to go with them. He wasn't going to let a baby ruin his dreams. Mom never heard from him since.'

I swallow. 'Did you ever think about... trying to track him down?'

Lenny frowns and shakes his head. 'Mom's still in Chicago, where he left us. Never moved. He could have found us.'

'Did he... *make it big*?'

Lenny shrugs. 'Michael Stoneham. You ever heard of him?'

'No. But I'll bet he's heard about you. I'll bet he'll get in touch soon.'

'Well he'll be twenty years too late.' He looks at his cards. 'Mom... was ill. Well, you know what I told you; I'd come home from school, and... she wouldn't have moved from the broken armchair in front of the T.V, except to fill her vodka glass.' He looks down. 'I learned early to cook for us both and to clean a bit. But, I was pretty useless. But... it was the least I could do, or try and do, to make up for ruining her career and losing her Mike.'

'You don't believe that. If she carried on touring with Mike, would she be where *you* are now? Mike isn't.'

'She's doing ok now though. When I was sixteen, she met this guy, Jim. He helped her get better a damn sight better than I could. I noticed for the first time she had blonde hair instead of dirty brown. Jim moved in. I moved to acting school. Then I joined Debbie Rutland; acting agency. They got me extra parts in T.V shows and movies. They put me up for *Blood*. My first speaking part. *Two whole* scenes, it started out as. I had *eight lines* in a Hollywood Blockbuster. For some reason they upped it a little. I had a character, with a name.'

'I bet your mum was proud.'

'I can't believe, you know, I got noticed so much for that movie.'

'You... swept everyone away, Lenny. You're a good actor.'

'I had a few scenes. That's a big deal to an unknown like me, but it's hardly in the same league as—'

'But look where it led. You're the most talked about person in the world now.'

'I don't know about the world.'

'Everyone can't wait to see your next film. What's it called?'

'*Buzzard Block*.'

'*Buzzard Block*.' I pour some coke into plastic beakers and hand one to him. I raise mine. 'Here's to *Buzzard Block*.'

Outside, the rain continues beating on the tent. The wind is howling and the river is picking up pace. I'll have to walk over the bridge and up the soggy bank, through the back garden and sneak into the house without being noticed. I'll just wait until the rain stops.

The rest of the world is fading. Nothing exists except our cosy little place.

I remember how Barry, the flight attendant, made me relax on the aeroplane; how he'd made me laugh to ease the tension. I pick up the pack and face Lenny. 'Wanna see a trick? Pick a card, any card. And don't look at it.'

I awake to sharp digging in my side. I sit up, my body stiff. He must have pitched the tent on stones. Or glass. I look at my watch. It's just before 6am. Beside me, Lenny's blond eyelashes flicker. His chin shows the slightest stubble. His face is concentrating, but peaceful. His chest rises under his coat. I could stay here all day.

I realise I hogged the sleeping bag all night. I try to put my hair in place and wipe the sleep out of my eyes. A spot has erupted on my chin overnight. I pull my jumper up and squash down my neck.

He opens his eyes. They meet mine and he smiles. 'I couldn't wake you up to make you go back home in that rain last night.' I want to dive on him and kiss him.

We pack everything away so I can be in bed before my parents stir, and so he can catch his train before anyone misses him.

MICHELLE WOOLLACOTT

We cross the bridge, him with his camping equipment and me with my cardboard *cell-phone* box. Mud covers my trainers and the bottoms of my joggers.

'I won't be able to call you at seven now,' he says at the top of the bank. 'If you put it on charge now, I'll be able to call you at, like…'

I look at my watch. 'Ten-ish? I'll plug it in as soon as I get in.'

He kisses me, apparently not minding about morning-breath, spots, and un-brushed hair.

I leave him watching me as I tiptoe into the house.

In my room, I run to the window and see him walk away, holding his tent under one arm and pulling his hood up with the other hand. As much as I want to watch him until he's out of view, time is short. So rip the phone from the box to plug it in and hurry into my pyjamas. I hide my muddy clothes and the phone-box under my bed. The sun is rising, clearing the damp. The river is nearly still. There is almost no sign of the night's rain.

I lie motionless until I hear my parents stir. I pull up the covers and sink into the sheets just as Mum opens the bedroom door. 'Morning!'

I feel Lenny's kiss on my mouth and his warm arms hugging me to him as we fall asleep.

A sharp dig from Jodie's elbow makes me realise where I am. Mr Banton is eyeing me impatiently. I turn to see everyone else in the class is too.

'Well, Amy?' The English teacher strides to my desk and peers down. 'You haven't even got your book open on the right page. Come on, Act two, scene one. Do you even know what I just asked you?'

I sink into my seat. 'No, Sir.'

'Do you *want* a GCSE in English, Amy?'

'Yes, Sir.'

'Then I suggest you stop staring into space and start participating.'

ALL THAT YOU WANT

I'd told Jodie first thing; 'He came to my house last night; he couldn't contact me before in case anyone found out; we spent all night together and he didn't try anything. He's going to phone me at ten o'clock tonight–'

'Well, we'll have to wait till ten o'clock then,' she had replied, cynically.

Will he bother with me after he hadn't got anything last night? After he'd seen me unprepared, without the Hollywood-glamour-planning? With no-make-up, messy hair, joggers, spots, bad breath…

I can picture the phone, plugged in beside my bed. He'll call…

3:45pm. After school, I walk next door's dog. I've been helping them out since Sarah went to college. Six long hours and forty-five minutes to go.

5:00. I arrive home and have tea, ignoring Beth's subtle digs at the dinner table. He'll ring.

6:00. I have a bath. 6:30. I try to do some homework. 6:45. I put the T.V on. 7:30. I try to go to sleep. I'm not used to so little sleep as I had last night. If I can sleep now, I'll be wide awake at ten, and in the meantime I won't be watching the clock. I lie in bed. The phone remains on the bedside table staring at me. I turn away. I know he'll ring. A CD seems like a good idea. I choose my Westlife. *Don't you know that dreams come true…* and immediately turn it off. I switch the TV back on. I turn it off and plod downstairs to phone Jodie. Her mum answers; Jodie is in the bath. So I phone Sarah at college. No answer. I phone Annie. She is out at band practice. I don't care if he doesn't ring. I help Mum sort the washing; I start the ironing. Mum is wide eyed. It doesn't look like Beth has said a word to Mum and Dad. Maybe she thinks she dreamt it. Or maybe one of us did.

Why would he ring after my morning breath? After I said nothing interesting last night… He's not that fabulous, anyway. Even if he has got a gorgeous face, even if he surprised me with a midnight feast… So what if he came all this way to see me…

9:50pm. I smart up to my room and switch on the phone. It takes ages to turn on and I pace the floor. The phone bleeps. I jump. It is a message, telling me to delete it, turn the phone off and then back on. I do as I am instructed. The phone takes an age to turn back on. I stare at the screen. I stare at the bedside clock. 9:56pm. I sit cross-legged on the bed. I put the phone in front of me. I run to close the bedroom door, and the curtains.

A shrill ring comes from the phone. I dive onto the bed and press the phone to my ear. 'Hello?' I breathe.

The phone continues to ring. I look at this strange noisy thing, willing it to shut up. I realise I have to press the green button. I push it. It stops ringing. Slowly, I bring the phone to my ear.

'Hello…?' says Lenny.

9

I don't know how I did it. I manage to persuade Mum and Dad that Grandma and Grandad, my dad's parents, are too old to travel all the way to us for Christmas, and that we should go and stay with them, in London. Something drove me beyond myself.

London, December 2000

Grandad, Grandma, Mum and Dad have gone to bed. Beth and I are in the box-room. My sister insisted on having the bed and I am on the floor. For once, I didn't argue. It was over an hour before she finally stopped wittering and fell asleep. I didn't hear a word of what she said. I wait until I can hear her breathing at its heaviest.

There is no other sound in the house. I have to be careful because my grandparents' house is old and it creaks. Beth and I learnt to avoid the creaks when we were younger, when we would sneak downstairs before everyone else was awake to take chocolates from Grandad's chocolate box. I use those techniques now. I open the box-room door at just the right speed. I step at the edge of the landing, not in the middle. I step over those stairs I know groan. I tiptoe to where the keys hang in the kitchen, open the back door and step out. I close the door and turn the key. I'm out.

It's been a month since I've seen him. Now, Lenny stands before me and I laugh. He is wearing a long coat, big hat and sunglasses.

Despite my jeans and jumper, I'm cold in the December night. In my haste to leave the house, I've forgotten my coat.

'Is that all you're wearing?' he whispers putting his arm around me. I sink into him and let him lead me. We've got a handful of precious days together.

We make our way to his trailer, barely speaking as we walk so as not to draw attention to ourselves. I grip his soft hand and he clasps his fingers into mine. I have not bitten my nails for about two months and run a finger over my smooth thumbnail. Even in his guise, that unmistakable gait does not leave him. I wonder if he has been trained to walk so confidently or if it is naturally in him.

When we arrive, I realise making films isn't as glam as all that. I am faced with a tiny room, containing a single bed that folds down from the wall. There is barely room to turn around, let alone for two people to stand. But the rain beats on the thin roof and I feel safe and snug in our little den. There's nowhere I'd rather be. Lenny switches on the gas-fire and it smells damp, yet warm as the dust heats up.

Lenny removes his coat, hat and sunglasses, revealing his flawless face, those emerald eyes and his golden hair. He pours us some soda water from the rickety excuse for a fridge, and we perch on the hard board posing as a bed.

'Thanks...' I sip the water. It wets my throat, which I hadn't realised was dry.

He grins at me. 'I'm so glad you made it.' Lenny and I have spoken every night since he gave me the phone. 'I've missed you.'

I grin, blushing. I've been counting down the days until this trip to London. I take him in a moment longer, then tell myself to be cool. 'So... can I see your script?'

'I don't know about that,' he grins. 'I can't let anything be leaked.'

I give him my sweetest smile.

'Well... if you let out any spoilers, I *will* have to kill you.'

I pretend to zip my mouth. 'So what's it about? *Buzzard Block*.'

'It's... just your average romantic-comedy. Boy meets girl, boy's company is going to buy girl's apartment block, sorry, *flat* block, to expand his business, leaving all the residents homeless.

ALL THAT YOU WANT

'But of course,' I guess, 'when they meet, she doesn't know that he works for the company, and he doesn't know that she lives in Buzzard Block. Am I right?'

He raises his eyebrows. 'Spot on. He doesn't know she is one of the residents his company is going to make homeless.'

'I see. And they find out, fall out, realise they error of their ways, and live happily ever after?'

'Something like that. Classic, mistaken identity... the girl, Alli, is a single mother of a three-year-old, and if she gets kicked out of her apartment, she'll have to move in with her sister, hours away from London. So she plots to find a rich guy who lives in the city, who she can get close enough to for him to ask her to move in with him by the time she has to move out of her place.'

'I see. So he finds out her plan the same time she finds out that he's behind making her homeless -'

'Uh-huh, by which time of course, they realise they love each other-'

'And dance off into the sunset.'

'After a big fall-out, and a public declaration of their love to win each other back.'

'Ok. Like, *You've Got Mail... Ten Things I Hate About You... Never Been Kissed*. And you're playing the hero's best friend?'

He looked at me. 'Didn't I tell you?'

'What?'

He moves to a rickety cupboard and takes out the script. He passes it to me. I fidget on the hard bed.

I flick through it. 'Wait, Lenny... you're Fred. Fred's the... main guy...'

Lenny shrugs. 'I guess they liked me.'

I throw my arms around his hunched shoulders. 'Well done!'

'Thank you.' He blinks those sandy eyelashes. 'So are you going to help me, or what?'

I move back from him on the rigid bed and thumb through the script. 'Sure. Which scene?'

He takes it from me and looks through. 'This one. *Outside the Playgroup*. Fred's gone to pick up Josh, but Alli's ex, Bill, has turned up as well. You read Bill and Josh, and I'll answer you with my lines.'

'Ok.' I begin. '"Daddy! Hey Fred."'
'"Hey, Josh. So, this is your Daddy?"'
'"Yes. And you are." Sorry, I mean "And you *are?*"'
'"Fred Hutchins, a... friend of Alli's."' Lenny holds his hand out to me.

I laugh and shake it.

'Take it seriously.'

'Sorry.'

He carries on. '"I guess there's been a mix up, buddy. Your mom asked me to pick you up."'

'"Come get you."'

'What?'

'The line is, "your mum asked me to come get you."'

He looks at me. 'Potato potaaahto.'

'You asked me to help you learn your lines; I'm correcting you if you make a mistake. Carry on.'

'It's Bill's line.'

'Oh.' I look down at the script. '"Run and get your coat, Josh. Pause. So you're—"'

He laughs. 'You don't say *pause*!'

I laugh at myself. 'I'm not the one who needs to learn it. I'm helping *you* here.' I deepen my voice to make it sound manly. '"So you're the next mug, eh?"'

'"What? I've just come to get Josh."'

'"Collect" this time; "I've just come to *collect* Josh".'

He shakes his head. 'How can I get into character when you keep—'

'I'm helping you.'

'You're *nit-picking*. Carry on.'

'"That your Merc there?"' I pronounce the 'c' in Merc as soft.

'It's Mer*ck*. As in Mercedes.'

'Oh. Well *I* don't know anything about posh cars. Besides, it should be a soft c in Merc, because it's soft in Mercedes. "Is that your Mer-ck there?"'

He looks at me.

'Come on,' I encourage him.

'I can't remember my line now.'

'"What?"'

ALL THAT YOU WANT

'I can't remember my line now.'

I laugh. 'No, that is your line; "What?"'

'Oh. "What?"'

'"It figures, with her about to lose the flat and everything. Oh you didn't know? Found herself a nice safety net for her and Josh to move in on."'

He's taken aback. '"Move in?"'

I look at the line again. 'Did I read it wrong?'

'What? No, why?'

'You're... shocked.'

'*Fred*'s shocked.'

'Oh, you're- I thought...' I feel stupid. I've just been *reading* my lines, not *acting* them. Now he thinks I'm useless. I look at the script. It feels like an audition now. '"She'll spring it on you soon enough. *Oh Fred*".' Bill is mimicking Alli now. I have to change my voice into a high-pitched, man –taking- the-mick-out-of-a-woman's voice. '"*Oh Fred, we've got nowhere to live. We'll have to move to the Cotswolds to stay with Julia. I'll have to uproot Josh, just when he's settled into playgroup. You know how hard it is for him to make friends. What are we going to do Fred? Hey Joshy."*'

He is laughing at me.

I look at the script. *JOSH returns with bag and coat*. The last sentence wasn't mimicking Alli. I feel my cheeks flare. '"Hey, Joshy."' I wait. The next person to speak is Josh –me again. '"Am I going with Fred or Daddy?"'

'"You go with your Daddy."' Lenny's voice is quiet and hurt. '"I'll let your mommy know. You take care, kid."' He says that last line with regret, as if he isn't going to see the little boy again.

I stare at him. 'You're...' but I can't think of the word.

'I'm what?' he grins. Now he is Lenny again.

I shrug. 'A good actor. You deserve this.'

'Thanks. You're not bad yourself.'

I tut. 'For an actor you're not a very good liar. I sounded like a robot.'

He laughs. 'No, you didn't.'

'Poor Fred. What a bitch that Alli is.'

'She's just looking out for her kid. She'd do anything for Josh, and that's what makes Fred fall for her.'

I smile. 'You really understand your character, hey?'

'It's my job to.'

'No, you're really getting into it. You really like soppy films?' I grin.

'No, it's my job to become the character!'

'You're not fooling me. I'm bringing *When Harry Met Sally* over tomorrow night, and don't pretend you won't enjoy it.'

'You make me watch that and I'll make you make you watch *Lethal Weapon*.'

I laugh. 'Ok. Put it on now, and tomorrow we'll watch a film of my choice.'

He pulls out a plastic tub that holds his DVD collection from the top of the wardrobe and drops it onto the bed. He plucks out *Lethal Weapon*. I look through to see what else the container beholds. Half of them are awful cop how-many-people-can-we-shoot, we-hate-working-with-a-partner-but-we'll-be-best-friends-at-the-end action films. I wonder why on earth I'd agreed to this. But the other half is horrors.

'*The Sixth Sense?*' I pull it out of the box. 'I haven't seen this yet. Is it meant to be scary?'

'You like horrors?'

'Don't look so surprised. I may be a girl-'

'Well, shall we watch that instead?'

'Yeah. And I won't make you watch *When Harry Met Sally*.'

He grins. 'Sounds good to me.'

After the film, Lenny turns to me, nuzzled into his arm. 'I'd better walk you home, I guess. Wait, wait.' He untangles himself from me and opens the small wardrobe and takes out a selection of jumpers. The first is a black sweater that looks expensive. 'Better not. If anyone sees the label, they might ask questions.' He turns to me. 'Not that you're not worth my designer sweater.' He holds up a plain hoody, dark-green with a zip and no distinct marks. 'This one's *high-street*. No-one will bat an eye at this.' He hands it to me.

'Except to wonder where I would get a man's hoody from.'

His eyes glisten. 'Let them wonder.'

The streetlights guide us back to my grandparents'.

'I can't believe that ending.'

ALL THAT YOU WANT

'I can't believe we've found a **type of movie we both like.**' The stars reflect on the Thames.

I suppose the DVD is better quality **than a video.**

He holds my hand. The coat, glasses **and hat have gone back** on again. 'Tomorrow night, you'll have to **bring some of your** homework so I can help you.'

'What?'

'It's the least I can do to repay you for helping me with my script.'

I groan. But I can't think of a better way to do homework.

$(2x + 5)(3x - 4)$

'Why did you have to bring *algebra*?' Lenny asks.

'GCSE maths. Got to be done.'

I hid the hoody in the bottom of my suitcase when I got in last night. Knowing it was there all day, it was hard not to smile to myself.

I scribble for a few minutes and come up with $6x^2 - 23x - 20$. 'There. Is that right?'

He looks at me, bewildered. 'You're smart, Amy Minor.'

I laugh. 'Thank you, Lenny Hunter. I don't know if it's right.'

'You didn't need my help after all. I wouldn't know where to start.'

I laugh again. 'Alright. You're as bad at maths as I am at acting.'

'We're even,' he grins.

Only a few more days and I'll be going home. Who knows when I'll see that grin again. I wonder if he will even *want* to see me again.

'So... when are you going home?' he ventures, as if reading my mind.

'Boxing day.'

'When does school start up?'

'Tuesday the second.'

He quickly counts in his head. 'Seven days after you leave London.'

'Yeah. It would be too much for my grandparents to have us any longer. Plus Mum and Dad have got to go back to work.'

MICHELLE WOOLLACOTT

'If just *one* of you stayed it wouldn't be too bad on your grandparents.' He raises an eyebrow. 'Beth's eleven, but you're not a kid so you would be no problem for them; they wouldn't need to worry about you. You could do your own thing...'

'What, do... you want me to stay longer?'

'What do you think?'

'Even though I'm rubbish at helping you with your lines-'

'And you were going to make me watch a *chick-flick*. Maybe I don't want you to stay after all.'

'I couldn't anyway. They'd ask why...'

'I know. Do you think... you could come back up here in your next school break?'

I frown. 'I'll try and think of some kind of way.'

He leans in to me. 'We'll put our heads together.' His forehead touches mine. I breathe. He kisses me.

Take that, Kay Summers. I *am* worth something.

10

It is Christmas Eve. Grandma, Grandad, Mum, Dad, Beth and I are on our way to have lunch. We make our way through the bustly London streets, pushing through hectic last-minute shoppers, all of us wrapped up against the cold. Before we reach the café, an office building catches my eye. It's time. I stop.

Dad tuts. 'Come on, Amy.'

'Can I just go in for a minute and talk to someone–'

Grandma is confused. 'That's the local newspaper office, dear.'

'She wants to be a journalist,' Dad tells her.

'Oh. Well, let her go and find out what goes on, so she can decide if she likes it.'

'We'll be next door,' Mum tells me. 'They'll be busy today so don't be long.'

They hustle into the café and I step into the newspaper office. It is filled with the quiet buzz of computers and smells of new paper and polish. I take a deep breath and focus on the plan Lenny and I conjured up together.

'Can I help you?' asks a woman behind the front-desk. She peers at me above narrow-rimmed spectacles and appears to have no eyebrows at all.

'Hi –I was wondering if anyone was available to discuss a work experience placement.'

'Is someone expecting you?'

'Um... no.'

'Well, I'm sorry, Miss, but we're very busy at the moment. I don't think anybody's going to have any free time. Maybe if you come back in the New Year. Or drop in a C.V.'

MICHELLE WOOLLACOTT

Just then a large middle-aged man walks in behind me, arms piled high with papers. 'Daniel,' he yells. 'I want that college Christmas party report on my desk pronto. Katy, I should have had those reviews *yesterday*.' He drops the pile of files, scattering them all over the floor. 'Why can't anything go right?'

I run over. 'Let me help you.'

'Those were in alphabetical order!' He takes a deep breath. 'Thank you. Sorry, it's the time of year. Harry Sanderson.' He holds out his plump, clammy hand. 'Editor.'

'Amy Minor.'

'Is Beatrice helping you?' he refers to the no-eyebrowed receptionist.

'Actually, I came in to offer *you* help. Voluntarily. I thought, this time of year, an extra pair of hands might come in useful…?'

He frowns. 'Voluntarily? What's in it for you?'

'Experience. I want to get into journalism. I can be around until the first of January… over the busy period.'

He holds half the files in his hands and I have the other half in mine. We stand up.

I can do this. 'You look like you could do with a coffee,' I persist. I don't know what's come over me. 'Let me make you one, then you can think about it while I put these back in alphabetical order. When I've done it you can tell me yes or no. What do you say?'

He raises an eyebrow. 'The coffee machine's over there. White, no sugar.'

I do know what's come over me. And he begins with L.

'How are you going to do work experience, Amy, in London? A hundred miles away from home, when you've got school?' Mum and Dad start on me as soon as I walk in the door, for making them wait at the table half an hour while the queue grew and the waiters became impatient, so now probably isn't the best time to bring up my work-experience opportunity.

'It would only be for the rest of the Christmas break; they need help this time of year. Until the beginning of January. I can't turn down work experience, can I?' Christmas music and tinsel fail to mask the stress of the waiting staff, but I hope the

ALL THAT YOU WANT

season's tidings might go in my favour with my parents. 'I thought you'd be pleased I'm thinking about my future.' I know exactly what I'm doing, asking them in front of Grandma. 'It's going to look far better on my C.V., working in the big city than at home. It will open more doors for me. Think of the contacts I'd get-'

'Where would you stay?'

'You're sixteen Amy. We're not having you staying in the city.'

The waitress arrives with our food.

'Thank you.' I hope the sugary tea might sweeten dad up. 'Merry Christmas,' I add to the waiter, attempting to spread the goodwill.

'Well I think it's very enterprising of her,' pipes in Grandad. 'Shows initiative.'

Beth and I are in the box room getting ready for bed.

'You want to stay in London to see *Lenny* don't you?' Beth jibes.

'Mind your own business. Get your shoes off my pillow.' There is no more space in the room than for the single bed against the wall and my mattress on the floor, so if we want to stand up, we have to stand on my make-shift bed. I topple with my sister's every step, and get a knee in the chin as she climbs onto the bed. 'Ow!'

'Move over then!'

'I can't move over!'

'You better be nice to me, or I'll tell everyone.' Beth reminds me.

'No-one would believe you.'

Suddenly we hear dad's raised voice from downstairs. 'Mum, she's *my* daughter, and I'm not leaving her in this city.'

Beth and I creep to the top of the stairs.

'She's sixteen,' comes the retort from Grandma. 'When your father was her age he was fighting for his country. She's growing up. We were *married* when we weren't much older than her. She'll be leaving home before you know it. At least she knows what she wants to do with her life which is more than most young people can say these days.' I realise my fate lies with

67

Grandma. If she gets her way with Dad, as she usually does, she'll double my time in London. She continues; 'If she's serious about this journalism business we should be supporting her. She won't be *on her own in the big city*; she'll stay here with us. We don't see enough of our granddaughters. We'd be more than happy to help out. Make us feel useful.'

'Mum...' Dad tries.

'She'll stay on here another week after you all go home. It's just one week. She'll be back before school starts. Now, do you want to tell her or shall I?'

At the top of the stairs I grin like the Cheshire Cat. 'Nice one, Grandma.' I hug my sister. 'Call me Lois Lane.'

Beth pushes me. 'Get off me.'

ALL THAT YOU WANT

11

Beth keeps her beady eyes on me.
　It's Boxing Day. Grandma and I stand at the front door as Mum, Dad and Beth pack their cases into Grandad's Volvo.
　I ignore my little sister. 'Safe trip back!'
　'Be good for Grandma and Grandad,' Mum tells me.
　Grandma and I watched as Grandad drives them off to the train station.
　Grandma drapes her arm round me. 'We've got you for another week then, kiddo.'
　I hug her. 'Thank you, thank you, thank you. You don't know how much this means to me.'
　'Anything to support our granddaughter,'
　'I think I'll go to bed early, ready for tomorrow.'
　'Sensible girl.'

I lie in bed in my jeans with my make-up on. I have the bed now Bethany has gone.
　Eventually I hear my grandparents totter upstairs.
　When the noises from the bathroom and master bedroom stop, I wait half an hour.
　I creep out of bed, smooth down my hair, slip on my shoes and sneak onto the landing. Feeling my way along the wall, I pass my grandparent's room.
　The door opens behind me.
　I stop as the floral wallpaper springs to life.
　Grandad squints as his eyes adjust. 'What are you doing out of bed, Love?' His striped pyjamas are creased.
　'Just going to the toilet.'
　'Pardon? I haven't got my hearing aid in.'

69

MICHELLE WOOLLACOTT

'The loo,' I say louder, pointing to the bathroom door.
'Oh, me too. Why are you still dressed? You've got an early start.'
'I'll get changed now. You go first.' I nod to the bathroom. 'Night, Grandad.' I step back into the box-room and close the door.

I hear the toilet flush, footsteps on the landing and then my grandparents' bedroom door close.

It's now or never. Silently, I open the box-room door again and creep downstairs.

Lenny meets me round the corner and we walk to the caravan.
'Did you get out unnoticed?' he asks when we are safely inside.
'Eventually. Grandad had taken his hearing aid out,' I grin.
'First day at the paper tomorrow?'
'Yeah. Do you mind if I just, have a sleep? Want to be fresh-'
'Sure. I'll set my alarm for what, 5:30?'

We lie down on his single bed. I breathe him in and hold his hand, pressing against his warm body. His lips brush mine. Those green eyes smile at me and I close my own. I feel his body tight against me and this is the best way I've ever fallen asleep.

The open-plan newsroom houses at least ten desks, all adorned with varying attempts at Christmas decorations. Some have made huge efforts – in one case I can barely see the reporter beneath the tinsel - while others have hung a token holly-leaf on the corner of their computer, or dangled mistletoe suggestively above a desk. I knock on Harry Sanderson's door.

It opens. The editor is red faced and sweaty. His tie hangs over his shoulder. His collar looks to be strangling him. He eyes me, confused.

'Amy Minor...' I give him.

His expression doesn't change.

'We spoke last week... I came in and... you said for me to start today... work experience?'

ALL THAT YOU WANT

'Oh... yes... take a seat. I'll be with you shortly.' He gestures to a seat beside the reception desk and disappears back inside his office.

Perching on the edge of the chair, I peer over the desk to smile at the blonde woman - with non-existent eyebrows who tried to get rid of me last week - but can't make eye-contact because she is on the phone.

Tired remnants of tinsel hang around the editor's office. I stare at his door.

I test the pens I brought and throw away those that don't work.

I go to the toilet.

I write the date in my notepad.

A suited reporter with mistletoe above his desk leans back cheekily as a young girl passes him. She playfully bats him away. Then, an older woman approaches. He leans towards her, apparently expecting her to wave off his advances, but she dives onto his lap and plants a snog on his face.

Wolf-whistles and laughter erupt from around the newsroom, and I fight back a smile from my seat at the edge.

Half an hour has gone and Harry Sanderson has not emerged from his fort.

As I shuffle to stop my tights riding down, I spot the coat pegs by the front door. Picking up my coat, I walk towards them.

'I was just about to suggest that.'

Turning, I and am greeted by the sharp green eyes of No-Eyebrows peering over her desk.

'You might be better to come back another day. Mr Sanderson is very busy.'

'But...' I hover, not knowing whether to hang up my coat and persevere or to put it on and leave. Then I think of falling asleep in Lenny's arms last night, and remember why I'm here. 'Could you just... ask him if he wants me to stay... or if I should just go home?'

No-Eyebrows sighs. She huffs into Harry's office and yanks the door closed behind her.

71

I hold my coat and shuffle between the seat and the door. I should just go. I was kidding myself I was good enough to do this.

No-Eyebrows re-emerges. 'He said go in.'

I stare. Throwing my coat onto a peg, I run into Harry's office.

Mr Sanderson, sitting at his messy desk, is just as red-faced and harassed as he had been thirty minutes ago.

'Anna, would you take these to the photocopier and get me thirty-five copies of each?' He puts the papers on the end of his desk and looks back at his computer.

I blink. 'Sure.'

The photocopier is in the corner of the main office. I do as I've been asked and return to Harry.

'Thanks, Anna.'

I push my hair behind my ear. 'It's… Amy.'

His face and neck grow even pinker. 'Sorry. Amy. Could you do me a huge favour? It would make my life easier if that filing cabinet was organised. Actually, before that can you make us a coffee? Leanne, the girl by the corner, will show you where the coffee machine is. Mine's white, no sugar.'

I tell myself to focus on why I'm here, and convince myself I can put up with anything.

When I reach the coffee machine, the brunette woman, who Harry pointed out as Leanne, looks up. 'Oh, are you making coffee?' She stands and calls, 'Who's for coffee?'

My heart sinks at the chorus of, 'Me please,' from the twenty-strong staff.

During the next two hours, between sorting through Harry's files and making a second round of teas, I remind myself I matter. This is about more than just seeing Lenny at night. Lenny thinks I am worth something and he's right. What would he think if he could see me now, downtrodden and making teas? I haven't dared make one for myself, but I can taste the smell that wafts in the air. I hand them round the main office and step into Harry's.

'Hi. White, no sugar.'

'Thanks. So, how you finding your first day?'

ALL THAT YOU WANT

'Good... good.'

'Good.'

My shoulders stiffen. I feel my chest rise. This is my chance. 'Actually, Mr Sanderson... I'd really like to... be more involved, you know, in the journalistic side of things... to maybe, shadow someone...'

His eyes focus outside of his office door that I've left open. 'Leanne!'

The brunette's arms are piled high as she runs to the door. 'Make it quick, Harry.'

'Take Amy with you.'

I stare at him.

'Don't just stand there girl, you'll make Leanne late.'

I don't need telling again.

'No. You stay here this time. Tidy up the files or something while I'm gone.'

'But the Greenpeace story has to be done by the end of the day-'

'I'll be back in time.' She shoots out of the door, leaving me standing there with the mugs.

Placing both drinks down, I sit in Leanne's seat. On the computer screen is an e-mail. It's from James.

'Hi Gorgeous. Come to my flat a.s.a.p. We can make up properly xx'

I fly out of the door. I look both ways down the street. But the little sneak has gone.

Deflated, I drift back into the office. I fall into Leanne's chair and sip the bitter coffee. I grimace. I had meant to drink my tea. But the hot bitterness fills me anew.

'Right,' I place the mug down and sit up straight. I can do this. I'm Amy Minor, girlfriend of Lenny Hunter. I open a new document and begin to type.

Just before five, Harry emerges from his office and strides over to me. 'Where's Leanne?'

'She... had to run out. Some hot story.'

'Oh. She get the Greenpeace article finished before she went?'

'It's here. It's done.'

He leans over my shoulder. 'These photos are bit dodgy.'

'And then, she ambled back in at five thirty and Harry was all full of praise; "*Well done on the Greenpeace article, Leanne,*" and do you know what? She lapped it all up.'

We are sitting in Lenny's caravan drinking lemonade. The dim light from the lamp catches his stubble makes his cheek bone golden. I've never been so glad a day is over. If only I could ditch the office and stay in here for rest of my stay.

He looks at the newspaper article, with one name, which is not Amy Minor. 'You're a good writer, Amy.'

'Huh. No-one's gonna take the work-experience girl seriously. The scatty, self-absorbed editor doesn't even know my name.'

ALL THAT YOU WANT

'Well you've got to make him know your name; you've just got to show them you can write. Because you certainly can't take photos.'

I thump his side.

'Ow,' he laughs. 'Go on, show them. Write something, then take it to the boss and see if he'll print it.'

I raise my eyebrows. 'What do you suggest I write?'

He grins. 'How about, an exclusive interview…'

'With who?'

'With the star of blockbuster-in-the-making, *Buzzard Block*,' he cries

'Who, Jenny Green?' I tease.

He digs his elbow into me.

'Ow!'

'I'll talk to the director tomorrow and see what we're allowed to disclose. We can't tell you media folk just anything, you know.'

'Mr Sanderson…' I step into his office, sheet of paper in hand.

'Make it quick. I want to be out of here early. We've got the New-Year's-Eve party to sort out, and Leanne's let me down on the film reviews.'

'I've written a piece… it might fit in place of the film reviews.' Gingerly, I pass him the paper for scrutiny.

He casts his eyes over it. I hold my breath for the verdict. He frowns. 'An interview with… How did you get this?'

I smile. 'I used my journalistic skills.'

'Ok, I haven't got time to hear it, I'm just glad you got it. We're going to run it.' Clutching my interview, he dashes to the door. He turns back. 'Amy, will you do work experience here again in your Easter holidays?'

Beyond the hedge we can hear the electric bustle of London at night. The air is icy. The city is waiting for the countdown.

'Who'd have thought it,' Lenny says, 'you, a journalist.'

'You'd better believe it.' I wave the article under his nose. 'It's right there in print. What a wonderful, fair editor Harry Sanderson is.'

Lenny laughs. 'That's not how you described him a few nights ago. What was it, scatty? Self-absorbed?'

'No! Would I ever say that about the brilliant guy who put my name in print?' I giggle.

I told my grandparents I was going to the paper's New Year's Eve party. Grandad wanted to drop me there at eight and pick me up at twelve-thirty. That was fine. Where I am in between, who knows? Nobody at the paper has noticed me enough in the office; why should they notice if I'm at the office-party or not?

I stayed at the party for twenty minutes, then slipped out.

On meeting Lenny I laughed because he wore his ridiculous black disguise again –his long coat and twenties hat. But nobody noticed him. We made our way to the river and are now sitting on the bank wrapped in gloves and scarves.

We'll watch the countdown and then Lenny will walk me back to the party in time for Granddad to pick me up.

Sitting close together to keep warm, we can see our breath in front of us. Lights sparkle up from the black water.

'You know, you couldn't have done it without me,' Lenny grins, holding the printed newspaper article in front of him.

'It's not what I wrote *about* that makes it a good story. It's the way I wrote it,' I tease. 'I could have written about anything; I've obviously got talent.'

'Well, it helps to have an interesting subject matter.'

'Who wants to hear about you?' I joke.

He puts his arm around me. 'We're both on track for our dream career now.'

'You're there, Lenny.'

'Well. Nearly there, maybe. And you will be soon.'

'Lois Lane, eat your heart out.'

'I guess you can't be that bad if they've asked you back.'

This is definitely the beginning of something.

From over the hedge, the chant begins. 'Ten! Nine! Eight!'

I am excited for what the new year will bring, as Lenny and I join in. 'Seven! Six! Five!'

He squeezes me closer to him.

'Four! Three! Two! One! Happy New Year!'

Lenny throws both arms around me. 'Happy new year.' He kisses me as the fireworks crackle in the water.

13

Kiantown, Spring Term 2001

'Yea we just lay there. Just went to sleep. It was… nice,' I tell Jodie down the phone.

'Ah, it's so sweet, just to lie their spending time together.' I can hear she is smiling.

'You're softening to him now,' I laugh.

'Now I know he's treating you properly.'

'Amy,' calls Mum from the kitchen. 'Will you come and set the table?'

'Gotta go. Dinner's ready. Happy new year!'

My family sits around the table in the middle of the hot gravy smell.

Beth keeps her little eyes on me all through dinner. 'Did you have a good time in London, Amy?'

I saw at my pork chop. When we were little, Mum used to cook us fried chicken or Cuban food. Over the years, her cuisine has gradually become more integrated. Now, her full weekly menu comprises of traditional British meals.

'Yeah,' I reply to my glowering sister. 'I really enjoyed working at the paper. I really think it's what I want to do.'

'Lucky they've asked you back at Easter isn't it?' Beth stabs her fork into a carrot. 'Remind me, why can't you work for the papers around here?'

I'm floating in a bubble and she is not getting near me. I smile sweetly. 'Well, Bethany, London will open more doors for me. It's… where everything's happening.'

'Listen, Darling,' Mum says. 'We're really proud of you to be asked back to work there again at Easter. But, listen, just

ALL THAT YOU WANT

remember how old your grandparents are. It might be a bit much for them having a teenager there for two weeks-'

'Mum, I won't give them any grief,' I smile, assuredly.

'What your mum's saying,' Dad chips in, 'is, just make sure you pull your weight. Don't make extra work for them.' He puts his knife and fork down. 'Right then girls, will you wash up please?'

Beth pushes her chair back. 'It's Amy's turn.'

'I don't care whose turn it is. Sort it out between you.' He and Mum retreat to the living room.

Beth closes the kitchen door and leans her back against it. The eleven-year-old scowls up at me with her piggy eyes. 'You know you're doing it or I'll tell. I don't even have to say it anymore.'

I cross my arms. This is wearing thin. 'Beth, I'm sick of this. I'm not letting you hold this over me anymore.' I am above everything. 'Just go and tell them. No-one will believe you.' I walk towards the door, which Beth is still standing in front of. I reach around her for the handle.

My little sister doesn't move. She stands at her full height, up to my armpit, and opens her mouth. 'Mum!'

'For God's sake, Beth, grow up. You're at secondary school now.'

Footsteps move towards us along the hall. Beth moves away from the door and Mum opens it.

'Why *are* you shouting, Beth?'

'Amy's going out with Lenny Hunter.'

Mum laughs. 'Amy, you know better than to wind your sister up.'

I laugh and start to run the water. 'She came up with this one on her own.'

Beth puts her hands on her hips. 'I saw them. He came up to her window like Romeo.'

I add a squirt of washing up liquid and the warm apple smell steams into the kitchen. 'I wish.'

'Ok,' Mum says. 'You can play your game after you've washed up.'

'But, Mum, they got together when they met in America! Why do think she wants to go to London? How do you think she got that interview?'

I scoff and turn off the tap

'Bethany, I won't tell you again. Wash up so you can do your homework.'

I pick up a tea-towel. 'I'll dry.'

Mum turns to leave.

'But Mum...'

'Beth, get on with it.' She closes the door.

I hand my sister the rubber gloves. 'If you think *Mum*'s laughing at you imagine how stupid you'll look when you tell your friends.'

Beth scowls and sinks her hands into the washing-up bowl.

Sitting in English, I stare out of the window. It's raining.

From my seat I can see the gym. I used to sit in this seat after the bell had gone, taking my time packing my things away, waiting for the year above to disperse out across the playground after their P.E. lesson. Now, I laugh to myself at the idea.

'Amy Minor?' Mr Banton calls.

I catch myself laughing. 'Yessir?' I rip my forehead away from the window. Only now do I feel the cold.

Even after almost five years I haven't stopped noticing how Banton's moustache wriggles. 'Would you care to give me the answer?'

I look frantically around the classroom. All eyes are on me.

'Do you even know what I just asked you, Amy?'

I feel like that squirming caterpillar on Banton's top lip.

'This is your GCSE, Amy, not mine. You might want to pay attention if you want to pass this exam.'

Jodie mouths to me, 'Iambic pentameter.'

I know she is making up the first thing that comes to her. I look down at my *Romeo and Juliet*. 'Sorry Sir.'

He turns back to the board.

Jodie's brown eyes grin at me.

Banton has asked me to stay behind after the lesson. I sink into my chair as the rest of the class leaves.

The English teacher sits in front of me, his upper-lip wriggling. 'Do you want to tell me what's going on?'

'What do you mean, Sir?'

'Amy, you're fantastic at English. I've always seen great potential in you, since you first started in year seven. When my daughter was your age, she became distracted, just like you have been. It's not just your exams, Amy. I'm concerned about your well-being. If you'd rather talk to Mrs Baker, that's fine; it doesn't have to be me. As long as you've got someone you can talk to about what's on your mind. *Have* you got someone you can talk to?'

'Yes, Sir.'

'Good, good, I know exam pressure can be difficult. But you're a bright girl, Amy. If you put your mind to it, you could have a great future. You just need to focus. You've worked too hard to let distractions get in the way now. Especially if it's over some boy. In my experience, it's usually a boy. Am I right?'

I don't know what to say. Then it comes to me. I tell him about the paper in London.

Well, of course, that changes things. What initiative I've shown. How *wonderful* that I'm trying to make a head-start for my future. No *wonder* I've been distracted. What an exciting and pro-active thing to do with a young person's free time. But of course, I must still concentrate on my studies. And I *must* bring in some of my articles to show him.

I leave the classroom wondering how I managed to wriggle out.

'I've never known Banton to be so caring and concerned in nearly five years,' Jodie declares. 'Maybe he's pushing for results. That's all that matters to teachers. Statistics.'

I giggle. 'I don't know, he seemed quite genuine. Showing his fatherly side, maybe. He was comparing me to his daughter. I can't believe that newspaper stuff came to me.'

'Who'd have thought it, Jodie laughs. 'Old Banton: The stuffy old-school teacher with a secret fatherly side.'

'I'm just glad I got away,' I twinkle.

I pass through the living-room to pick up some school books. Mum, Dad and Bethany sit in front of the TV.

'Stick the film on, Beth,' Mum asks my sister.

Mum and Dad have bought this new DVD player and are dying to trying it out.

Beth is making her way to the set when I notice the screen 'Wait, wait.'

She looks at me and rolls her eyes. 'Oh, she's obsessed with him.' Since our little head-to-head over the washing up, she's given up trying to tell anyone what she's privy to.

An interviewer and his interviewee sit across from each other on plush couches. Behind them, the walls are white, and box-shelves stand, holding a single item on each.

'Come on, Lenny,' the trendy presenter plugs. 'Spill. There must be a special lady in your life.'

Lenny Hunter is sitting bolt upright with his body pointing purposefully toward his relaxed acquaintance. His eyes, however, occasionally flick in the direction of the screen. He is looking right at me.

'Well... I really don't have much time for romance... My schedule keeps me busy.' He is dressed gorgeously in a white shirt and dark jeans. His skin and hair are flawless, while his eyes sparkle at me. His smile gives the pretence of a laid-back aura, but I know Lenny. He is tense. I swear he sneaks me a secret glance.

Beth huffs. 'Can I just put the DVD on?' She is asking our parents, not me.

I shrug. 'Enjoy your film,' and I retreat with my books.

'Don't you want to watch it with us, Ames?' Mum calls.

'Work to do,' I reply. They're just like videos anyway, surely.

In the bedroom, I text Lenny. 'I saw your interview. Call me when you get chance.'

I float on my coursework for an hour or so until he rings.

'I was terrible,' he confesses. 'As always.'

'You were great.'

'You have no idea how many takes they had to do. It's always the same; I look at the camera. I get, "Mr Hunter, would you mind facing the presenter? Pretend the camera isn't there."

ALL THAT YOU WANT

But the more I try to ignore it, the more aware I am of it. The take they finally got was the best I could do.' He laughs.

'Well, you would never know. You looked like you were taking the whole thing in your stride.'

'I was still glancing at the cameraman. I can't help it,' he babbles. 'And sometimes, I answer the questions too shortly, with yes or no, when I'm meant to answer if the interviewer's not there. Like, they'll say, "Tell us what it was like working with Jenny Green?" and I'll say, "Yea, it was cool," when what I should say is, "Working with Jenny Green was..." I don't know, something better than "cool".'

I marvel at this perfect being stumbling over what he portrays with such ease. It's hard to comprehend he struggles with *any*thing.

I move to my wall calendar and cross off another day until I return to London.

The highlight of spring-term is Sarah coming home from college for half-term. Her chocolate hair has grown.

'Sarah!' I hug my next-door neighbour as she tumbles out of her mum's car. 'I've missed you.'

The older girl does not return the embrace. 'Well, I was home at Christmas but you stayed in London.'

'I know.' I shuffle. 'I'm sorry.' I have been a little wrapped up, I suppose. 'We'll make up for it this week though. We'll... have girly video nights and go shopping.'

Sarah's face softens. 'I suppose I can't be peed off just because I've missed you. Good on you, Ames, doing this work experience. I'm proud of you.'

I grin. 'So tonight then, chick-flicks and chocolate?'

*

Jodie, Annie and I stand at the top of the steps outside the main school doors. The sun shines brightly. The white shirts we left for school in this morning are covered in blue and black ink scribbles. So are the leavers' books in our bags. We've ignored the teachers' stern reminders that we have to wear our school shirts for our exams in May.

MICHELLE WOOLLACOTT

We wear our hair in pigtails and have drawn black eye-pencil freckles on our cheeks. We are all donned in mini-skirts and coloured stripy tights.

At the bottom of the steps, other year-elevens are squealing and shouting. A lot of it has to do with the bottles that clink in their bags. Some of them are just high on freedom. They squirt each other with water-pistols and throw water-bombs and flour-bombs at each other.

The fire bell has rung three times today. The final time the bell rang was just now. The end of the day. It will be the last time we will hear it. The last time we have come out of these doors.

More year-elevens burst out of the doors behind us and charge down the steps.

'Come on girls.' Jodie links both of our arms. 'Watch out world, here we come!' We run down the steps with the swarm, into the chaos, ready to get drenched.

All we have to do now is come in after Easter for our GCSEs. Meanwhile, I get to spend two blissful weeks in London.

London, April 2001

'Well, Amy,' Harry Sanderson says, beetroot-faced. We are sitting opposite each other in his office. A bead of sweat runs slowly down the editor's forehead. 'I appreciate your keenness and willingness to come back and volunteer with us again. You're a quick learner and a good writer, and we really like you. We would love for you to come back and work with us again in your summer holidays. But, it's not fair for us to keep you so long unpaid. And, unfortunately, there are currently no vacancies for paid work.' The drip rests on his eyebrow.

I force a smile. 'I understand.'

14

That night in the caravan, Lenny puts his arm around me. His hair is a little lighter from the sun. 'It's their loss. They'll be sorry when you're successful-'

'No, I can't expect it. But how am I going to come back to London in the summer holidays?'

He looks at me. 'You have to come back.'

'Yeah, how?'

'Well… just run away and live under my bed.'

'Huh.' We've got two measly weeks together and then what? How will I get to see him again if I don't have the paper as an alibi?

'You can work for another London paper,' he declares. 'Harry will give you a reference. We'll write you up a C.V and send it to all of the newspapers and magazines around here. And I'm sure you can butter up your parents.' He squeezes me. 'We'll get you back here.' He reaches into a drawer and pulls out a pen and paper. I feel a surge run through my body. He wants me here.

Kiantown, Summer Term 2001

The examination hall is deathly silent. The words on the question-paper swim before my eyes, the letters as disobedient and wayward as a year-eleven on her last day of school.

Lenny was brilliant at my C.V. I lost count of how many papers we posted it to.

I told Grandma, Grandad, Mum and Dad that Harry had asked me back for two weeks after my exams. That will give me a bit of time. All that is left now is to wait to hear back from the other papers. I don't even care that I'm deceiving them.

The year-elevens surround me in silence, focused on their own little tables and I wonder what would happen if we all burst into a raucous anarchy.

I stare at the question paper, forcing the letters to come to order and make sense.

London, Summer 2001

'Amy Minor? I'm Suzie Strite, editor of *The Capital Gazette*. Come through.'

It is my first morning back in London and I have said goodbye to my grandparents and headed 'off to the paper.' What I hadn't mentioned was that I have an interview at an entirely different newspaper.

Ms Strite's office is minimalist and smells new. Floor to ceiling windows look out to the surrounding sky-scrapers. Suzie Strite is in her early thirties with blonde curly hair. She wears a smart suit and is slim and manicured. She takes a seat and gestures for me to do the same. 'So you're looking for temporary summer work.' Ms Strite scans my C.V. She looks at me. 'You're... s-sixteen?'

'Yes.'

'Sixteen and you've done this?' She looks down at the article on her lap that I sent with my C.V. 'So... was this work experience organised through your school?'

'No, I arranged it myself.'

'This is good writing, Amy.' She holds up the Lenny Hunter interview. 'I called you to interview because of this. And your... get up and go is extremely impressive.'

'Well, I really want to be a writer.' *I really want to stay in London...*

'Is that your portfolio?'

I hand her my folder with the articles I wrote at Easter.

Ms. Strite looks through them.

'Well thank you, Amy. You're a very talented young lady. And you make opportunities for yourself; you realise that things don't just fall into your lap. It was lovely to meet you. We'll be in touch.'

ALL THAT YOU WANT

The sun warms my arms and the grass tickles my bare legs as I sit in the park, re-reading the same paragraph of *High Fidelity* over and over. Every now and then a quiet breeze blows my mousey ponytail. My grandparents think I'm at work for Harry Sanderson.

I can't read this book with the heavy sounds of traffic all around me.

My second and last interview is for this afternoon. It is already Friday of the first week. All week I've spent my days sitting in parks and wandering the streets, a still outsider while the city rushes around me. The nights in Lenny's caravan have been on a timer. Only a week left after this. If I don't get either of these jobs, I have no excuse for being in London. I look at my watch. Another hour before I have to make my way to the interview.

I just hear my phone ring below the constant noise.

'Amy? Suzie Strite, from *The Capital Gazette*.'

*

Grandma's mug smashes on the chess-board patterned kitchen floor. 'Oh Amy, you gave me a fright.'

'Sorry.' I find the dustpan and brush and begin sweeping up the shattered blue china.

'What are you doing home at lunchtime?' She passes me a plastic bag.

'I've... got something to talk to you about.' I drop the broken pieces into the carrier and put them in the bin. 'Where's Grandad?'

'Gone to get a paper.' She tears off some kitchen roll. 'What's happened, Love?'

I take a piece from her and mop up the spilt tea. I don't look at her. 'Harry Sanderson —you know, the editor- has... employed somebody who can be there all year round. So... they don't need me anymore.'

'Oh, Darling, that's rotten.' She squeezes my arm. 'Let me make another cup of tea.'

'But the thing is...' I stand up. 'He... Mr Sanderson... felt bad about it, so he's passed my details on... to another newspaper.' I pass my grandmother two fresh cups.

'Oh that's brilliant! So you'll be doing work experience at a different newspaper while you're here?'

'Well, not work experience. They're... going to pay me.' I take the milk from the fridge.

'Oh well done, Darling! That shows what they think of you!'

'Well, the thing I wanted to talk to you about is...' I sit at the table and push my hair out of my eyes. 'The contract would be... for the whole summer...'

Grandma turns to face me. 'The whole summer? But... you're only supposed to be staying with us for two weeks...'

'I know.' I shake my head. 'It's too much to ask, I'm sorry.' I can't believe I'm lying to her like this, my sweet grandmother who only wants to help me with my career.

Grandma sits with me. She sips her tea. There is a twinkle in her eye. 'Well... I suppose... it would be a shame to give up this chance. Wouldn't it?'

'Yes... but, well... it would be an amazing opportunity,' I say slowly. 'And... I'll help around the house, and I could... give you money for keeping me now I'm going to be paid...'

Grandma smiles. 'How can I say no to my granddaughter's *amazing opportunity*?' She winks. 'You leave your mum and dad to me.'

'Really?' I put down my tea. 'Thank you!' I hug her, pushing down the pang of guilt and allowing elation to engulf me.

That night I run to Lenny. 'I've got *The Capital Gazette* job!'

He picks me up. 'Amy! That's great!' He hugs me tight and kisses me. 'Well done!'

We begin to stroll.

'I already knew you were a good writer, and now they see what I see in you.'

'But I tricked my grandparents. I'm taking advantage of them aren't I?'

'Yep.'

'You're not supposed to agree.'

He laughs. 'No, your grandparents like to think they're doing something good for you. It's not hurting them.'

We reach the caravan and step inside. He squeezes me tight. He smells of the cheap aftershave I bought him for Christmas. I

ALL THAT YOU WANT

can't believe he's actually wearing it. 'I've got you all summer,' he grins, 'even if you did con your grandparents for it.'

'Two whole months.' This is longest time we'll have ever spent together.

He smiles at me, his arms strong around my waist. His normally light-brown hair is now almost totally sun-bleached. 'I've got something to tell you.'

'What?'

'Well... sit down.' We sit on the bed. 'We're going to finish filming *Buzzard Block* soon.'

'Oh. So... you'll be going back to the States.'

'No,' he grins. 'I've got a part in another British film.'

'Oh, well done!' I hug him. Then I stop. 'But, your first film was... Hollywood. Don't you want to go for another big, blockbuster, Hollywood film?'

'No, not if means I can't be with you.'

'You're... doing this to be with me?'

'Yes,' he says. 'Because... I love you.'

The words hang in the air, then shoot me in the chest.

He shrinks back into himself. 'Is that alright..?'

I dive at him and throw my arms around him. 'I love you.' I look at him and I know I do. Suddenly I want him in a way I've never wanted anyone before. I want his arms around me. I want to feel his body. I want to be part of him more than I ever have before. I kiss him. I push him down.

He hits me away with a pillow and we are play-fighting, laughing and writhing. My ponytail has fallen loose.

Before I know it I am undoing his shirt to reveal his beautiful chest.

He holds my hand. 'Are you sure?'

I nod. 'Yes.'

The summer is glorious. Working for the paper means I am out in the sun almost every day. Each day lifts the grey from the buildings and warms my face, clinging to me, wrapping me as the sky-scrapers stretch around me. Every day sweat trickles down my back. I am continually dazzled by the reflection from car bonnets and food-wrappers on the ground. Scents of sun-cream mixed with exhaust fumes fill the air. The ground and the walls are burning to touch. My pearly white legs are as dazzling as my white strap-tops. Soft-tops and double-deckers cook in traffic-jams. The parks are always filled with picnickers. I envy the kids paddling in fountains and streams.

I embrace the work. I know this is the job for me. Just as Lenny knows his job is for him.

But what I love more than the days is the cool relief of the nights.

In mid-August I receive my exam results. I will be joining Sarah at college. Suzie says I can come back at Christmas and Easter. Everything is going right.

And then those planes hit those towers and the world changes.

15

College, Autumn Term 2001

Annie, frightened, hair on end; Jodie, eyes wide and eager; and me, somewhere in between, lug our cases off the train onto the swarming platform. We have arrived at college.

My wild eyes scan the chaos. Hundreds of sixteen and seventeen year olds, whose small towns don't offer sufficient quantity or quality of further education, have all flocked to the little county city, my contemporaries and I among them, and every one of us, it seems, today. We are all hermit crabs who have outgrown our old shells, running naked and frantic about this train station, desperate to find the comfort of a new home.

Through the bedlam, my eyes fall upon my new shell. Between the hoards of students, I see the soft chocolate hair and the beaming smile of Sarah.

We push through the crowd towards each other, and her familiar arms encase me.

Kay appears behind her, cold eyed. Thomas is beside her, grinning and waving at us.

While Sarah moves to greet Jodie and Annie, who have caught up behind me, I move to make efforts with the Ice Queen. She stands rigid, her posture as spikey as her features, and permits herself to be hugged.

'I'll take that.' Thomas reaches for Jodie's suitcase.

'But you're holding *my* bag,' Kay indicates to the over-sized handbag Thomas is carrying.

'But I've got two hands.' He holds out his free hand to prove it.

Kay grabs it. 'To hold mine.'

'But...' Thomas begins to protests but decides against it.

'Come on, girls,' Sarah beams, grabbing my case. 'Let's show you your new home!' She links my arm and forces us through the hubbub and I feel like it's the first day of school again; with Sarah guiding me, I can do this. We glide on, with Jodie swinging her curvaceous hips and Annie pushing up her owl glasses beside us, and Kay –her black straight hair not blowing an inch out of place- dragging Thomas behind.

Sarah helps us haul our baggage up the stairs of the student flats. Kay trails behind, arms folded.

When we reach the top, Sarah fumbles with her key. 'This is it!' she exclaims, bursting through the door.

We find ourselves standing in a barely decorated corridor, whose carpet needs vacuuming badly. On either side are two doors. Sarah opens the first. 'This is mine and Kay's room.' She uncovers a messy twin room with bright duvets. Books and clothes are scattered about, and posters and photos decorate the walls.

Sarah steps to the next door. 'And this is your room!' She reveals a bedroom housing three single beds. The walls, floors and desks are a blank canvass for us to make our mark. 'Why don't you get yourselves unpacked, then we'll get a takeaway?' our mother-hen beams. The three of us bundle into our new room.

On the coffee table in the sitting room lie the remains of our Chinese food and half a cheap bottle of wine. Thomas has returned to his own shared flat.

It is early evening and we sit, stuffed, on the shabby sofas, wine glasses in hand, and I don't think any of us could manage another mouthful of egg-fried-rice.

'Well, of course, Thomas is going to propose to me as soon as we finish college. I told him we've got to finish our studies first.'

Jodie laughs. 'So you've told him when he's got to, spontaneously, ask you to marry him?'

'There's nothing wrong with a man knowing who's boss,' Kay retorts.

Nobody speaks for a moment.

ALL THAT YOU WANT

'Anyway, what about these terrorists? They're saying they might target London next,' Kay tells us. 'Amy, I don't suppose you'll go back to do that journalism anymore, then?'

'What do your parents say about it all?' Sarah asks me.

'My mum and dad think we can't let extremists dictate our lives,' I tell them.

Jodie pipes up beside me; 'Amy can't put her life –and her career- on hold because of some might-be's and suppositions.'

Kay raises her eyebrows. 'So you're still gonna go to London in the holidays?'

'Try and stop me.'

'I hardly think it's worth risking your life,' Kay continues. 'There are newspapers and magazines all over the country. You don't have to work in London.'

'So don't go to London then, Kay,' Jodie almost spits. 'But don't tell Amy what to do. It doesn't affect you. Since when do you care about Amy, anyway?'

'Hey, hey,' butts in Sarah, ever the diplomat. 'We're all entitled to our opinions. We'll *worry* about you, Ames, that's all. But it's your decision.'

Kay tries to say something but Sarah spins her head round.

'Let's talk about something else, eh?' Her voice is soft but her eyes bear into Kay.

None of us speaks for a few seconds. Annie chews on some prawn toast and keeps her head down.

'I might need your help, Annie,' Sarah begins. 'I'm helping my little brother with his homework. He e-mails it to me. The trouble is, I'm a bit out of touch. You guys might remember more than I do about GCSEs.'

'Oh, yes, of course,' Annie nods.

Kay scowls. 'Let him get on with it by himself. We all had to.' She eyes me over the top of her wine glass. 'I got an e-mail from Matt today. He's in the second year of his apprenticeship up in Newcastle.'

Sarah darts her eyes to her companion. 'Kay!'

I smile. 'It's all right; you can talk about him in front of me.'

Sarah frowns.

Kay smiles coolly. 'So how *is* your love life, Amy?'

Sarah shoots Kay another look, but the witch keeps her eyes on me.

I laugh. 'Nothing to report.'

'You can't stay a virgin forever, Sandra Dee.'

Jodie and I exchange a glance.

'You know,' Kay continues, 'Thomas and me are going to move in together after college. And Sarah and Alec are going strong.'

'Well I'm thrilled for you both, but I don't need a boyfriend to be happy.'

'Annie and I aren't seeing anyone either,' Jodie puts in.

Kay smirks. 'Annie's always too busy with her studies, and band, and church, and Jodie, you're seeing a different boy every week.'

This term is going to be a long slog after the breeze of summer. I am already living for Christmas.

Sarah gives me a cheeky smile. 'We'll find you a fit college boy up here, don't you worry, Sweet.'

I roll my eyes. 'Sarah!'

'On a completely separate note,' Sarah grins conspicuously, 'a gang of us might go to the cinema next week, if you guys wanna come?'

Kay spins round to Sarah. 'I thought it was just us?'

'Well, we'll sort it out nearer the time.' Sarah waves a dismissive hand. She looks at me. 'I promised your mum I'd look after you. We'll sort you out,' my surrogate sister grins, clinking her glass against Kay's, then raising it to me.

My heart sinks.

It's not long before Jodie has stalked out the student hang-outs and eyed up the lads. She prowls through the college corridors like she's in a night-club. I wish I could 'own it' the way she does.

Lenny and I speak every night.

Lectures have begun and Annie, Jodie and I are in our bedroom working on an English assignment.

Annie sits at her neat desk while Jodie and I lie on our stomachs on her bed, books sprawled out in front of us.

'That Iago is one devious character.' Jodie chews her pencil.

ALL THAT YOU WANT

'Othello's not stupid enough to fall for it though, is he?' I muse.

Annie turns to us with her innocent eyes. 'Maybe Iago will repent in the end and admit he was making it all up.'

There is a knock at the bedroom door. Kay pokes her head round. Her face looks different. It takes me a moment to put my finger on why. Then I realise. She is *smiling*. 'You guys up for the cinema tonight? Alec is coming, and Thomas. A big group of us! It'll be fun.'

Jodie and I look at each other, then at Annie.

'Yea, we'll come,' Annie smiles.

'Cool, great, can't wait.' Kay skips out of the room. She actually *skips*.

'You see,' Annie smiles through her big owl lenses. 'She's making an effort.'

Jodie and I look at Annie, then at each other.

'And Iago might turn out good in the end,' Jodie mumbles.

The five of us girls stand outside the cinema in front of a big poster of Lenny Hunter's face, and the title, *Buzzard Block*.

Three guys; Thomas, Alec and someone else, emerge from around the corner. Alec puts his arm round Sarah.

'Is Dad eating properly? Are you checking?' Sarah asks Alec.

'Oh yeah –we had beef last night,' he reassures her. 'Burgers.'

'Alec!' Sarah hits his arm.

'No,' he laughs. 'It was bourguignon; beef bourguignon. With loads of veg,' he grins.

Sarah raises an eyebrow.

Floppy-haired Thomas beams at the three of us first-years. He manages to hug Jodie, Annie and I all at once. 'Hey!'

Kay pulls him away and hits him with a big –too big- snog.

Thomas retreats and put his arm around her. 'Hey, Beautiful.' He turns back to us. 'Um, we brought Gary.' He nods towards his friend. 'Gary, this is Jodie, this is Annie. And *this is Amy*.' His voice notches up on the last four words.

Gary is attempting to rock the Justin Timberlake cornrows-look. 'Good to meet you all,' he says, but he fixes his eyes on me. He steps right in front of Lenny's giant beautiful face,

97

covering most of it. But no matter how much he tries, the cornrows could never eclipse Lenny Hunter

Sarah pipes up; 'Gary, Amy was in London over the summer, working for a newspaper. Guess who she interviewed?' She taps the face on the board behind us.

Thomas' skinny friend pulls at his leather collar. 'Lenny Hunter?'

I feel my cheeks redden. 'Al*right*, Sarah.'

My friend presses on. 'Tell Gary about it, Ames.'

Kay links Thomas' arm and stalks inside, followed by Sarah and Alec.

Jodie tries to rescue me by linking Gary's arm, but he snatches mine in one glide. I turned back in panic to Jodie and Annie, who stand open- mouthed, but before I know it, Gary has whisked me through the doors as slickly as the hair on his head.

Lenny's flawless face takes over the big-screen in front of us.

The cinema is nearly full. Our group fill a dark row near the back. I am sitting between Gary and Jodie.

Jodie offers me the sharer popcorn and I offer her a sip of giant coke. Our arms become tangled as I reach into the box she is holding and she sips from the big cardboard cup in my hand. Giggling, we untangle ourselves. The salty taste makes my tongue curl up. 'I thought you got toffee?'

Suddenly, I feel a hand on my thigh. I spin round and stare at Gary.

'What's so funny?' he presses.

'Nothing; we just got tangled up.'

'*I kinda like this girl*,' Lenny's sexy Chicago accent floats from the screen; from another world to right here in the room. I wish I was with him.

Gary leans in, gel dripping down his temple, and with stale popcorn breath whispers into my ear; 'I'd like to get tangled up with you.'

My body is rigid as he leans closer and his bony hand begins to press into the flesh of my upper leg. His shiny forehead is almost touching mine. His spiky fingers crawl upwards. Too far.

I jump up, knocking the cardboard cup into his lap.

Gary leaps up and yells. 'Crazy bitch!' His crotch is drenched.

I squeeze past everyone without looking at them, but all eyes are on me.

I barge down the steps and finally burst out into the fresh air.

The entourage is hot on my heels. The only person absent is the sleaze-bag. Probably trying to dry his trousers in the gents'.

I am shaking. No man has ever scared me like that before.

Sarah, holding Alec's hand, is first to reach me. 'Did you spill it on purpose?'

My face grows instantly hot. 'He's a creep! Tommy, you have bad taste in friends.'

Kay is next. 'You didn't have to throw a drink over him.'

Jodie is fast behind them. 'He was trying to put his hand up her skirt. And I don't want to know what he was whispering in her ear.'

I'm shaking.

Jodie takes my arm and tries to calm me. 'Ok, remember; men are like mini-skirts.'

But I can't laugh. My heart is still beating fast. I shake my head. I don't want to be here. 'I'm going home.' I turn and flee.

16

The next morning I am the first up. I'm waiting for the kettle to boil and I'm simmering that Sarah could try to set myself up with that creep, but I try to remind myself she meant well.

There's a knock at the door. It's Thomas with an armful of flowers.

'Come in.' I lead him into the kitchen. I stick the flowers in the basin and take out another mug. 'Are these for Her Majesty?'

'Well, you know... to say sorry for last night... the night being ruined and everything.'

'It wasn't your fault.'

'It will be somehow. I brought Gary along, to set you up with, which I'm sure you guessed... and it didn't work out, so everyone missed the film.'

'I doubt you were the master-mind behind the little scheme. You were just doing what you were told, bringing that creep along.'

'Well, I'll still be in the doghouse.'

'Thomas, you're a good bloke. You shouldn't let her push you around.'

Thomas shuffles.

'I wonder if he had to walk home with that damp patch on his jeans?' I giggle.

Thomas laughs. 'Or, can you imagine him in the men's, with his crotch up under the hand-dryer.'

We are both tittering as Kay graces the doorway, arms folded. We immediately stop.

She glares at me. 'You know Gary only tried it on as a favour to Thomas. You don't actually think you're desirable, do you?'

I pick up my tea and slink past her. 'I'll leave you to it.'

It's early evening and Kay and Sarah are studying together in their room.

I tell them I'm reading in my bedroom. I close the door, take my phone from under the mattress and head to the window. I text Lenny. 'I'm free if you are.'

A minute later the phone vibrates.

I answer instantly, whispering, 'Hello?'

'Hi,' comes that voice.

'Sarah and Kay are in the next room, so I have to be quiet.'

'What about Jodie?'

'On a date.'

'I should have known. And Annie?'

'Band practice.'

'You haven't really told me much about Annie. You always mention her in passing but she always seems to be in the background.'

'She's a very, kind of, in-the-background type of girl. Very sweet, very dependable. Reliable. But, she's always quiet. Keeps herself to herself.' I sit on the bed. 'She plays the saxophone. She likes her choir practice. She's something on every evening; she goes to drama club and Christian Union —she's quite religious. What else do you want to know?'

'Well... how's college?'

'Oh, good, the lessons are ok. Sarah and Kay are on my back, prying about my love-life. They've already tried to set me up on a date with a creepy guy.'

'Really?'

'They took me to see your film. I didn't get to see the end because he was such a creep. I had to run out,' I try to laugh and push away the shakes. 'What about you? How's it going on set?' I've been deliberating whether to tell him about Gary. But I decided, why keep any secrets? But I leave out any mention of Matt Scotts.

'Ok, we're getting into it. There are some cool people. I'm getting to know all the cast and crew. We've been for drinks around *London town*. We're going through scripts, running through the first few scenes. Yep, it's all getting started. You are still coming at Christmas aren't you?'

'Yes. Two and a half months.'

'It seems like a lifetime. I'm just keeping my head down at work and hoping it'll go quicker. Keeping busy.'

There's a knock at the door. Sarah opens it just as I stuff the phone under the pillow.

'We're going to get fish and chips. Want anything?'

'Oh, no thanks, I'm fine.'

'Alright. See you in a bit.' She closes the bedroom door. In a few minutes I hear the front door close. I pick up the phone. 'Sorry, Lenny. Are you still there?'

'Yup, still here. Did you get interrupted?'

'Yeah. Sarah and Kay are going to the chippy. Sorry to put the phone down.'

'It's alright.'

'So what are you up to?'

'Just in the caravan, looking through the script. Gotta pack up my stuff soon. I've got some news. So...'

I lie back on the bed and remember his lips on my neck.

'You'll never believe it. I'm moving into a hotel room in a couple weeks. The high-life. So when you come at Christmas, we'll be in luxury.'

'Wow. What's the room like?'

'It'll be beautiful. I won't tell you anymore. It'll be a surprise.'

I giggle. 'I'm really happy for you. You're doing so well.'

'I know, I know. It's all good. So... tell me more about Annie.'

'Why?'

'Because I want to know about your life, and about the people you spend most of your time with. Because I love you, Amy. Because I'm interested. I... want to be able to picture you, and know who you're with, and to know about your past. I know your school-life and your friends mean a lot to you. I want to know all about you.'

I melt into the bed. 'Ok, well... Annie. Annie, Annie. She's always kept her cards close to her chest. There was only one time she really let her guard down. And never again.'

'What happened?

She sat next to this boy, Sam, in French. He was a bit of a... I don't know... he was really cool, really popular, outgoing, bright. Not in our league at all. Annie was always too scared to speak to him.

But then something happened to Sam. Something shook him. He drew into himself. He lashed out at public property –damaged shop-windows in Kiantown square. His schooling started to suffer. He completely changed. I suppose Annie wanted to help him. It took all the courage she had to speak up and offer to help him with his French homework.

At first he didn't want to know. But she persevered. She reached out to him. So they started to spend time together. First it was just French. Then it was English and Maths as well. I suppose Sam was lonely. He went from having loads of mates to having no-one.

It's funny how people can turn on someone like that. They wanted to know him when he was on top. But as soon as he had a real problem, or "went all weird", as some people said, they shut him out. I'm glad I was never in with them. I might be able to count my real friends on one hand, but at least I know they're my real friends. They wouldn't ditch me when the going gets tough.

Anyway, that's why Sam gave in to Annie's help; he didn't have anyone else. She may have been helping him with homework, but she liked to think she was helping him through a tough time as well. Sam would never admit it, but Annie did help him. But after a while, he started to get picked on for hanging around with her. And he wouldn't ever stick up for her. He would just keep his head down. Eventually, after a few months, he started to get over his tortured-soul image a little bit. Sam had it in him to be cool. He calmed down, stopped being "all weird"; started to laugh off his "friends'" taunts. He began to give it back to them; to banter. And then it turned into a joke. They could see the old Sam coming back. He had to, I suppose, to survive. But, the more he started to get back in with them, the less time he spent with Annie. She held on for as long as she could; tried to arrange study meetings with him, but he was always too busy with his old friends.

Eventually, Sam acted almost as of the whole thing had never happened. He stopped even, really, acknowledging her.

'Poor girl. She put herself out there, and he treated her like that,' Lenny laments.

'She's the… the introverted bookworm who wore her heart on her sleeve.'

'Complicated guy. Didn't know when he had a good thing.'

I wish so much I was with Lenny right now and could hold his hand. And feel his chest against me. That we could just lie together and fall asleep.

I hear the latch on the front door and a waft of salt and vinegar disperses into the flat. 'Sarah and Kay are back with chips. I'm gonna go and pinch some. Night, Lenny. I love you.'

'I love you too, Amy.'

17

It's student night at The Basement club. Jodie and I are shaking our booties to *Stuck in the Middle with You* by Louise - Jodie with ease and sexiness, while I am clumsy and awkward. Two lads stand at the side of the dance-floor, noticeably watching her – and she gives them a show. I imagine Lenny approaching to ask me to dance.

On the way here, Jodie told me that Grace Harris in our English class told her Greasy Gary had tried it on with her, and tried putting his hand up her skirt too. She also heard a similar story about the barmaid from the student bar.

The room is filled with a smoky scent and I can taste it.

In a dark corner of the room, I spot Sarah talking to a guy in a white t-shirt who I don't know. They are both looking in our direction. I ignore them and continue to dance. Jodie winks at a nearby bloke. The lights are dim and club is buzzing.

I feel a tap on my shoulder. It's the white-t-shirted guy Sarah has been talking to. He smiles at me and his teeth are as white as his shirt. He is built like he plays rugby.

'Do you want to dance?'

Under other circumstances I could find him good-looking. I can see Sarah over his shoulder, watching from the side of the dance floor, grinning at me. I look at the white-t-shirted-rugby-guy. 'Sorry, I'm with my friend.' I gesture to Jodie.

The music is loud so he leans in, putting his hand on my waist. 'Can I get you a drink, maybe?'

I lean back. 'Sorry, I...' I nod towards Jodie again.

All of a sudden, she grabs me and turns me to face her. At once, my best friend is planting a soft, sloppy snog on my mouth.

Once she's let go, she turns to the poor rugby-player guy - who stands as open-mouthed as I do - and says, 'Sorry, mate.' She wraps her arm around my shoulder and sticks out her ample chest.

He holds his palms towards us and backs away, but he is smiling. 'Hey, if that's your thing, that's your thing.' He grins and turns away.

Jodie and I look at each other and burst into laughter. I feel the blood boiling under my scalp. I am sure Sarah is still watching from the side of the dance-floor.

*

It's week later we are at a house-party for an eighteenth birthday.

It's approaching midnight and the flat is filled with students drinking, dancing, kissing, smoking - or lying passed-out.

Jodie has been pressed up against a guy from her class, talking in his ear for the last few minutes. Now, she peels herself away from him and joins me in the living-room doorway.

Alien Ant Farm's version of *Smooth Criminal* plays loudly. It is difficult to hear what anyone is saying.

'Nothing could live up to the original,' I shout so Jodie can hear me.

She points to an armchair and I follow her gaze. We laugh at a guy who has tried to sit on the arm of a chair but has completely missed, and has subsequently landed on the floor.

Just then, another drunk guy sways towards us. He is big and struggles to stand. He begins to dance up against me. His eyes are glazed and I am sure he's had more than booze.

I can just make out Jodie's voice through the music. 'Get off her!'

I try to push him off but he is leaning all his weight on me to prop himself up. My spine digs into the doorframe. Before long, he flops onto me and I fall sideways to the floor.

My head and my coccyx bang onto the carpet. The drunkard is unconscious on top of me. His weight is so great on my chest I can't catch my breath. I rasp and writhe but my ribs are crushed. I can't push him off. I know who's doing this is.

In an instant, Jodie is there, along with some other more sober party members, rolling the dead weight off of me.

I'm raging hot. I struggle to my feet, assuring the small concerned crowd that I'm alright. But I look past them all, even past Jodie, scanning the packed room for one face. I stride through them all, determined to seek her out.

I reach the kitchen doorway, searching. Then, my eyes fix upon her. While others mill about laughing and chatting in my peripheral vision, she is pouring coffee in the corner, probably doing her mother-hen routine for some poor soul. I'm burning up.

'Sarah.' When I've said her name, I realise my voice must have been raised, because suddenly all the eyes in the kitchen are on me. I don't care. 'Sarah, that guy just *collapsed* on top of me. This has got to stop.'

I quickly realise they are all squeezing past me to get out of the room as a rant is pouring out of my mouth.

Sarah is irritatingly composed and level-faced, patronising me with that motherly look I usually let her get away with. Well not this time.

'First you set me up with Greasy Gary, who tried to *touch me up* in the cinema. Then, you send a rugby-guy to try and dance with me in the dodgy Basement.'

'Rugby? No, no, he's a Chemistry major. Don't let looks deceive you.'

Blood prickles in my scalp. 'I think what he is studying is beside the point. And now, tonight, you send a drunk, who's *off his face*, on *God knows what*, to try it on with me. Did you really think he was a suitable match? Am I really so sad and desperate in your eyes, that even the most *pathetic, paralytic, drunken loser* is good enough for me?'

Sarah has put the kettle down and is backed against the work top, as though pinned there by my bombardment of words. 'You don't have to raise your voice…'

Everyone else has left the room and someone has closed the door. It is just her and me now.

'I do *not* want to be set up with any guys, Sarah. I'm happy as I am. I'm happy in myself. I'm happy in my life. I'm fine. My life is fine. Just because you and Kay have a bloke each, it doesn't mean that's what everyone needs to be happy. I've got enough going on my life without having to fight off all these *losers*.' My voice is growing less controlled with every second. It pours out at her, as if it won't stop.

I don't feel as though I'm in the room. It's as though I've left my body and exited the kitchen with the others, and am standing in the living room, with the music blaring, staring at the closed kitchen door, unable to hear my own cascade of words as they are drowned out by the overpowering background noise.

I can't remember the last time I was this mad.

18

'They're beautiful,' Jodie exclaims as I hand her the white lilies.

'Congratulations on your new job,' I beam.

'It's only a bit of waitressing at the college caf,' she laughs, looking through the kitchen cupboards for a vase.

'But it's your first job!' I take in the apologetic bunch of flowers, with only one of the four heads blooming. 'The rest will open up in a day or two. It's better to get them while they're like that; they'll last longer.'

'Yes,' she grins, filling the vase. 'I'll put them in the window so they can get the sunlight.'

I follow her into the bedroom where she sets them down on her desk beneath the window. 'There. This pretty thing will have some friends in no time. Thank you, Ames.'

'Well, great news about the job! I've got to get to a lecture. See you when I get back?'

'I've got my first shift tonight.'

'Ok, you'll do great! See you later.'

As I open the door, Sarah is in the hall, on the phone. 'No, Dad, you need to pre-wash it if it's got coffee stains. Pre-wash. You can get a spray...' She stops when she sees me, and stares coldly. We've barely spoken since the party.

I equal her look. 'Bye,' I snap.

'Bye,' she barks back.

Kay emerges behind her and glowers at me. 'After the way you spoke to Sarah at the party, you're lucky to still even be living in this flat.'

I spin away from them and leave.

Lucky to be living in the flat... A two-bedroomed box for five girls, which was at first full of excitement and freedom, can sometimes feel a little claustrophobic now the novelty has worn off.

Standing outside English class, bag slung over my shoulder, I wait with the others, as we always do, for our lecturer.

I'm standing beside Sally, who I usually sit by. She is leaning against the wall with her back to me.

'I don't know why we bother to get here on time,' I laugh to her. 'Mind you, the one day we turn up late will be the one day he's early…'

Sally steps away from me and joins another group. I am left pulling my shoulder-strap up, standing alone.

Derek Blight walks past us along the corridor; the boy who's eighteenth it was at the weekend.

'That was a hell of a party,' I call to him.

Derek scowls at me and walks on. I suddenly wonder if I've got something on my face today.

At last, Tony Peek, our English teacher, scurries along, his face as red as his hair. I'm still not used to calling teachers by their first names. He unlocks the classroom and we file in. I make my way to my usual place and pull out my chair. A scrap of paper lies on the seat. I pick it up to sit down and casually read the scribble.

My whole body is hot. *Amy Minor is a dyke.*

I try not to look at anyone as I struggle to stop my hands trembling. I slam the note face down on the desk. My cheeks are burning red. Sweat prickles under my hairline. I realise the class has hushed and Tony has begun to talk but I can't hear a word he is saying.

As soon as we are dismissed, I race home as fast as I can walk, keeping my head down all the way.

I burst into the flat. 'Well I've told Thomas, he just has to take me shopping for a new dress, because it's his fault it's ruined.' I hear Sarah and Kay in the kitchen but I run past them to the bedroom. I fling open the door to see Jodie planting on some lip-gloss. I need her.

'Jodie… you're not gonna believe…'

'I've gotta go, Ames.' She is tugging on her coat.

ALL THAT YOU WANT

'But I need to talk to you.'

'First shift, remember. I don't wanna be late.'

'Oh, yes. Yes, good luck...' It is only now I notice she is wearing her new uniform – with the top buttons of her blouse undone. 'Where's Annie?'

'Drama club.' Jodie darts out of the room. 'See you later.' I hear the front door slam.

For a moment I stand in the middle of the empty room. Then I run to close the bedroom door.

I pace to my bed and reach under the mattress for my mobile phone.

Standing away from the door where anybody might hear, I dial the number and wait. I need an ally.

After an age of rings, I reach a generic answerphone. I clear my throat. 'Hi, it's me. I know I'm meant to wait for you to call me. But I just really wanted to talk to you. I miss you. Christmas seems ages away. Anyway, ring me back when you get this. Please. Oh, I saw your interview on Four. You were ace. Anyway. Speak soon. Lots of love.' I hang up.

I return the phone into its hiding place, pull out my books and sit down to study. I hear someone move into the hall. I keep still and sink into my books.

Then I hear Kay's voice, just outside my door. 'Hi Mum, it's me. I'm sure you must have tried to ring but it's been so mad around here... oh, you haven't... Well anyway, we went to this mad party the other night. Oh, there were people smoking and drinking. It was outrageous! I didn't take any of the drugs. I don't think. I – oh ok. Yeah, course you have to. Speak soon then, I'll...' Then there is a pause. I'm sure I hear Kay sigh and put down the phone.

I remain alone in the room. Beside me on Jodie's desk stands the vase with the single flower, waiting for the others to open.

About an hour later, I am in the middle of studying hard, surrounded by books and papers. There is a knock at the bedroom door. I turn to see it creeping open. There stand Sarah and Kay. I try not to gulp.

Their arms are folded. Sarah holds a sheet of paper in her hand. She does not look about to apologise.

I force myself to meet their stares and the pair enters purposefully, yet delicately.

Sarah sits on the end of the bed opposite me. Kay remains standing, her arms still crossed.

I have to twist my body from my desk to look at Sarah. Her face is crumpled.

She clears her throat. 'Amy, I need to ask you something.' She speaks softly. Too softly. 'Amy... have you... have you been using Kay's laptop?'

I frown. 'Why would I?' I hiss.

She swallows. Gingerly, she hands me the A4 sheet.

I unfold a printed e-mail. 'What?' I read it aloud. '"Matt, I never stopped loving you. Please give me a chance..."' I spin to Sarah. 'I didn't write this.'

'There are at least ten e-mails on there, Amy. It's not normal.'

'But...' Burning simmers behind my eyes. I shoot a look at Kay.

Sarah signals for the towering beanpole to leave.

She swaggers out, pulling the door behind her so sharply that my notes fly off the desk, scattered and disorganised all over the floor.

'Amy?' Sarah asks.

'My work...' I cry. 'It will take ages to sort out this mess.' I drop to my knees and begin sifting through the chaos of strewn papers.

'Amy...' Sarah falls to the floor. 'We'll sort it out together.'

The room is large and open. There is a tidy desk in front of me and a metal filing cabinet against the beige wall. A slatted blind covers the window and a Venus flytrap actually stands in one corner. An involuntary laugh escapes me, causing Ruth Hart to peer at me over her half-moon spectacles.

Sarah must think I have a tangible problem to bring me here.

The college counsellor is what I expected. She is probably in her early fifties and wears her specs on a chain. Her greying bob frames her face and her lilac turtle-neck is tucked into her high-waisted pencil skirt. Although slim in the face and lower arms, she bears the slight overhang of middle-age. She looks like one

ALL THAT YOU WANT

of those icing-piping bags, where you squeeze one end leaving it empty and wrinkly, and the middle is full to burst.

I can't believe Sarah made me come here.

The small woman sits opposite me in an easy chair in front of her desk and crosses her ankles.

'So Amy, what brings you here?' She clasps her hands in her lap.

'My friend made me. She made me... She thinks I have a problem. She brought me here.' I hunch in my chair.

'Do you think you do?'

'No.'

'What problem does your friend think you have?'

I can hear an imaginary fly buzzing around the room. 'She thinks... I'm still obsessed with this guy from school.'

'But you disagree?'

'I'm not.'

'Why would your friend think that?'

'Because... I liked him for... all the years through school. And he moved away, about a year and a half ago, and she doesn't think I've been interested in any guys since.'

'And have you? Been interested in guys since?'

In my mind the fly buzzes dangerously close to that flytrap. It would be so easy to tell her, in the confidentiality of this room. 'No... but, I'm only seventeen. And she keeps setting me up with these creeps. I don't have to be with someone to be over Matt. To be happy.'

'Are you happy?'

'I was. But... now everyone at college thinks there's something wrong with me, and, I don't care about them, but Sarah...'

'You care what Sarah thinks?'

I nod. 'She's only trying to help. But, she's got it all wrong. She thinks I'm mad, bringing me to a... psychiatrist.'

'I'm a counsellor. You and Sarah, you live together now, at sixth form? Dynamics can change once you live with someone. What about these e-mails?'

'Kay must have written them.'

'Kay... Summers.' She consults her notes. 'Why would she do that?'

113

'She's never liked me.'
'Why do you think that?'
'She's jealous. Of my friendship with Sarah.'
'And Kay has a good relationship with this Matt Scotts?'
'They lived in the same village, back at home, growing up. Jesus, it was a school girl crush. Why can't they forget it?'

I feel that burning behind my eyes again. The fly is almost touching the tip of the trap and I want to just tell her.

The counsellor hands me a tissue. 'What's making you so upset?'

'Sarah. We're not like we used to be.'

It's beginning to get dark as I walk back through the college corridors. By now the halls are sparse of people, but I am certain the few students I pass avert their gazes from me.

I jump at a touch on my arm and look up from the floor. It's Thomas.

'You alright, Ames?'
'Oh, yeah.'
'What's wrong?'
I force back the tears.

'Hey, hey,' he sooths. We move in to the wall to let a couple pass. We watch them exit through the bottom door and the corridor is empty.

I take a deep breath. 'Sarah. Sarah made me see the college counsellor.'

'What? Why?'
'She thinks... I dunno, she must think there's something wrong with me.'

'There's nothing wrong with you, Amy. You're just a sweet girl who fell in love with the wrong guy.'

'I'm over it, Tommy, and she won't believe me.'

'Course you are. And you'll meet someone in good time.' God, even Thomas doubts me. 'Maybe, I don't know, maybe Sarah thought talking about things might help, that's all. Get it all out of your system.'

'Tommy, I didn't send those e-mails.' God, what if Matt actually received those e-mails...

'Amy, I've gotta go. I'm meeting Kay after a late class.'

ALL THAT YOU WANT

'Sure. You don't want to be seen with me.' I push past him.
'Wait… Amy…. You're going back to the flat?'
I nod.
'Ok. I'm not really meeting Kay. She's at the flat.'
I turn. 'What are you doing then? Thomas, you're not meeting a secret lover?' I tease.
'No. I'm having a meeting. A… sky-diving meeting.'
'You're going sky-diving?'
'Who'd have thought it, eh?'
'Are you sure?'
'There are lot of things you don't know about me, Amy. I've done two tandem sky-dives. After this, I want to do a bungee-jump.'
'Are you winding me up?' But I look at his face and I don't think Thomas has it in him make something up with such sincerity. 'Well, who knew? Thomas, the secret adrenalin junky.'
'I'm raising money… it's, I don't know, a release. A way to get things out of my system.'
And suddenly I understand. Thomas, ever the downtrodden, submissive, lapdog, has to have a crazy cathartic hobby. Otherwise how could he keep it all in?
'You rebel. Maybe I should join you,' I laugh. But I know I don't have it in me.

After wandering aimlessly for an hour, I eventually face up to heading home. Home, ha. I open the door as quietly as I can, wishing I could sink into the walls.
From the kitchen drifts the aroma of tomato pasta sauce. And wafts of voices. I stand still.
'So, I told Mum she needs to take him to the vets.' The voice is Sarah's. 'But *will* she listen?'
'It's only a scratched paw,' Kay tuts.
'But what if it gets infected? Maybe I should go home this weekend and check. But I don't want to leave Amy at the moment.'
'I don't know why you bother with her,' Kay retorts. 'We've had nothing but trouble since she arrived. Why don't we just tell her she's got to find somewhere else to live? We can go back to the way things were. We didn't have any of this drama last year.'

'Kay, she needs help. I'm not about to turn my back on her.'

I hurry on, hoping to reach the bedroom unnoticed.

Sarah sticks her head out of the kitchen as she hears me pass. 'We're making pasta. Do you want some?'

'I've eaten,' I lie, not stopping until I've reached the bedroom and rammed the door behind me.

No Jodie. No Annie.

Then I spot the note on my bed. I step warily towards it, remnants of the *Dyke* letter at the forefront of my mind.

I exhale as I read Jodie's round smiley handwriting. *Gone to work @ the caf. Going out with fit waiter after! Annie @ band practice. See you later. J*☺ *xxxxxxxxxxxxxxxx*

I reach under the bed for my phone. Watching the door, I dial the number.

Once again I am greeted by the answer-machine. This time I don't leave a message.

I sink onto the bed and the pasta smell drifts under the door. My stomach gurgles. I don't know how I can convince them of a truth I don't even believe myself.

On Jodie's desk, the single lily remains alone, waiting for its companions to show their heads.

19

A tree hammers at the pane of glass. I am in my bedroom at home. Bethany runs towards the window and I tell her, 'No!', but she flings it open wide. Branches fly in, wrapping themselves like arms around my sister's mouth. Her frightened blue eyes call to me but the wooden limbs continue to grow. Now they are coming for me, entwining themselves around my face. I try to take a breath but the spindly branches squeeze tighter.

In front of me, Sarah and Kay are laughing and making pasta. There are no branches near them. They stir a big pot of spaghetti with tomato sauce and dish it into bowls. It is so vivid I can smell it. Sarah turns to me, smiling, and outstretches her hands to offer me a bowl. My stomach growls but I can't speak to say yes. Sarah and Kay can't seem to see the twines and they think I'm not hungry. Giggling, they tuck into their meal and I try to shout. The tree is growing stronger and tighter, and now it is beginning to wrap around my whole body. Sarah and Kay eat and laugh.

I look to Beth at my side. The tree is encasing her now, covering her freckled face, and soon I won't be able to see her at all. I can't move to help her. I am as constricted as she is.

'Aaahhhhh!'

The scream forces me to sit bolt upright in bed. 'Bethany?' I call. But the window is in the wrong place; I am not in my bed at home. There are two single beds beside me.

The clock reads 7:02am. Outside, it is just becoming light.

'Aaaahhhhhhhhhhhhh!'

Jodie and Annie sit up this time. They stare around the room in their sleepy state, looking for the origin of the scream.

I jump up and they follow. We pad down the hall in our pyjamas and push open the door to the other bedroom.

The scene stops us in our tracks.

Sarah is leaning over Kay's bed, lightly touching her shoulder and shushing her.

'Aaaahhhhh!' Kay is sitting up in bed and staring at us.

One side of her hair is still a perfect bob. The other side has been cut off almost to the scalp. On her pillow lies a scattered pile of black hair along with a pair of kitchen scissors.

Through her hysterics, she fixes her eyes hard on me, like a bull to a rad rag. 'That bitch! She did it when I was asleep! Look what she's done to me!'

I can't speak.

Kay is seething like an angry rhinoceros. I am sure she is about to charge out of the bed at me.

Sarah tries to rub the animal's back. 'Amy? No! Why would she?' she soothes.

Of course I didn't. Did I? We watched a film last year where the guy has two personalities, and when the suppressed side emerges, he does things he can't remember doing.

'She's crazy! She's jealous, because I'm close with Matt and you, Sarah!' She is a caged elephant who's been stabbed with a needle and is about to burst out.

I can't move.

I swear she is foaming at the mouth like a rabid dog. 'I'm calling the police!' she screams.

I turn and barge through Jodie and Annie and race out of the room, wishing I could run all the way to London.

20

That night, I push open the flat door with more force than necessary. My extremities are icy and my bottom is numb from sitting on the hard cold seats in the police station all day.

Laughter floats from the kitchen and Kay pokes her head out of the door. I choke on the elaborate mist of perfume that surrounds her. She is dolled up and has had her hair cut into a drastic but stylish pixie 'do. 'They let you out then?'

'They had no proof,' I shoot back.

Sarah appears behind her. Her face is just as caked in make-up and her hair is piled up on top of her head. She wears a little bag over her shoulder to match Kay's. Her smile falls as she sees me, turning into a pitying gulp. It's the worst look she's ever given me.

My eyes water as I cough at the chemical that has invaded my throat.

The pixie links the beehive's arm. 'Come on, let's hit the town!' she steers her towards the front door.

Sarah looks back over her shoulder, then allows herself to be led away.

I curl up in bed, alone, hugging my knees until I fall asleep.

Several nights later, everyone is out and I sit at my desk. Jodie tried to nag and guilt-trip me to go with her to this stupid party but there was no way. I've got too much work to do. The flat is cold. I open my notebook to a new page, click my pen and begin to write.

Well I got my wish. I always wanted to stand out and be noticed. Now I can't walk into a classroom without people sniggering. I daren't step into the canteen without everyone going quiet. When I shuffle through the corridors, pulling my skirt down around my knees like an idiot, scrunching my grubby little-girl's fingernails up my sleeves, I feel their eyes bearing into me. They all think... what? I'm a lesbian? I'm a mad stalker? I'm a frigid, asexual freak?

Nobody knows if half the people at college ever date or not. Why is everyone so fascinated with my love-life – or lack-of?

Lenny hasn't called for over a week. It's only a week. And three days. He's just got other things to do... important things. Scripts to learn. Friends to go out with. Gorgeous actresses to party with... He'll call me when he can. We've got to be careful. He can't let anyone know about me.

The summer feels like a distant dream. It did happen. It did. There is nothing wrong with me. And I didn't cut off Kay's hair.

So what if I don't always want to go out with Jodie. What, to be a latch-on while she flirts with all the guys? To sit in the corner, sipping coke, pretending not to notice the odd looks and the whispering?

Jodie sounds like Kay these days. She says she wants me to go out with her because it will do me good, but I know her agenda. Well she can find another tag-along to sit dumbly in the corner while she flaunts herself like a tart.

I don't mean that. I wish I could be confident and beautiful like Jodie. I've never told my best friend I envy her, but she must know.

I'm happy to stay in with my college work. It's important. Even if Annie's got more of a social life than I have. Who would care if I was at the party or not? I'm fine here, thank you, with my dowdy hair, my grey eyes and my spotty chin. I'm not interesting. I'm just that weirdo with nothing to talk about because I'm not allowed to talk about what's on my mind. I'm a dirty little secret. That's fine, I won't be around. I'll just stay here and study English and be a great journalist and get away from all this in just another year and a half. It's not that long.

My phone must be on the blink.

I screw up the paper and toss it into the bin.

The following week I enter the flat after college and can hear Kay and Thomas talking in the bedroom. I creep unnoticed into the kitchen and begin to make myself a sandwich.

ALL THAT YOU WANT

As I raid the fridge for cheese, I hear the latch on the front door. Hoping it might be Jodie, but fearing it will be Sarah, I step cautiously into the hall to greet the newcomer.

My chest falls. Sarah steps in soundlessly, laden with supermarket shopping bags. It seems I'm not the only one in this flat who moves noiselessly these days.

Sarah eyes me silently as she sets down her bags, with that piercing, pitying look. She is drawn to the voices drifting from the bedroom she shares with Kay. Slowly, she removes her jacket and scarf and hangs them on a coat peg.

We can hear Thomas' voice. 'I can't believe Amy's... so... what's the word? Unstable.'

Sarah creeps closer towards the bedroom door. Through the cheap wood, Thomas and Kay speak freely, apparently not having heard either Sarah or me enter the flat.

The minion continues. 'She always seemed such a sweet girl.'

'*Sweet?*' comes the pixie's retort.

'I just mean... I can't believe...' Kay's lap-dog stammers. 'Poor girl. I know what she did to you was shocking, babe, but she's not herself. Sarah was right making her see that shrink. I hope this is just a phase and she'll get better. Amy...'

'*Amy, Amy, Amy.* It's all I ever hear. *Poor little Amy.* My own boyfriend and my *best friend* are more concerned about her than about me. Can't we just have *one* conversation that's *not* about that girl? What more do I have to do to get her out of our lives?'

Sarah's body stiffens in front of me.

Beyond the door, Thomas' voice mimics Sarah's body language. 'What do you mean, "what *more*"?'

Sarah's eyes are fixed on the bedroom door. I can see something growing inside her.

Thomas' voice emerges again, venturing a little further. 'Did you write the e-mails?'

Then we hear Kay's stabbing laugh. '*Matt I love you. I don't think I can live without you.*'

Thomas, usually the bleating sheep, is not laughing. 'You didn't cut your own hair off as well?'

The witch's wicked cackle is too much to bear.

Sarah throws the door open, ripping off the illusionist's mask.

121

The unwitting duo spin around.

'Sarah!' Kay's bag of tricks has spilled out over the floor.

I am not going mad.

Sarah almost pounces on the sheepish Kay. I've never seen her this wild. 'Why did you do it?'

'I... don't know.' Kay's crumpled body reaches towards the tower of Sarah.

'You cut your own hair off and you don't know why? And you say *Amy*'s wrong in the head.' She is a bear on its hind legs.

'I... just don't want to lose you, Sarah. She takes up all your time and...'

'If you don't get on that phone right now and tell the police what you've done, you'll lose me altogether. You'll move out. When I see you I'll treat you as a stranger.'

'I'll get on the phone.' Kay jumps towards Sarah. 'I'm sorry...'

'Just do it.'

Kay crawfishes along the hall and scampers into the living room.

Sarah, Thomas and I stare at each other.

Sarah clears her throat. 'I'm sorry, Amy.'

21

A few days later, I force myself to face the canteen between lectures. I try to ignore the smells of chips and cleaning fluid as I balance a pasta salad and a bottle of water on my tray. After paying, I squeeze through other students –I'm sure they are whispering- to look for somewhere to sit. In front of me stands a lanky bloke with cornrows and a leather jacket. He has his back to me. As I pass him, he steps back, not seeing me, and I trip over his heel. My tray is sent flying. Pasta splatters over the floor and the bottle splits, spraying everywhere.

I land on the cold floor, breaking my fall with my hands and knees. Pain shoots up to my elbows.

The hall is silent. If they weren't pointing before, they certainly are now. All of a sudden, laughter explodes around the room.

I turn to the boy who tripped me. He towers over me with his lunch tray. The tiny eyes are the same that leaned into me at the cinema. He smirks at me. 'Fucking dyke.'

I scramble to me feet.

'What if she is?' a voice rises, loud and challenging, soaring above the laughter and bringing the room to silence.

All eyes spin to see Sarah.

'You narrow minded prick.' Her words are unrelenting, stabbing into the skinny punk, who seems to visibly shrink. 'She isn't, by the way. She just said that to get creeps like you off her back. Don't take your bruised ego out on her.' Her voice keeps the room hushed.

The boy gulps, his tray wavering in his bony upturned hands, his face reddening as all the eyes in the room turn on him. 'I didn't mean to trip her up. She walked into me. I'm not a prick.'

Sarah strides towards him. 'Don't you think you owe her something?'

'An apology?'

'More than that.' The girl stands head and shoulders shorter than the boy, but in this instant she appears a giant compared to him. She plucks the sandwich and juice carton from his tray. 'I think this should do it.' Without waiting for a reply, she glides towards me with his lunch in her hands.

So Gary treats girls like objects, but then is publically shot-down by the fairer sex. I wonder if Gary is like my dad – under his mum's thumb.

From somewhere in the room comes a slow clapping.

I look to see it is coming from the white t-shirted-rugby-player/chemistry guy from The Basement. Not all of them are creeps. Maybe he'd be good for Jodie. I had thought he was a rugby player but he studies chemistry. I had judged Barry the flight attendant as gay, but he had just split up with his girlfriend. Who else could I be wrong about? Surely I hadn't misjudged Kay?

Gradually, others start clapping too.

Mr Cornrows stands for a moment with his empty tray, then drops it and scuttles out of the canteen.

A cheer rises around the room.

Grace Harris from English approaches. 'Good on you,' she tells Sarah. 'The creep had that coming.' She turns to me and smiles.

Sarah looks to me, half bowing her head, and gestures to an empty table. 'Can I sit with you?'

I stand for a moment, not knowing what to say or do.

Then I smile and pull out a chair.

22

Tonight, Kay is out doing Sarah's laundry – Kay has already shopped for her brother's birthday present, organised her wardrobe and created a study-plan for Sarah today.

Meanwhile, Sarah has spent most of the afternoon cooking me a meal like a sorry boyfriend.

They all know I'm innocent. But Lenny doesn't have a clue. He hasn't phoned for weeks.

Jodie is helping Annie choose an outfit for her drama-club ball. They take up the bedroom, laughing and parading about in wigs and masks. Jodie throws a black feather boa around Annie and they dance. I see them through the open doorway, a window into our shared space that I am not a part of.

This flat is too small.

The smell of onions takes over every part of the tiny apartment. There is no room for me.

I grab my phone and dart to the door. I charge down the hostile stairwell and out into the car-park. The only sounds are the sporadic breeze and the intermittence of distant traffic. I find an ignored corner, perch on the railings and make the call.

It rings. Then... the too familiar answerphone.

This time, I do not hang up.

I half-look around, not really caring anymore if anyone hears. Still, I don't say his name.

I wait for the beep, then let it tumble out. I tell him how the set-ups crescendoed. I tell him how everyone at college began to shun me. I tell him about the looks, the whispers. The only piece of information I hold back is any mention of Matt. Instead, I simply explain that Kay had taken my lack of dating as fuel to cause Sarah concern. I reveal Kay's secret tyranny. I spill out all (excluding the e-mails); how she planted worries in Sarah's ear; how she framed me for cutting off her hair. 'I got arrested,' I hiss into the phone. The answer phone cuts me off. I've been talking for too long.

Behind me, traffic continues to hum, metallic and uncaring.

I dial his number again, and once more wait for the beep. The cold rail digs into my backside. I hear a rustle and spin round. But it is only a lifeless crisp-packet. I continue to talk to no-one, telling him *not to worry*; the truth has come out. We found out Kay was behind it all. She is grovelling to Sarah, while Sarah is crawling around me. 'All *that* went on,' I tell him. 'But I know you're too busy. Let me know how *you've* been, when you have time to fit me in.' I hang up, seething.

I stare at the inanimate phone, expecting an instant reaction. But there is no stir at my tirade, not a glimmer of acknowledgement that my world almost came crashing apart and is now building back up again.

I throw the thing into my pocket and stomp back through the apathetic car-park, pulling my skirt down around my knees on the way. The ground remains docile. There is not a glimmer of life or emotion in the concrete space. My ponytail half-flitters in the inanimate breeze. If I screamed right now, no-one would come to my aid.

'Amy...' Sarah calls as I re-enter the flat. 'Dinner in five?'

I grunt the affirmative, not halting in my march to the bedroom. In an act of rebellion, I slam my thumb on the off button and heave up the corner of the mattress. I throw the phone into its hiding place and slump out to the aroma of Sarah's spaghetti bolognaise.

We endure an evening of sullenness. Sarah misinterprets my brooding and pads around me. I let her. 'I know it will take time to get back to how we were, Amy. I'm trying my best. Have some more salad?'

The spaghetti tastes rubbery and the meat metallic. Sarah has gone to great efforts with what is usually my favourite meal, but my taste buds won't respond. Finally, I skulk off to bed.

I'm surprised I've lasted the evening without checking my phone. Jodie is at a party with some guy but Annie is already

ALL THAT YOU WANT

tucked up when I dive into the covers. Silently, I reach under my bed and jab the on button, ready to be greeted with silence.

I wait for the stubborn thing to warm up.

Then... it vibrates. I have, not one, but two answerphone messages.

I leap out of bed. Tucking the phone into my waistband, I tear to the bathroom. I yank the door but it's locked. All I can do is pad the hall.

The door flies open. 'Al*right*,' Kay scowls, sauntering out.

I dodge past her and slam the door. I throw my back against it and rip open the message, jamming the phone into my ear.

'You have... two... new messages.'

Yes, I know that.

'Message... received today... at... nineteen... fifty-six... hours...'

And then it comes. At first, I don't take in the mood as I revel in his voice. It has been so long. Those golden tones seep through my dehydrated skin.

After a few minutes, when I have got over the hit, I begin to take in the content.

'She lets Kay treat you like that? The girl has... persecuted you... For her own sadistic satisfaction... because she's jealous of your friendship with Sarah. God, Amy. It sounds like she doesn't want Sarah to have any other friends. And... and Sarah bought into it,' he rants. 'Ok, so the girl was manipulated. But even when she found out Kay had invented all these lies, even then Sarah didn't show Kay the door.'

I slump onto the toilet seat. I am unprepared for this unslaught.

'Why does Sarah even want to know Kay anymore? Honestly. If she can just sit on the fence and let Kay think it's acceptable... How can you let it go, Amy? You don't need people like that in your life.'

And then his voice crackles and he's gone.

It takes every ounce of strength not to phone him back.

'Message two... received today... at... twenty... 0 four... hours.'

'Amy, I'm sorry. I should have been there for you through all this. We've been working all-hours on this movie... nights,

127

weekends... I have a far bigger part than I've ever had before... But it's no excuse. I had no idea you were going through all this. Please, call me back as soon as you can. I miss you so much. Call me, right away. I love you.'

I remain on the toilet seat and take it in.

'Amy... come on, I'm bursting!' Annie's voice breaks me from my trance. I don't know how long I've been sitting here.

I stand from the toilet and jerk back the lock. 'Sorry,' I murmur to my hopping friend in Disney pyjamas.

She doesn't wait for an explanation and darts into the bathroom.

I wander back to the bedroom and climb into bed, then push the phone under the mattress in my daze.

The impassioned rant was not of someone who had forgotten about me. He has been working hard, that's all. He's had no time to party with sexy actresses – he has been working day and night, put under the spotlight, gruellingly repeating lines, surrounded by people, catching a few hours' kip here and there in his pokey caravan. I can believe that; I know Lenny. I trust his feelings for me, really. As soon as he discovered I was in trouble, he was there, straight on the phone.

I'm still not going to ring him back right away.

The following evening, I turn on my mobile to discover five answerphone messages.

'Amy... call me. I've been such an idiot. I can't believe I haven't made time for you. You've needed me. You gotta believe me - I've been watched all the time. But I... I got my priorities right today; I've made endless excuses to get away from the set, back to the trailer, to call you. You need to know I care.'

Three of the messages follow those lines, while the other two rage about Sarah.

I resolve the best tact is to defend my friend. I reason this is the appropriate response; I don't wish to play the needy girlfriend, whining about why he hasn't called me. But his baiting of Sarah... that, I have to put a stop to.

I text him to ask what time he will call tonight.

He responds immediately, with '8 o'clock xxxxxxx'
So I make sure I'm ready.

Perching on the secluded railings at the back of the car-park, I switch on my phone at two minutes to. I find more missed calls, and immediately the phone vibrates.

'Hello?'

'Amy?'

I try desperately not to melt.

'I'm so sorry. You wouldn't believe the hours I've been working... they're always watching me, Amy... As soon as I get a break... my head hits the pillow... I've been a walking zombie...'

I stop his ramble, telling myself to be hard. 'Listen. I don't care about that. I know I can trust our relationship, even if we don't get to talk every day.'

There is a beat. Then, 'Really? You're not mad at me? You know... you know, don't you, what you mean to me?'

'Yes, I know all that. I know you would have called me if you could. But what I can't accept is the way you're talking about Sarah.'

'Amy... you can't let her... how can you have someone like that in your life?'

I take a deep breath, and remind myself he is only saying this because he cares. 'But, you don't know her. She's always been there for me... she took me under her wing at school - before that even, we played in our back gardens together; she stopped me from running out into the road. You don't know what she's been through.'

'Amy, that girl *allowed you* to be arrested.'

'Look-'

'No, you need to give her an ultimatum. Kay or you.'

He is trying to protect me. There's nothing for it. I need to make him understand.

23

Her parents split up when she was thirteen. Her dad moved in with his new woman.

I didn't see Mrs Chine leave the house for at least a week. I'd look through the curtains and spot Sarah, over the wall, coming home with shopping bags or hanging out the washing in their garden. Then, she'd disappear for a few days at a time to visit her dad.

But Sarah and her brother ended up spending more time at their dad's new place. So I'd have to walk to school by myself. I'd meet her at lunchtimes and she'd tell me how goo-goo eyed her dad and his new girlfriend were. She said they were so wrapped in each other, they forgot they had kids. Her dad's girlfriend had two sons, so Sarah was lumbered with mothering all three boys.

I look around the deserted car-park, the phone pressed to my ear. I know I shouldn't be revealing Sarah's past but... it's Lenny.

Sarah would cook for them, wash their school uniforms and make sure they did their homework.

Sarah's mum went from a nuclear family to living alone in a matter of weeks.

My mum would send me next door to walk the dog for Mrs Chine, to check she was ok. She wouldn't even answer the door, so I'd creep into the house and grab the lead, calling to Sarah's mother upstairs in her room. She'd never answer me.

Then, she seemed to move into a new stage. One day, she emerged from the front-door, in overalls, and began painting the front of the house - something her husband had put off for years. She chose a brilliant sky-blue.

ALL THAT YOU WANT

With her new resolve, Mrs Chine climbed the wall-ladder, paintbrush in hand, stamping her feet with each step.

Well, you can guess what happened, with Sarah's mum in that state. From our front garden, Beth and I watched, my sister with her dolls and me with my magazines. So it must have been summer. I can still see the front of the house, half of it the pastel colour of a beach-hut, and the other half the dull grey that used to be white. The ladder stood between the two colours. We watched from our picnic blanket, the fresh-paint smell wafting across the wall. And Mrs Chine came crashing down to the ground with a piercing yelp.

Mrs Chine had broken her wrist. The doctors said she was lucky that was all it was. She was in a cast for six weeks. Sarah had to come home to nurse her. Not that the daughter had intentionally stayed away, it had just turned out that way, I suppose, because she, subconsciously, must have felt her dad was the parent in need of looking after.

Well, after that, her dad had to wake up. He stayed with his new girlfriend —he's still with her now- but they both had to face up to the fact they had been so wrapped up in themselves they'd been neglecting their kids. Sarah's return to her mum's — and so her absence from her dad's place - made them understand how much the girl had been doing for the boys —well, for them all.

'So, you see, the point I'm trying to make is, Sarah has it in her to help people; to be motherly —and to keep the peace,' I tell Lenny down the phone. 'She wants to look after Kay *and* me, just like she wanted to be there for her mum *and* her dad, without taking sides. Sarah is fiercely loyal to her friends.' And I do love Sarah, really, I realise. 'I may not be as grown-up as I'd like to think, but I'm mature enough to put up with Kay. I couldn't make her choose between her two best friends. Do you see?'

He sighs. 'Amy, you're a good friend. I fall more in love with you every day.'

A few days later, I receive a letter through the post.

'Post-mark says London, Amy.' Kay leans across the table, munching her toast. 'One of your magazine people?'

I snatch the envelope and slope out, mumbling, 'Maybe my editor.'

Kay howls. '*Maybe my editor*, daahhhhling!'

I shove the bedroom door closed and jump onto my stomach on the bed. Annie is at her desk, concentrating. 'Don't mind me,' I murmur.

She half-nods, not looking up.

I tear open the envelope and read the scrawl.

A love-letter....

Dear Amy

I miss you so much. I wanted to explain myself after berating your friend. I don't know, it just seemed easier to get it down on paper.

I meant what I said. You are a good friend. But you need to believe in your own worth. Don't believe you deserve to be treated like that. I wish I could be there. You have no idea how helpless I feel, sitting in this tin box, hundreds of miles away from you. It makes me mad.

I just wish you had more confidence in yourself, that's all. Don't stand for any excuses.

You don't feel worthy of Sarah's friendship. You think you should be grateful for her. That's a load of bull. Admit it, you do. You feel inferior to Sarah. And to Jodie. You don't feel good enough to have them as friends. But let me tell you, anyone who's fortunate enough to have you in their lives ought to realise it.

Especially me. I am so... blessed... to have met you, Amy. You need to hear it sometimes. You put yourself out for me. You put up with all that ill-treatment at college; all the sneaking around; being apart for months. You make the effort to come to London each school-break. I hate being away from you, Amy. And I hope you understand how much you mean to me. Because people who don't realise what they have in you, those so-called friends, well, they don't deserve you. I can hardly believe you came into my life. You're kind, loyal, beautiful. You have a huge heart. I fall for you even more every day. I just want you to know what you're worth, Amy. Stand tall. And be proud to be Amy Minor.

Can't wait to see you at Christmas.

All my love
L xxxxxxx

ALL THAT YOU WANT

24

I have resolved to confront her.

It's the end of October half-term. Sarah and I have spent most of the week with our respective families and have barely seen each other. Now, I take a separate train back to college than the rest of my friends.

This niggling has been gnawing at me. Much as I love her, she can't think it's ok. I'm not Kay's outlet. I find a reclusive seat with a table, not seeing anything else, and pull out my notebook and pen.

Dear Sarah,

I know we made up. But I just need to know.

Why do you stand by Kay? She sucks all the energy from you. She demands so much attention. She doesn't want you to have any other friends. You've seen her true colours now, so why do you want anything to do with her? Or don't you care that she basically started a hate campaign about me, spreading rumours... trying to turn you all against me? Do I really mean that little to you, that you can essentially give her the ok? She can do anything she likes to me, according to you. I really thought you and I had a stronger friendship than that. That you would look out for me.

Kay has had her moments throughout the years, but this is something else. Making me see a shrink? Convincing me I was going mad? Calling the police on me? How can you allow someone to remain in your life who could put me through that?

She has to be deeply disturbed to go to such lengths to try to get rid of me, just because I'm a friend of yours and I take up a bit of your time. Kay takes up more of your time than even your boyfriend, or your parents —your family, or any of your other friends. What has she really got to be jealous of?

I'm not just being selfish; I also don't think she's any good for you. It's not healthy, Sarah. You don't need that spoilt brat in your life.

Finally I take a breath. I can't believe I've spilled it all out. I watch the blurred fields race past the window and I know that letter is it. No revisions, just a tumble of stream of consciousness. There's no way I could say all that to Sarah face-to-face. I'd get tongue-tied and she would interrupt me, so I sign the rough and final draft.

Love, your friend, Amy xxxxx

The train is slowing into the station and finally the images become clear.

When I arrive at the flat, I see her coat in the hall and hear the TV in her room. A quick inspection of the apartment confirms she is the first back. It's a rare fragment of time when the others are away, leaving just the two of us at home, and I know I have to seize it. I am *not* weak.

I dump my bag in the hall and don't even bother to kick off my shoes. I take a deep breath and barge into her room.

She is lying on the bed and spins round. 'I thought I'd locked that.'

I stop. 'Why would you lock the door?'

Then I take in the scene. She is in her pyjamas, sprawled on her bed, surrounded by empty chocolate wrappers, an open box-set on the floor and some American drama on her TV.

She gulps.

I don't think I've ever seen level-headed Sarah look guilty before. 'What..?' is all I can manage to stammer.

'Ok... you caught me.' She sighs, sitting up. 'On the first day back, this is what I do. I make sure I'm the first one here; I lock the bedroom door. I don't answer the phone to Mum or Dad, or brothers, or Alec. And I... have some me time. I... I indulge.'

I don't know what to say. I've never seen Sarah act selfishly.

'I spend all my time looking after everyone else,' she adds defensively.

ALL THAT YOU WANT

'Yeah, you do. You deserve it.' I shake it off. I've come in here for a purpose. 'I have something for you.' I throw the letter at her, without thinking, and spin out of the room, pulling the door behind me.

I take my time unpacking in silence, bracing myself for the aftermath.

Eventually, as I'm hanging the last of my clothes in the wardrobe, I hear her door open.

She appears, still in her red flannel pyjamas and dressing-gown, looking at me earnestly.

I stop and gulp at her.

She moves to sit on the bed with the letter in her hand.

I close the bedroom door and sit with her.

'Amy,' she begins, her eyes tired. 'You can't ask me to choose between my two best friends. I know she hasn't treated you well - and I've had long conversations with her that you weren't in on. I've made her take a long hard look at herself, believe me, about what she did to you. So don't tell me I don't care about you.' She rubs her eyes. 'Yes, I was sucked in and manipulated. And I'm sorry for that. But you must see, I only had your best interests at heart. I tried to help you, didn't I? I organised the meeting with the counsellor and tried to set you up on dates to try and help you get over Matt. Well... you can understand why I would believe you were...' she lowers her voice, '*obsessed* with him, Amy. You were besotted with him for five years.'

'Four actually. I haven't thought about him since he left.'

'Even so, the lie wasn't far from the truth, so you can see why it was easy to be taken in.'

'I don't blame you for that, Sarah. Anyone would be taken in by those lies. But it was... when you found out the truth. You put Kay in the doghouse for a day or two then, basically, went back to normal. Don't you think what she did was bigger than that?'

'You don't know her like I do. You don't have a relationship with her like I do.'

'Because of how she is to me! You think I want all this drama? Don't make excuses for her.'

'Amy, you have to understand.' Sarah sighs. Her freshly painted toe-nails show signs of her indulgence. 'I don't know if I should tell you this. But I need you to understand. You need to know I do care about you, and to understand why I can't just ditch her. I can trust you, can't I?"

'Yes...' I am intrigued now. Am I about to find out some deep secret about my arch-enemy? Some weakness?

'Honestly, you can't breathe a word to anyone. Not even Jodie. Especially not Jodie. *You'll* understand. Maybe even have sympathy. But Jodie...'

'Jodie looks out for me. She won't let anyone treat me that way.'

'She'll use this as a fuel against Kay. Maybe I shouldn't tell you. I shouldn't have started this. Forget it.'

'No, it's ok, I won't tell Jodie.' My intrigue gets the better of me.

'You won't tell anyone?'

'No-one.'

'Promise?'

'Yes. I promise.'

'Ok. Well, the thing is,' she clasps her hands. 'I don't suppose you ever knew... Kay has a twin sister..?'

I frown in disbelief. 'You're joking, right? So it's not Kay doing that stuff, it's her evil twin? Sarah, please.'

'No, Amy.' Sarah is deadly serious. 'Her sister had an accident.'

Kay and Carla were five. They were playing catch in their garden, and Kay threw the ball over her sister's head.

It landed in the pond. Carla leapt in after it and... she fell and banged her head... face down.

Kay just stared at the back of her motionless twin, blood and hair floating on the shallow water. By the time Kay alerted anyone, her sister hadn't been breathing for too many minutes. She was saved, but suffered severe brain damage. She was left unable to walk, talk... move.

She is now wheelchair bound. She has to have her head supported and is fed through a tube. When you hold her hand, she is limp. When you watch her parents carry her, it's as if she is boneless.

ALL THAT YOU WANT

I don't suppose you would have ever been to Kay's house so you wouldn't know about Carla. All of Kay's parents' time is taken up with caring for her. They never have spare time for Kay. She's left to her own devices.

I stifle a scoff at that.

You may find it hard to believe, but she is far from spoilt.

Once a year, Kay's parents put Carla into respite and they jet off on holiday. They used to send Kay to stay with her aunt for the week, but when we were in year eight they decided she was old enough to stay home alone.

They stocked up the fridge for her and left her a wad of cash and a phone-number for her aunt – not even the phone number of where they were staying. And they swanned off to sun themselves.

Well, naturally, Kay had a house party. Got absolutely wrecked. Invited half the year.

I remember that party. I remember wishing I could go and feeling so jealous because Matt was going to be there.

'People trashed the house,' Sarah tells me. 'I couldn't stop them. Kay... lost her virginity to Thomas. I couldn't stop that either.'

In the morning she made a half-hearted attempt to clear up. She left a luminous-purple condom wrapper on top of her bedroom bin.

Then, she waited. Loud music still rung in Kay's ears so prominently on their impending return, she was almost sure her parents would hear the ghosts of the records. The tastes of cigarettes and alcohol still filled her dry mouth, despite brushing her teeth. She was positive they would smell the telltale signs on her breath. Her head – in fact, her whole body - ached, inside and out.

Mr and Mrs Summers flounced back in from their holiday, Kay's mum's hair sun-kissed, her dad still in his shades. They swept over the smell of bleach smothering the stench of stale cigarettes; they breezed past the red-wine stains half-covered by an out-of-place rug; they ignored the glasses piled on the draining board and the gaps in their wine-rack. They didn't say a word.

They told Kay about their luxurious hotel and brushed off Kay's claims that a few people had been round and it had got a little out of hand, with, "oh well, Maude will be over to sort it out in the morning". The cleaner didn't mention the condom wrapper, or the cigarette butts in the plant-pots or the stains on the carpets and the sheets.

Her parents went to fetch Carla from respite and life carried on pretty much as normal.

Sarah has grown again in my eyes. I look at her face and see the endless wisdom and compassion that extends far beyond her years and I remember why I feel safe with her. I am reminded why a whining brat like me is lucky to have her on my side.

'So next time, Amy,' Sarah pulls her dressing down around her. 'Next time you call someone *spoilt*, maybe, Amy, if someone seeks attention, they might not be getting it from where they should.'

25

London, Christmas 2001

I've been feeling prickly all day at the office and it still hangs around me tonight in the caravan.

'Sorry the hotel has been delayed... I told you I'd be in there by now.'

I don't care about the stupid hotel. I care that he is happy to hide me away in a box while he carries on with his blissful life.

The golden hamster runs in his wheel, a frantic rattling sound vibrating through the mobile home. The scent of musty sawdust scatters through the air.

'I got him to keep me company when you're not around.' Lenny places the newly filled water bottle into the cage and flicks his blonde eyelashes. 'A guy can go stir crazy around here sometimes.'

'So you got another poor creature to keep prisoner,' I mumble. I am perched on the cold bed while Lenny shows off his new pet.

'He's not a prisoner. Look; he's free to run around.' He produces a clear plastic ball and unscrews it. Opening the cage, he reaches for Samuel and pops him into the sphere. He re-attaches the two halves and places the orb on the floor. The hamster immediately begins rolling around the uneven carpet. Lenny jumps onto the bed beside me to avoid being run into. There is a desperate rattle of paws against the plastic.

'You think being in that bubble makes him free?' I muse.

Lenny's body tenses beside me. 'If you're peeved about me not answering the phone when I was working, Amy, you know you wait for me to call you. I have the phone hidden and switched off except for the times we've arranged to talk - the times we know it's safe.'

I shake my head. 'Do you actually love me, Lenny? What is this, a fling? A bit of fun? 'Cos I sure haven't been having much fun the last few months.'

'Of course I love you. Where's this coming from? I thought we'd gone beyond the bit-of-fun stage. If you were only a "bit-of-fun" do you think I'd keep this up, not seeing you for months, then snatching a few precious nights together? You're all I think about, Amy.'

Samuel's claws tap around the floor.

'I thought love was meant to be forever, didn't you?' I ask. 'Do you want to be with me forever? Hiding forever? Do you see us together when we're old and grey, hiding out, snatching time together every few months?'

'I hide to protect you.' He gestures towards the door. 'There's a lot of crap out there that comes with being in the spotlight.'

'Are you ashamed of me?' I demand.

'Why do you want to come out all of a sudden?' he snaps. 'You want to have your name all over the papers?'

'So you think I'm with you because I'm, what, a gold-digger? You think I want to go public because I'm after fame? I thought we knew each other by now, Lenny. I thought we trusted each other? I could have told everyone already if I'd wanted to.' I stop and turn my body to face him. 'Lenny, I want to be with you all the time.'

'I miss you every second when I'm not with you, Amy.' He holds my hand. 'I just don't want to subject you to all the crap that would go with being with me. Do you want to be photographed, gossiped about, judged, picked apart, scrutinised?'

'And you think all this hiding and secrecy is the easy option, do you? My friends think there's something wrong with me for not being interested in any college guys. I've been set up with *creeps*. I've been *groped*. I've been *passed-out on-*'

'I'm sure you've got all the guys after you at college.' He is cold. 'It must be hard to say no.'

ALL THAT YOU WANT

'How dare you. It's not like that at all. They only do it to please *Saint Sarah*. Don't you trust me? I've been taken to the bloody college counsellor to *"talk about my issues"*. They all thought I was going mad. Have you got any idea what it's like for your friends to look at you like that? I could have stopped it any time by just telling them the truth. *"Guess what? The reason I'm not interested in any college guys is because I'm in love with Lenny Hunter. I've been seeing him in secret for over a year."* But I didn't. I've never told *any*body apart from Jodie - and Bethany found out by accident and I managed to silence her. I put up with all that for us. And you think I want to come out about us because, what, I want the glamour? I want to be famous? I thought you loved me as much as I loved you. But I'm just your dirty little secret.' My stomach won't unclench and the lump in my throat won't be swallowed. 'Sarah's my oldest friend. She's like family to me and I can't tell her this huge thing that's going in my life. She's been so worried about me and I couldn't tell her I was the happiest I've ever been.'

The hamster is running into a wall, then turning and running straight into the next boundary in this little globe. I feel his frustration.

Lenny doesn't seem to notice it. 'Amy, I haven't seen you since summer. We've got this precious little time together and I don't wanna waste it arguing.'

My chest is tight and I struggle to catch my breath.

'Here, let me get us a drink.' He steps over to the kitchen area.

Samuel bangs into the caravan door.

Lenny has his back to me. 'Those paps are like *vultures*, Amy. They'll look for any juicy piece of meat.'

Before I know what I'm doing, I've sprung to open the door and am unscrewing Samuel's ball. Gently, I tip the sphere, and Samuel is leaping down the steps and darting into the darkness.

'What are you doing?' Lenny is dashing past me down the steps. He scurries back in to grab a 'flashlight'. Then he is scrabbling around outside again.

Slowly, I move to the bed and collect my coat and bag.

Lenny is still scrambling frantically about outside. 'Samuel!' he is hissing.

I step into the doorway.

Lenny shoots round and glares at me. 'He'll be eaten by city foxes. He'll be torn to bits.'

'At least he'll be free,' I murmur, but I feel a pang of guilt for the small creature. I step down from the caravan and begin to help Lenny search. After some minutes, we hear a rustling from nearby bin-bags. 'Over there,' I point.

Lenny scrambles around the bags with his back to me. After a minute, he turns to me with the animal in his hands.

I retreat back into the caravan and open the cage for Lenny to place the hamster inside.

Then he closes the cage door.

'Trapped again,' I murmur as I head for the door. I step out and begin to walk away.

'Where are you going?' he demands.

'Home.'

'I'll walk you. You can't walk through London on your own at this time.' He grabs his coat and his keys.

And his big hat, to stop himself from being seen with me.

We walk through the city in silence.

We reach my grandparents' back yard. I keep my head down and push open the gate. 'Bye.'

'Amy,' he calls me back. 'I don't get it. Don't you want to be with me anymore?'

I turn back a final time. 'I can't carry on hiding like this,' I tell him. I move through the yard to the house.

I continue to work for the magazine for the rest of the Christmas holidays. And I spend my nights inside my grandparents' house.

26

College, Spring Term 2002

It's a Friday evening. Sarah and I are sitting in the living room with cups of tea. We have the curtains drawn against the relentless sheet rain.

Sarah pulls a video out of her bag. The generic blue and white rental case doesn't give anything away. 'I got *Buzzard Block*. Seeing as we missed most of it at the cinema.'

I force a smile. 'Great.'

Sarah fusses around the TV, setting up the film.

I'm cold from being outside but now my cup warms my hands. I take a sip. Hot, sweet tea trickles down my throat, but doesn't settle my stomach.

I don't want to make it difficult for her to be friends anymore. But I can see she is still trying to make amends. I can't muster any way to reassure her.

I haven't spoken to Lenny since I got back from London.

The living-room door drifts open and Kay and Thomas peer at us. They look like a pair of drowned kittens, their hair flat and water dripping down their faces. I don't think I've ever seen the usually self-assured Kay looking so washed out.

'Oh,' says Kay. She holds a video case in her hand. 'I see you had the same idea as us. Don't worry; we'll go to Thomas'.'

As if on cue, a crack of thunder roars outside.

Sarah turns to me for permission.

I keep my face blank.

She turns to Kay, who still hovers in the doorway, shoulders hunched. 'Well, come and join us. It's pouring down.'

Thomas flicks his hair awkwardly.

Kay gingerly pads over to take a seat.

'Sit down,' Sarah half-smiles. 'We've got *Buzzard Block*. Then we can watch yours afterwards. Have ourselves a bit of a film fest.'

Thomas slowly sits down too.

Sarah takes Kay's hand and mine, either side of her. Her fingers are still cold and her sharp silver ring digs into my palm. 'Look. You are my two best friends in the world. You should be getting on. We should *all* be getting along. I really want us to put all of last term behind us and move on. What do you say, Kay?'

The snake shrugs. 'Fine by me.'

Sarah turns to me. 'Amy?'

I keep my face blank and stare ahead. I don't have any fight in me for this. 'Yeah, sure. It's all forgotten.'

Kay looks at me. I can tell whatever she is about to say will be hard for her. 'Will you come and watch Thomas do his sky-dive?'

My eyes are wide. I don't know which part of this causes me most disbelief. 'Yes... I'll come...'

'That's settled then. Video night, great,' grins Sarah, picking up the remote. 'Because I got too much popcorn.'

Jodie and I are food shopping. I don't think I'm much help to her in the supermarket. Apart from nagging at me to read the list to her or to take my turn pushing the trolley, Jodie is digging at me about how quickly I've forgiven Kay.

'And how can you let *Sarah* off the hook, come to that? She treated you *appallingly*. She believed Kay over you. It's always been the same, all through school. You've had to compete against that conniving bitch.' She stops to throw endless tins of beans and spaghetti-hoops into the trolley, in true student style. 'And even now, when she's discovered the truth, about what a bully Kay really is, she still doesn't throw her out of her life, like a good friend should.'

'Jo, I don't have it in me. I can't keep it up. You forget, Kay and Sarah have been friends for years too. Yes, Kay has always been jealous, and Sarah's always been stuck in the middle. And yes, you would think she would shun Kay after last term. But she never would. She'd forgive her anything. I accepted that a long time ago. She might give the bitch a hard time over it, but

ALL THAT YOU WANT

ultimately, she'll always forgive her. She's an old mother-hen, and really, all Sarah was at fault for was for caring about me.'

'Well if some *skank* treats *you* like that, my best friend –and you're supposedly Sarah's best friend too- I would want nothing to do with that person ever again. Sarah is too good at sitting on the side-lines.'

'She just wants to keep everyone happy. I'm resigned to the fact I have to put up with Kay if I want to keep Sarah as a friend. She means too much to me. To be honest, I'm so tired of all this fighting, and of the atmosphere in the flat. I'm tired. I'm ready to… just keep the peace with Kay; to try and get back on track with Sarah.' I stop. 'I have too much else to think about to bother with some petty feud between housemates.'

Jodie stops in the middle of the aisle, causing a middle-aged-woman to almost crash her trolley. Ignorant of the back-up she has caused, Jodie flings her arm around me. 'He'll see sense, you wait. He'd be nuts to let you go.'

I still haven't spoken to Lenny since I came back from London.

Suddenly realising we have stopped right in the middle of the aisle and are causing a hold-up, she begins to push the trolley forward. 'Come on. Let's have big fat jacket potatoes tonight with loads of cheese and beans.'

As soon as we are back at the flat, I run to the bedroom to check my phone, as I do every day, while Jodie takes the shopping bags to the kitchen.

I flinch as I pass Kay, sitting in the living room with the door open, flicking through a magazine. Sarah may have Kay on a short leash right now, but she still believed all the lies; she still allowed herself to be turned against me so easily. I'm sure the trust will come back. I won't always feel tense in my own home. The college whispers will stop soon enough. They'll soon be bored of, *"Did you know she had to see a shrink?" "Did you hear she was arrested?"*

In the bedroom, the screen on my phone shows I have one answer phone message. I put the mobile to my ear.

I hear Jodie yell from the kitchen, 'You could come and help!'

'What?' shouts Kay. 'Oh, look at this, Lenny Hunter's got a new bird.'

I hear what sounds like Jodie dropping a can of beans on the kitchen floor. She darts to the living room.

I listen to the message in bedroom but crane my neck to hear what's going on in the sitting-room.

'I'm sorry,' pleads Lenny's voice down the phone. 'She was upset, that's all; I found her crying. I was just asking if she was ok. Ignore the tabloids...'

I drop the phone and run into the living-room.

Jodie is standing behind Kay's chair, leaning over her shoulder.

Kay is laughing at the glossy mag. '"*Len's Mystery Missus*",' she reads aloud.

I stop dead in the doorway, fearing we have been exposed.

'She's a runner on the set of this new film, apparently,' Kay continues from her throne. 'A nobody. A very lucky nobody, who was in the right place at the right time.'

Jodie tries to shrug. 'You can't believe anything you read in those magazines,' she breezes. 'These journo-types will do anything for a story, won't you, Amy?' She forces a laugh.

I stride across to Kay.

'Here.' She hands me the mag.

I am shaking as I am confronted with a photo of Lenny and a girl. She has her back to the camera but she is young and slim with long blonde hair. She wears a tight black vest top, which shows off her curves, over a low pair of jeans. In the background is the Thames.

Lenny's arm is around her bony shoulders.

27

In the bedroom, Jodie hugs me as I cry.

Annie peers in. 'What's the matter?'

'She's homesick.' Jodie grabs her jacket from the bed. 'Let's go for a walk, Ames.'

We sit in the cafe on the corner. The aroma of coffee, crispy bacon and cigarettes fill the air. New music plays around us.

'What's this song?' I ask.

'Daniel Beddingfield,' Jodie tells me. *'Gotta Get Through This.'*

I stir my tea but don't drink it. 'He could have any girl he wanted, Jo.'

'Yea but he wants smelly little you. I bet it's innocent. The papers are bound to twist things for a story.'

'How could I seriously think he was only interested in me? God, I'm an idiot.' My stomach is lurching.

'He's the idiot.' Jodie picks at her pink iced bun.

I gulp. 'How are things with the waiter guy?'

'Oh, I binned him.' Jodie waves a hand dismissively.

'Why can't it be as easy as that for me?'

'Because, in your case, it's love.'

My chest is aching. 'I don't know what to do.' I shake my head. 'I'd better phone Suzie and tell her I'm not coming back at Easter. And Grandma and Grandad.'

'Now you *are* being an idiot. Go to London. But don't go for him. Go to work at the paper. Don't give up your career dreams because of him.'

I look at her. 'You know what, you're right.' I steal a piece of Jodie's bun and pop the sickly sweetness into my mouth.

So, for the spring term, I concentrate on my work. I think about my career. I am going to be a successful journalist. I am going to know everything there is to know about English –about literature, language, grammar, punctuation, spelling…

With my head in my books, Jodie enters to bring me a cup of tea. 'Stop itching; your hands are red-raw.' I hadn't noticed my eczema had returned. It must be the weather. I keep the curtains closed to stop the sun invading my skin.

I finish my assignment two weeks early and ask Jodie to hand it in for me, because I need to get on with the next one. She buys me a pot of E45 and tells me to stop biting my nails. I'd thought I had grown out of that habit since… well, around my sixteenth birthday, I suppose. But apparently not. I'm sure I over-hear Kay mutter, 'Eeeeeyoow. Forehead fingers.'

I finish the next assignment a week before it's due. I ask Jodie to take it, but she says no. She says it will do me good to go into college myself. I know it's really because she's too busy with whatever new guy she's seeing. But I say, ok, I will. Then I ask Annie and she takes it for me.

When Jodie comes back, she tells me to stop scratching my head or all my hair will fall out. The eczema must have moved. This weather. Down the back of my chair is a clump of hair. I grab my handheld mirror to look at the back. I move it around where I've been scratching. I lift the hair and see my scalp is red-raw. Is that..? I am sure that is the beginnings of a bald patch. I feel a stab in my chest and shake my hair into place, trying to erase the hideous sight.

My phone has been turned off since… well, since the beginning of term. I want no distractions. My career is important. I only go out of the flat for lectures, and wear Lenny's hoody to cover any hair loss –because it's the only garment I have with a hood, not because it's Lenny's- and gloves to protect my hands from the elements and hide my stubby nails. The trouble is, it's getting warmer.

People at college don't really speak to me. I'm sure everyone is starting to forget the mad girl.

ALL THAT YOU WANT

London, Easter 2002

My phone buzzes on the bedside table. I am in the foetal position in my grandparents' box-room.

Still asleep, I cancel the call.

It buzzes again.

I cancel it again. And again.

I pick the wretched thing up and, with one eye open, hold it under the covers. I try to press the off button, but before I can, the phone rings again, so pressing the red button only cancels the call.

Immediately, it rings once more.

This time I answer. 'Will you stop phoning me? You'll wake my grandparents up and I've got work in the morning.'

'I'm outside the back,' he whispers. 'Please meet me. Please. Or I'll keep calling.'

I try not to melt. 'You'll have my grandad down there in a minute.'

'He hasn't got his hearing aid in. Just meet me, please, for five minutes then I'll let you get some sleep. Please, Amy.'

I haven't heard that voice in too many months. 'Five minutes.'

I wear my big dressing-gown around my nighty as I step through the back door. The night is cold.

He is standing by the gate, looking smaller than before.

I try not to laugh at his *Matrix* coat and hat. There is a general smell of dustbins. Somewhere nearby, a cat cries.

I fold my arms as a shield. 'You've got two minutes.'

'You said five.'

'It took me three to put something on and get down here.'

'Why weren't you here on Friday after college? I've been waiting here the past two nights. I thought you weren't coming.'

'I had to stay to support a friend who did a sky-dive yesterday.

As we'd watched Thomas tumble, free, through the sky, raising money for Carla, he was sending a subliminal message to his girlfriend. I'd glimpsed her face and Kay knew her boyfriend was doing something she could never do.

149

Observing Thomas in a new light, silently, I was reminded could never dare either.

'Anyway,' I say to Lenny now. 'I thought you'd be too busy to miss me, with your little friend.'

'Samuel? He… didn't make it long.'

I feel a pang of regret. But I remain stiff. 'I'm not talking about your stupid hamster.'

He swallows. 'Listen, Amy, that girl was just a runner who worked on the show. When I couldn't get hold of you, I went for a walk to clear my head, then I found her crying by the river. My first thought was to run away before she saw me. But then I recognised her from the set, so I asked her what was wrong. And she told me she'd written this script, and working on *Buzzard Block* was her big break.' His eyes are big and pleading. 'And she'd shown her script to the director. He blew her off; told her to come back in a year. So I tried to comfort her; told her that was just one director's opinion; that she shouldn't give up.'

I remain stiff. The cold air prickles my skin.

'Yes, I put my arm round her, but that was all. And that was the moment the pap snapped us. I swear to you, Amy, you're the only girl for me. You have to believe me. You're all I think about. I couldn't look at another girl.' He steps towards me.

I remain shivering on the door-step.

'I've been a complete idiot. I was stupid to put you through this for so long. I understand what you've been going through with your friends at college -for *us*. I know how loyal you've been. I don't deserve it.' He is shivering too, despite his layers.

I say nothing.

'I'm so sorry, Amy. I… I want to be an old man, living in our own little house together. I want to meet your friends and your family. I want to introduce you to my mom. She'd love you, Amy,' he smiles. 'I want to share your life and I want you to be in mine. We've done enough hiding and sneaking around.'

The wind blows right inside my dressing gown. Goose-pimples spring up on the backs of my legs. 'You could have any girl you wanted. You're a big star now, Lenny.'

'I want you. I want you and me. Forget everything that goes with it. I'm still that guy you shared a pizza with on the beach. I fell in love with you, Amy. And I've got this mad idea I want to run by you.' He steps closer and drops to his knees.

'What are you doing?'

He takes my hand and my icy fingers are instantly warmed.

'I want to share my life with you. Please, Amy Minor, will you marry me?'

A gust of wind rushes through my nighty to my ribs and I crumple into his arms. Here, in my grandparents' backyard, with the smell of dustbins and the yowling of cats, both of us kneeling on the cold cobbles, I have the best kiss of my life

28

'Who is he?' Suzie Strite remarks at the office the next day.

'Who's who?' I breeze.

'You've been bouncing with air-boots on all day, Amy. It has to be a man.' Her own blonde curls bounce on her shoulders.

'Nothing wrong with being happy.' I can feel my cheeks are glowing and my eyes are sparkling.

'Tell me! What are you thinking?' she persists as I gaze around her immaculate office. Suzie may be a meticulous high-flying editor, but she took to me straight away and I can be myself around her. It is nice to know someone like Suzie appreciates my worth when people like Kay are trying to bring me down.

'I was thinking,' I begin, still looking around the office where every detail has been planned, 'that your house must be like a show-home.'

She looks confused for a moment then takes in the environment to realise why I might have deduced that.

'I bet it's stylish and gorgeous.' I hit her with a bit of flattery to get her off my back.

'Well, thank you. But I have to confess, my house is a tip.' She raises an eyebrow. 'Nothing matches. Nothing has its place. Everything ends up where it's left. I suppose because my life is my work. I don't bother about —anyway! Very sneaky, Miss Minor. Trying to change the subject. I will get to the bottom of it,' she grins.

I beam back at her.

'Whatever you're taking, I want some.'

'Must be my great job, eh?'

Suzie smiles. 'Just make sure you spread it round the office.'

ALL THAT YOU WANT

Lenny doesn't take me to the caravan that night but to the plush hotel room he is now staying in. The ceilings are high and ornate, the en-suite bigger than my whole student flat and the bed so much larger than king-size.

'You're going up in the world,' I remark.

He begins to remove his big coat and hat.

I hand him the box I carried here. 'Careful,' I tell him.

He gently places it on the table pulls up the cloth to reveal two black-and-white hamsters, complete with wheel, shredded paper and an empty toilet roll. He looks at me. The thought had struck on me on the way home from the office, and I'd made a stop at the pet-shop.

'They may be in that cage,' I tell him, 'but they're in it together.'

He pushes me onto the emperor-sized bed and I sink into the luxurious sheets. 'I've missed you.' His kisses prickle my neck as he unzips my coat.

'Wait,' I say.

He sits up.

I sit on the plump pillow and pull my knees to my chest. 'Last night you made all those promises and tonight we're just hiding like ever.'

He shuffles beside me. 'Sorry. I know, I know. I've just missed you, is all. I have to tell you my idea. I've been thinking about it for months, and when I tell you I hope you'll...' He holds my hand.

I sit back and listen.

'I want us to come out; I'm dying for us to be together properly. But, we have to be careful how we do it. We can't let the media know we've been hiding all this time.' He puts his arm round me. 'They would make up so much stuff; come up with reasons as to why we were hiding; they won't just accept that we didn't want them in our business.' He pulls me in to him. 'You've got to get prepared for what it's gonna to be like. Everyone will want to know you. And there could be all sorts printed about you.'

'I don't care. The people who matter will know the truth. So what... how do you wanna do this?'

'Ok, so. Here it is. We stage a meeting; we, "coincidentally", bump into each other. We, of course, recognise each other from our first meeting; your competition, and from your interview. So... we get talking. We start spending time together in public. Then the papers can speculate all they like. Officially, that will be the beginning of our relationship.'

I nod slowly. 'Well, where are we going to stage this meeting? And when?'

'Well, you want to finish college first, right? I think it would be a good idea, before you're subjected to the press. You want to get your A-levels.'

'So... next summer?'

'It's only... just over a year to go. And we've lasted this long already, and after that we'll be able to be together for the rest of our lives. It will be worth it in the end.'

I lean into him. 'Another year and more...'

'I'm just trying to protect you. You've got to believe me. I know the press. You have to finish your education in peace.' He turns to me. 'So my idea is; I want to take you somewhere different from London. Don't you have a grandmother in Miami?'

'Yes...'

'So, after you've finished your A-levels, I was thinking you could take a trip to see her? I'll pay for it, but tell your mom and dad you're planning it now so there'll be time for them to think you're saving. Tell them you want to... have a two week break, to think about what to do after college.'

'As long as I ask Dad in front of Grandma...'

'And I'll be in Miami at the same time as you. Then, we'll both go to the same bar and "recognise" each other. We'll spend the evening together, openly, and the following two weeks as well. Then, I'll ask you to marry me properly. With a ring and everything.' He looks at me, eager yet sheepish. 'So... what do you say to my proposal?'

I meet his shy eyes and can't help but throw my arms around him. 'We're gonna be together for real....'

He smiles. 'No more hiding. So... is it a yes?'

'Yes! Yes, yes, yes.' I hug him tighter and let out a sigh. 'One more year...I can do this. I've only got to live with Sarah and

ALL THAT YOU WANT

Kay for one more term, then they'll finish college. Next year will be more bearable. I can get through this.' I smile at him.

He produces a bottle of champagne from the fridge. 'We're engaged,' he laughs as he pops the cork. We sip from the bottle. Bubbles trickle down my throat.

This wonderful man kisses my neck again and this time I don't push away.

Lenny and I are tangled in the magnificent bed-sheets and the hamsters are gnawing contentedly at the cardboard tube.

'Shall we let them out to run around?' Lenny steps over, naked, and opens their cage. 'Hang on, where's the ball?' He crouches beneath the bed in search.

I admire his body for a moment, then look to the cage from the sheets. 'Lenny, you've left the door open!'

He jumps up.

But the hamsters are still happily chewing their cardboard.

He looks at me, bemused, with the cage door hanging open. 'Looks like they don't want to get out.'

'They don't mind being locked up as long as they're together.'

He sits back beside me. 'What are we gonna name them?'

I grin. 'Daniel and Beddingfield.'

He frowns.

'Gotta get through this,' I laugh.

He moves towards me on the bed. 'One year.'

Spring Term 2002

Within a few weeks, the skin on my hands is clear. My hair has regrown. I have beautiful white tips on my fingernails. *No forehead fingers any more, Kay.*

'I can have painted nails on my wedding day,' I giggle to Jodie.

* * *

Summer Term 2003

As the months count down to The Day, I think, I ought to start looking after my body a little bit – I'll soon be on show. Healthy eating for me – salads and smoothies all the way. I make an appointment for highlights. 'No more mouse,' I tell Jodie. 'I'm going to be the fiancé of a movie star, Daaahling! Papped and in the spotlight.'

'In all the magazines,' Jodie beams. 'Every girl will want to be you. Just make sure you don't lose too much weight.'

I gaze at my reflection. I can still see a paunch in my belly. A while to go yet.

'The day we finish college,' I ask Jodie, 'will you come over to mine for a pamper night? We'll do fake tan, face packs, paint our nails, the works. Because, the day after that… I go to Miami…'

'Sure, and we'll stuff our faces with ice-cream. Put some meat on your bones.' She pinches my waist.

I gulp. 'A girl's night.'

Not long to go now.

29

Kiantown, June 2003

I have just finished telling them my secret.

Mum and Dad stare at me across the living room. They picked me up from my last day of college this afternoon and brought be home through the rain. Now it's early evening.

Rain beats ferociously on the windows, harsh and unrelenting, fighting to break in.

An empty wine bottle and three glasses sit on the coffee table. We all feel sober.

I clear my throat. 'Say something….' I urge.

Beth jumps up. 'I tried to tell you,' she yells at our parents. Her sea-blue eyes dance above her freckles.

My father places down his glass. 'Is all this true?'

I nod. 'The last year *was* easier without Sarah and Kay at college. It felt like an absolute age, but I got through it. I kept myself busy, as you know, with studying, reading a lot of books-'

'-and driving lessons,' Beth adds.

I reach for my mum's hand. 'I am so sorry to have kept it from you. The fewer people who knew about it the less likely it was to come out. But, I wanted to tell you the truth tonight, before-'

'Tomorrow she's going to Miami.' Beth helps Mum and Dad put the pieces together.

'Yes. We finished college today so-'

'So tomorrow the set-up meeting begins,' Beth puts in. 'He's going to be there, in Miami, and they're going to go public.'

Mum clasps her hands. 'Are you two girls having us on?'

'Of course not, Mum,' I tell her.

'Wait and see what happens in the next few days,' adds Beth.

'I just can't believe...' stutters Mum, 'you've been seeing him all this time. And now you're going to come out and live happily ever after...' A few frizzy hairs stand out from her otherwise composed ponytail.

'So, tonight I need to pack...'

Mum nods. 'Right.' She stands vacantly. 'I'll finish making dinner.'

Dad, Beth and I stand. 'Come here.' He hugs me. The taste of musty wool tickles my mouth. His arms are tight and safe. He reaches out and brings Beth into the folds.

Finally, I'm in control. I've battled through the uncertainties. I'm breaking through to the predictable; the plan; the happy ending.

I am an over-seeing eye. I know that right now, Jodie will be sitting at Annie's house, telling her the same truths I have just told my parents. I know that I will go up to my room to pack, then I will have dinner with my family. I know tomorrow I will be on a plane. I know there will be no more secrets and lies.

There's a darkness out there. It's fighting to come in, as I stand in the folds of my family, in the safety of my plan, in the comfort my truths, encased in the artificial light of the living room. I look to the window and all I can see is a black wall, but I can hear the rage and disruption just outside. Wind whistles violently through the gas fireplace. It is almost inside.

I push the feeling down, smile at my dad and his unconditional love –and at my sister and her unshakable smugness - and I advance up to my room to pack for my future.

30

I'm not sure if my parents know whether to believe me. They'll see over the coming fortnight.

Rain taps rhythmically as I pack a suitcase in my bedroom.

After dinner, I'll go next door and tell Sarah. When Jodie has told Annie, she'll come to see me.

Despite the June rain it is warm. I open the window and let the air in.

Although light fills the bedroom and touches every corner, I can see nothing outside.

I gather nail varnish, wax strips and face packs, and pile them neatly on the end of the bed ready for our pampering session.

Mum appears at my door. 'Can I come in?' She sits on the bed and pats it for me to sit beside her. 'I just wanted to say…' she struggles, 'don't let your Grandma Joyce feed you up on too much fried chicken.'

I laugh.

'I'm serious. It'll be all barbeques, Mexican food, fries, beaches.'

'Sounds terrible,' I grin.

She smiles at me. 'I moved away from Miami a long time ago, Darling, and I've changed a lot since then.'

'I know; you used to cook us all that exotic food when we were little –not that seemed exotic to us at the time. And gradually you moved on to cottage pies and roast dinners.'

'I know –because I soon learned I had to warm us all up. My clothes had to change too, from skimpy beach-wear to woolly jumpers. I don't suppose you remember your old Mum in hot-pants, do you? Don't look so horrified. I used to have quite a nice bum.'

'See, even your language has changed over the years.'

'Well, I have been here twenty years.'

'Why would you give up that lifestyle – the weather, the beaches, the food – for rainy old Kiantown?'

She smiles knowingly. 'For love, Darling. Some things are more important than geography. You'll be surprised what you'll do for love.' She strokes my hair.

'I just can't wait for Lenny and me to be together all the time, Mum. Nothing's going to keep us apart anymore.'

'I'm glad you've found happiness,' she beams. 'Well, I'd better dish up. And you'd better put the last bits on your case.' She totters back downstairs.

The case is packed. I close it and drag it to the bedroom door. I turn and look around my room.

For the first time in nearly three years I see the framed photo beside the bed. It's the photograph of the Kian Hill year ten and eleven end of year disco; the photo with Matt Scotts and I side by side. I hardly recognise the young girl staring back at me.

I smile. 'Bye, Matt.' I place the picture into the drawer.

I turn off the light and walk down the stairs, as the warm aroma of the roast floats up to greet me.

As I reach the bottom there is a knock at the door.

'Ames, could you get that?' calls Mum from the kitchen.

I open the door.

In front of me, his hair dripping wet, stands a familiar boy. But he is no longer a boy.

It is Matt Scotts.

31

The smell of warm chocolate fills the kitchen.

Dad dishes up crispy roast potatoes, juicy beef and boiled broccoli while Beth and I lay the table.

'I can't believe my big girl's finished college,' Dad beams.

Oh yeah, so I have. The detail is a tiny grain of flour in the whole cake.

'My mouth's watering.' Dad sits at the table and Beth and I follow suit.

It is like any normal evening. Normal family dinner round the kitchen table. Rain beating outside. Any minute now Mum will walk in and we'll eat, just like normal.

Except it isn't normal. There is an extra place set at the table. When Mum enters the kitchen, she won't be alone. She'll bring with her the person I was once in love with for four years.

Just ten minutes ago I'd stood at the front door, face to face with Matt Scotts.

My whole body had gone ice cold, then burning hot. It couldn't really be him, here at my door. To me, he hadn't existed for the past three years.

The face was a little more grown up. He had a little stubble on his face that was no longer accompanied by the odd spot. His body had broadened. He seemed taller. But those green-yellow eyes. That Roman nose. The line of his jaw. It was him alright. The boy whose photo I'd just removed from beside my bed. The person I'd sought to catch a glimpse of every lunch time, break time and lesson change throughout the whole of my secondary school years. How well I had known that face. And here it was; the dark hair shorter now; drenched with rain, at my doorstep.

I'd suddenly realised neither of us had said a word since I'd opened the door.

Mum had called from the kitchen, 'Amy, come and set the table please.'

I'd jumped, looked back to the kitchen, then back at him.

'Oh, who was at the door?' Mum had come out of the kitchen and walked towards us.

'Mum, this is,' I couldn't say his name because I couldn't believe it was him. I could see him there but how could it be..?

Matt, who hadn't moved or spoken since I'd opened the door, had held out his hand to Mum. 'I'm Matt Scotts. I went to school with Amy.'

Mum had smiled. 'Hello Matthew, come in.'

'Well... I... you're just about to have dinner.'

No, don't go, I'd screamed inside. Then I'd caught myself.

'Join us, Dear,' Mum had insisted. 'Amy's friends are always welcome.'

Matt had looked at me for guidance. I'd tried to keep my face neutral but it can't have worked because he said, 'Thank you, Mrs Minor.'

'You're soaked through, Dear. Come with me. Let me find you something to wear.'

And there I'd stood, the door wide, a sheet of dark rain curtaining the gape, watching my mum lead a dripping Matt up the stairs.

Matt Scotts had knocked on my door. Matt Scotts was in my home.

Dad, Beth and I sit at the table. My stomach tightens as I hear footsteps on the stairs. Maybe I'd imagined it and just Mum alone would walk through the kitchen door. Matt can't be here. But there is an extra place set at the table.

I have to be doing something as he walks in; can't just be still, just looking at him.

I grab the jug from the table and start to pour squash into everyone's glasses.

ALL THAT YOU WANT

The kitchen door opens and my stomach clenches even more. I spill purple juice onto the table, spoiling Mum's best white linen. I run to the sink to grab a cloth.

Mum is in the room. Dad's rugby shirt hangs off the boy that follows her.

I suddenly see the room through his eyes. Details I have overlooked for eighteen years are now new and cringe-worthy. My old-fashioned dad, unaware he has gravy on his chin as he babbles on, waving his fork dangerously. My dithery mum, flour in her fringe, fussing about the table. My sister, scoffing with her mouth open. Mail and dirty dishes scattered about the pokey kitchen. Me, in my old jeans with no make-up on. Hair pulled back into its thoughtless ponytail. My stomach clenches.

The cake smell is getting warmer; fuller in the room.

The summer rain outside is unrelenting, encasing us in the claustrophobic light of the kitchen.

'So Matt,' Dad cuts a piece of potato and pops it into his mouth. 'What do you do?'

Matt holds his knife and fork low. 'I've just finished an apprenticeship in mechanics.'

'Oh, so are you looking for work now? Or will you be able to work for the company you did the apprenticeship with?'

'No, I did it in Newcastle. After I finished school I moved up there with my mum and dad. But it's not, I dunno, for me. So I've just moved back. I'm staying with a friend for a while.' He turns to me. 'Urm, Kay, I'm staying with.'

I nod and stab a carrot. *Urm, Kay, I'm staying with.* The first sentence he has spoken to me in years. I can't speak back to him. He is sitting beside me which means I don't have to look at him. He is close enough to touch. His arm is beside my arm, his thigh just inches from mine. I can't turn to him. Instead, I stare at the dampened purple stain, the table-cloth turning translucent around the edges of the sunken patch.

'Oh, Sarah's friend Kay?' Mum asks.

'Yeah. Sarah was out at Kay's this afternoon; I gave her a lift home and I... remembered you lived next door. So I thought I'd say hi.' He quickly ads, 'I wanna catch up with old mates. Since I'm back.'

Mates?

163

'More gravy?' Mum drowns his beef.

I was eleven years old. It was my first day of school. Sarah had walked me in and we were waiting at the bus drop-off point for Kay. The September morning was cold. I wore my new blue fluffy coat right up to my chin and dug my hands deep into my pockets. I could see my breath in front of my face. The structure was a castle compared to the small brick building of primary school. The kids here were all bigger than me.

Kay's bus pulled in and I looked up at the window. Immediately my eyes fell upon the most astounding face I had ever seen. Those yellow-green eyes stared back at me, expressionless and deep in thought. Those eyes. I wanted to dive into them and see what he was thinking.

His hair was muddy chocolate, his skin golden apart from the first signs of teenage redness. His nose had a slight bend. He was flawless.

Another boy tapped him on the shoulder to bring him out of his trance and he stood to get off the bus.

I hadn't noticed the school-kids had been piling off and now Kay was right at our side.

Sarah and Kay had to practically drag me to reception.

That was it. I was hooked. I'd spend my lunchtimes watching him play football and my evenings thinking about him. I'd look out for him between lesson changes and watch him glide without bouncing, in that ghostly way he had that he was unaware of; otherworldly.

I was thrilled when I found out he was friends with Kay; they lived in the same village; had gone to the same primary school. I could barely speak when Kay introduced us.

But he was the year above me. Would never be interested. He went out with girls in his own year. Hung out with cooler people than me.

I'd never told him how I'd felt. For four long years he'd barely noticed me. And then he'd moved away. That was three years ago. I'd thought it would kill me.

But I'd moved on.

And now he is here. At my kitchen table. Sitting beside me. That boy I could never reach, is here, sitting beside me, calling me a 'mate'.

'So, lad,' this from Dad. 'I bet Newcastle's a bit different from little old Kiantown, eh?'

ALL THAT YOU WANT

I fidget in my chair. My knee knocks his and electricity rushes right through me. They all must be able to see it.

'What are you doing now, Amy?' he is asking me.

'I'm... going to Miami,' I manage to utter.

'Oh cool, when?'

'Tomorrow,' Beth puts in.

'Oh, good job I caught you tonight, then,' he smiles.

'She's staying with our grandma for two weeks and I can't even go,' Beth moans.

I can't sit here and listen to this small talk. I have to find out why he is here.

'Miami. Lucky you.' He is looking at me.

The cake scent from the oven is slowly changing to a black, burnt odour.

'Amy finished her A-levels,' Dad says, 'just today.' The kitchen is growing warmer and my cheeks are burning.

'Well done, Amy,' Matt says. He puts down his knife and fork. He's hardly touched his food. I've eaten none of mine. 'So,' he shuffles, 'tonight's a kind of, celebratory meal... I'm sorry to turn up unannounced. I'd better go.'

'No, no, don't be silly,' Mum says. 'You ought to stay and have some cake. Amy, you'll have some, Love? You've barely touched your dinner...' her comment is upbeat on the surface, but loaded.

Smoke is starting to waft from the oven.

Mum takes a deep sniff. 'Oh dear.' She jumps up.

The cake Mum places on the table in front of us is black all over. It has been in the oven too long. The sweet chocolate of earlier is charcoaled. It is too late for it to be saved. It has gone beyond the sweetness into tastelessness.

Beth leans into Matt and whispers, 'You don't have to eat it.'

Matt looks at it and looks at Mum. 'No, I'm sure it will be great.'

Mum takes a knife and begins cutting the burnt crust from the outside of the cake. Underneath, the soft spongy brown shows through. The sweet smell fights the burnt wafts. 'I won't be offended if you don't want any, Dear. It's probably gone beyond,' Mum pinks.

'No, no, it hasn't. It's still perfect underneath. The best things in life need time… to be cooked to perfection.'

In a sudden moment of mercy there is silence outside. The rain has stopped. I seize it. 'Matt?'

'Yeah?'

'Shall we go for a walk? Mum, we can have cake when we come back.' I am up and darting for the door before he can reply.

Matt slides back his chair. 'Thank you, Mr and Mrs Minor,' and he comes after me.

32

Matt has the same springless way of walking he always has, where he almost seems to glide above everything.

The night is mild after the summer rain. The grass is moist beneath our shoes and the river is quiet as we draw near. The glow from the houses in the cul-de-sac behind us guides our way. We reach the water and hesitate.

'Um,' I stutter, 'shall we go this way?' I point left.

He nods and we walk on. There is no moon to be seen. We step softly towards a large oak tree. I can't see it but I know it. The darkness turns it into a black mass block. The grass smells of summer rain.

'So… you've lost weight..?' he remarks. Then hastens, 'Not that you needed to, it's just… you're mum seemed worried…'

I stare ahead at the black block. God, was I really big at school? I hold in my stomach.

The sounds from the houses have gone now and all I can hear is my breath and our footsteps. My hands are stuffed in my jacket pockets. Although I am standing about a metre away from him I can feel him. To stand any closer would be too close. As I look to the top of the tree, in my peripheral vision I see his profile; his strong nose, his slightly parted lips, the slope of his forehead. I look down at my white trainers and faded trousers. In the corners of my eyes I see his wide dark jeans.

I look away from him, to my left, to my house and then to Sarah's, next door. Sarah has been at Kay's with him all afternoon. She's been with Matt. He's been right here. I'd been in Dad's car, on my way back from college, about to embark on my future. I was so clear, so sure, so on my way. Tomorrow I'll be flying to Miami, to see Lenny. All planned out. Matt Scotts couldn't have been further from my mind. He was the other side of the country, might as well have been the other side of the world. But he wasn't; isn't. He's right here. Right beside me. And I can't see him. Won't see him.

The clouds cover the stars tonight.

We walk further from my house, from my ideas; my plans.

The tree is getting closer, bigger.

The air is still and quiet. Neither of us has spoken.

'So,' he says finally. 'These marriage plans, big shock eh?'

My body stiffens. 'What?'

'Kay and Thomas. Didn't you know?'

I breathe. 'Oh, yes.' Poor Thomas, forever the lapdog.

'They'll be having an engagement party soon.'

'Is that why you're back? For Kay's wedding?'

'No, I don't expect they'll get wed for a year or so yet.'

'So... were you all talking about weddings this afternoon? At Kay's? You and Kay... and Sarah?'

'Oh, a bit. What else would Kay be talking about?'

We walk on.

'So...' he says, 'what are you going to do now college has finished?'

'Um...' All I can think is; 'I'm going to Miami tomorrow.'

'Yeah,' he nods. 'What are your plans after that?'

I'm going to marry Lenny.

'I mean, are you going to uni or anything?'

'Oh... I don't know really. I'd... like to get into journalism.'

'Cool.'

I swallow. 'Are you... happy... enjoying... what you're doing?'

'Yeah, glad the apprenticeship has finished. I'm qualified. Got a proper grown up job now. Well sort of. I'm still the newbie. The skivvy, really.'

The houses have left us behind now and we're nearly under the tree. We can see the leaves and the patterns in the bark. The branches are no longer one mass but individuals. As we come right beneath it we can no longer see its full shape.

The bridge is to our right. We step onto it.

I stop in the middle and look down. I can't see the water; only black. The branches hang above us, blocking out the sky.

ALL THAT YOU WANT

I grip the railing, no longer having to hide my finger-nails.

Matt stands beside me. We both lean on the wooden edge and look down at the invisible river. 'I'm glad I got to come and see you tonight.' He turns his head to me.

I keep looking down into the blackness. 'To be honest I'm surprised you thought of coming to see *me*.'

'I wanted to.'

I'm still looking down as I speak. 'Why did you come back?' I risk a look at him. I hold my gaze a little too long. I quickly look back down. 'I mean, you don't have to tell me if it's... personal or anything.' Something could have gone sour for him up there. But I can't help myself. 'Was there... a girl up there? Someone special? I mean... sorry. It's none of my business.'

'No, no. Erm, I mean, there's been... a girl or two in the last three years but no-one... special. Because... there was always someone else in the back of my mind, here at home.'

Kay. It has to be Kay. That's why he's come back now, when she's getting married.

I turn to look at him. Those deep eyes pour into me.

His dark hair has dried now. His chin is closer to me than I ever remember it being. Dad's rugby shirt hangs off him. The polo shirt is open at the neck, revealing his collar bone. He steps towards me.

The moon is emerging from behind the clouds.

A flash dances on his chest and my eyes jump to it.

He follows my gaze and holds the pendant. His hands are thick and cracked.

'I've just realised,' he murmurs, 'that I'm in love with someone. And that's why I had to come back. I don't know what she'll say, but... I've got to give it a go. You can't lose what you never had, right?'

'I suppose...' My throat is dry.

He takes my hand and that electricity rushes through me. He brings it to his chest. He places the pendent in my fingers, revealing it to be a silver locket. The chain is still hanging around his neck as I hold my thumbs on the catch. I open the locket. And I look at the picture.

It is part of the photo from the end-of-year ten and eleven school disco, three years ago. The photo I've had by my bed since then; the photo I've just put into a drawer. A photo with every girl and boy in Matt's year and in my year. This, in his locket, is a piece cut out from that picture. The cutting contains two people. A girl and a boy.

Matt Scotts and me, Amy Minor.

33

I pull away from Matt and dart off the bridge. The darkness is so dense. I can feel the wet grass beneath my shoes but I am running blind. I race towards the light of the houses. My toe stubs something hard. I trip. My knees hit the floor, then my hands follow. The world is on its head. I jump to my feet and continue to run. My toe throbs. My knees and the heels of my hands burn. My insides are all in the wrong place. I feel like Dorothy, whirling.

At last I reach Sarah's back door and bang hard. Her mother answers, looking tired. Sarah appears behind her with a huge knowing grin on her face, which quickly falls when she takes in my appearance.

'Sarah, come over to mine,' I plead.

She wastes no time and stuffs her feet half way into her trainers.

I run out of her back garden and into mine, with Sarah scuffing behind.

Once inside my back door, she kicks off the dirty shoes and is at my heels up the stairs. The house still smells of burnt cake.

'Amy? Hi, Sarah,' Mum calls as we pass her carrying a full basket of ironing.

I throw open my bedroom door and Smokey, Sarah's giant fluffy cat, darts out of the room.

'How did she get in here?' Sarah muses.

We feel a breeze and our eyes dart to the wide open window. I run to shut it, to keep the darkness outside. I run back to slam the bedroom door, just as Mum appears at it.

'Everything ok, girls? I've just let Smokey outside…'

'Oh yeah, she must have got up the trellis...' I go to close the door.

'How are you, Sarah, love?' Mum presses.

'Mum, I need to talk to Sarah, please.'

Mum frowns at me. 'Ok, Love. Your friend gone?'

'Yes,' I reply shortly.

'Ok.' Finally, defeated, she shuffles away.

I close the bedroom door and stand against it, staring at Sarah.

'Ok, this is not the mood I thought I'd find you in tonight. I thought... you'd be ecstatic by now.'

'Sarah, I need to tell you something.' I edge away from the door, satisfied that Mum has gone, and sit on the bed. I motion for Sarah to sit beside me. 'Something's been going on. You want me to tell you why I haven't been interested in any of those college blokes?'

She smiles. 'I think I know.'

'No you don't. You haven't got a clue.' I pull the pillow onto my lap and squeeze it. 'Do remember... when I went to Hollywood to meet Lenny Hunter?'

She frowns again. 'Yes?'

'Well... we got on really well and... we've been seeing each other ever since.'

Sarah's body stiffens.

'He's been making British films in London. He gave me this mobile phone. Sarah, it's been going on for nearly three years. But we're not going to hide any more. We're engaged.'

Sarah moves away from me on the bed.

'I'm going to Miami tomorrow for two weeks to, kind of, stage a meeting. We don't want the press knowing we've been hiding all this time because... well... it'll just cause too much hassle. As far as the rest of the world will know, we get together over the next two weeks. And... we're getting married in autumn.'

Sarah stands and begins to pace the room.

'I'm sorry I've been keeping it from you all this time, but, we couldn't tell everyone, not at first. But I want you to know.'

Sarah begins shaking her head furiously. 'No, no, no. Amy... this fantasy – this manifestation... I don't know if it's been a

ALL THAT YOU WANT

coping strategy for you because you couldn't have Matt... so you invented this... imaginary relationship... I don't know, but you need help, Amy. I don't know how to deal with this.' She makes for the door.

I run to grab her. 'Sarah? Why won't you believe me?' I push my weight against the door.

She reaches round me and tries to pull the handle. 'You can't seriously expect me to believe you've been having a secret affair with Lenny Hunter? Let me out. It's for your own good.'

Knock, knock, knock.

We both freeze.

'Amy, Sarah, it's me,' comes Jodie's voice through the door.

We both breathe out and I open the door.

When Jodie steps inside, tub of ice-cream in hand, I quickly close it again. She looks at me questioningly. 'Have you told her yet?'

'Has she told me she's been having a secret romance with a film star? Yes, she has. You haven't been taken in by this fantasy, have you?'

We stand in a spikey triangle.

Jodie shoots daggers through her hazelnut eyes. 'You're not going to turn on her again, are you? We're meant to be her friends, and you don't believe her?'

'A friend would *get help* for a friend with these delusional ideas.'

My two best friends are throwing words at each other at the same time and all I can hear is the clash.

I dart to my phone by the bed and tap a text. 'Call me please.'

In a few seconds my phone is ringing and the war of words falls.

I answer. 'Hi, Lenny,' I breathe.

Sarah stares at me.

'Hey, you. Can't wait to see you tomorrow.' He sounds so far away.

I gulp. 'I'm just telling my best friends about... about you, about the plan... Sarah and Jodie are here now, will you talk to them?'

'Yea, sure, put me on speakerphone.'

173

I do. I hold the mobile out towards them. Both girls step closer.

The gorgeous Chicago twang plays into the room. 'Hey Jodie, hey Sarah. I've heard so much about you. How are you guys?'

Jodie steps up. 'Hi, Lenny. You'd better look after our Amy.'

He laughs. 'Yessir. I sure will. Well, I guess I'll meet you guys soon. You can grill me in detail.'

Jodie smiles. 'We're just glad she's found happiness. Right, Sarah?'

Sarah stands open mouthed and manages to murmur, 'Er, yeah...'

I bring the phone back to my lips. 'Well, I'd better go. Lots to sort out. See you tomorrow.'

'See you tomorrow. I love you.'

I gulp. 'You too.' I hang up.

Our triangle stares at each other in silence.

Then, at last, 'I'm sorry, Amy.' It is Sarah who breaks the silence. 'I'm sorry for everything, sorry for doubting you... I... was just trying to help...'

I stop her. 'It's done now. New chapter.'

'But what about...' Sarah starts. 'Didn't... Did you get a... *visitor* this evening?'

Now it's Jodie's turn to be in the dark.

I close my eyes but a tear escapes. 'Yes. Matt Scotts came to see me.' I sink onto the bed.

Jodie stares. 'What?' She sits next to me, as does Sarah. 'What, why? Why's he here? I thought he was in Newcastle? What? What did he want?'

My trembling hand moves to the bedside drawer. 'He wanted to show me something... he had a locket round his neck.' Shaking, I pull the drawer open and take out the framed photo. The rows of faces smile at us from my lap. 'The locket had a cut-out of part of this photo. Two faces.' My fingers move among the many figures until they rest upon the two.

But Jodie has already guessed. She is a dart. 'What is he playing at? I suppose he told you he has feelings for you?'

'I didn't give him chance to say anything. I ran.'

Knock, knock.

We all freeze again.

'Only me.' Mum pokes her head around the door. 'Your friend Matt is here to collect his coat. Did you want to see him?'

I am stiff.

Jodie answers quickly, 'I don't think that's a good idea.'

Mum nods. 'I'll go and give him his coat then.' She closes the door again.

'I ought to go and give that rat a piece of my mind,' Jodie fumes.

'No,' I cry.

'Who does he think he is, coming back and trying to mess you about, when you're, you're *sorted*?'

'He's not trying to mess her around,' Sarah retorts. 'He's come back because he's in love with her. How was he to know she was having a secret love affair - that she's *engaged*?'

'He's... in love with me?' I whisper.

'Of course he is, Amy. He... realised it up there in Newcastle. He was talking about you all afternoon. He turned up, out of the blue, at Kay's, in a right state, asking us what to do. He said he couldn't bear it anymore, he had to come back and find out if he had a chance with you. He's going to stay with Kay, until he works this out. He wants to get a job down here and everything. He told us how he can't stop thinking about you, and that he wanted to come and tell you. But he was scared. I was furious with him for waiting for so long. For putting you through – well, I thought... putting you through torture for all these years and I told him to go for it - how was I to know? I thought it would make you happy. I thought it was what you wanted. I thought you'd be ecstatic to see him and to hear, at last, after all this time, that he feels the same way...'

I can't speak. I find a loose thread at the bottom of my top and I pull at it.

'Oh, Sarah,' Jodie shakes her head. 'You should have told him where to go. It's too late. Look at her; all this has done is mess with her head. She was happy. She was over it.'

'Matt Scotts was the object of Amy's desires all through school. I thought... I dunno, it was romantic that he finally felt the same way. I was excited for them. This is all she's ever wanted... How long can it last with a celeb? How real can it be?

He's gonna get bored, Amy, and realise he can have any girl he wants. A model, an actress, anyone.'

'Lenny's not like that,' Jodie retorts.

'Matt has been in love with you all these years, it's just taken him forever to realise it. He's gone off, got everything out of his system. But in the end he came back to you. He came all the way back down here for *you*. You never made that effort to follow him up there. You must mean a hell of a lot to him, Amy. I gave him the courage to come and see you tonight. I told him you wanted him. I assured him. Oh, Amy, take your happy ending.'

'Sarah, there's a man who's made Amy happy for the past three years,' Jodie retorts. 'He waited for her when she wasn't around; he's the only man she's ever been with. He helped her write her C.V; he took jobs in London just to spend some time with her.' Jodie turns to me. 'He adores you, doesn't he? He doesn't want all the models; he wants you. He's had plenty of opportunities to go off, if he'd wanted to. Why would he stick around, Sarah, for this long, if he wasn't genuine? Why would he want to marry her? Matt Scotts can't expect her to just wait around for him, moping. He's lost his chance. Amy's moved on. Her life is with Lenny. He'll treat her like a princess. Amy, he wants to live with you for the rest of your life.'

I'm wrapping the thread tighter and tighter around my index finger. My finger tip is bulging and blue.

'What it comes down to is,' Sarah says softly, 'Amy needs to know her own heart. It's how she feels that matters. You can only be in love with one man.'

'Can you?' I whisper. The cord snaps. I gently unwind it, back and back, freeing the blood flow once more.

'Look, let's make a pros and cons list for them both.' Sarah grabs a pen and paper from my desk. 'For Matt; pro, you loved him all those years. For Lenny, con, he kept you hidden for all this time.'

Jodie tuts. 'Lenny, pro, he treats Amy like she matters. Matt, con, he acted as if she was nothing.'

Sarah stands and walks to my book case. She runs her hand along a shelf of videos. 'How many times have we watched this on our girly nights?' She pulls out a Julia Roberts film, *My Best*

ALL THAT YOU WANT

Friend's Wedding. 'What is it Julia Roberts says to Cameron Diaz? You don't always want the fancy crème Brule. Sometimes you want plain and simple jelly. Or *Jello*, as they call it.'

'Do you know what I want?' I jump up and scramble under the bed. I begin to pull out shoes and suitcases and black bags full of soft toys. 'When I was at primary school, I used to sleep with Fred Bear. Then, when I moved to secondary, I decided I was too old for cuddly toys and I stuffed them all in a bin bag and they haven't been out since.' My pang for the old brown one-eyed thing is sudden and over-bearing. 'Right now I need something from before all this; from before I met Matt Scotts or - urgh!' I yell. As I pull out the last bin bag, a lifeless, grey mass of wet fur flies out with it. It has a pointed nose and sharp claws and a long strong tail.

'What...' Jodie cries. We are all on our feet now.

'A river rat...' I stutter.

'What? How?' Jodie splurts.

Sarah and I look at each other. 'Smokey.' I run for the door. 'I'll go and get a bucket or something to pick it up with.'

In the kitchen, I tell Mum and Dad why I need the bucket and the dustpan and brush. They chase me back upstairs.

I approach the inert creature and lie the bucket on one side. My parents and friends look on. I am about to push the body into the container with the brush, when the animal jumps up. I leap backwards. The rodent is darting for the door. Dad slams it shut. In turn, Sarah, Jodie and Mum leap onto the bed. The neat pampering pile topples to the floor.

I pick up the bucket bring it down on top of the vermin, forcing my weight onto it.

'Smokey must have just stunned it,' Mum says, still on the bed.

I pick up a yellow English text book and, with Dad's help, manage to slide it under the bucket, turning the pail quickly to keep the animal inside. 'Open the window,' I yell, ready to throw the creature, bucket, textbook and all.

'No,' calls Dad, taking it from me. 'I'll put it out.' He exits the room and heads downstairs.

Jodie gingerly steps down from the bed. 'You should have killed it, Amy. Now it'll be right outside your house.'

Sheepishly, Sarah helps Mum down from the bed. There is a squelch. Her slippered foot lands on a cucumber face-scrub sachet, splattering the frogspawn-like gunk over the carpet.

'So much for our pampering night...' Jodie murmurs.

We survey the room. The contents from underneath the bed are spilled around the carpet. The bed sheets are pulled out. My usually orderly room is now in chaos.

Mum puts her hands on her hips. 'Those creatures carry diseases, you know. We'll have to disinfect this room.'

Later, after Dad has returned from the back garden and my room has been practically fumigated, Jodie, Sarah and I set up camp in the living room. Beth insists on joining us – oddly wanting to spend time with me. We all take up Mum's suggestion of having something sweet to eat. With the cake ruined, we decide to make jelly to go with Jodie's ice-cream.

We sit on the siting-room floor in our quilts and sleeping bags by the soft light of the lamp and tuck into the sweet red simplicity.

Sarah licks her spoon. 'I'd take *"Jello"* over crème Brule any day, hey Ames?'

'Yes,' I nod. 'The question is; which one is *Jello*, and which is crème Brule?'

34

I lie awake listening to the others sleeping. The living room is alien with no lights on and I wonder how they can slumber so soundly when the world is unrecognisable.

Again, I re-live the moment I opened the door. The surge that went through my body – I was immediately back at school, turning a corner between lesson changes, and he would be right there. That rush of electricity that would go through me, tonight, returned.

That Roman nose. Those yellow-green eyes. The hair, soaked to his head. Could it really be the same boy from my school days? I remember a quietly assured lad who used to flick the curtains from his eyes and don his luminous sports jacket, gliding with the tide, oblivious to how he glistened.

The being who'd visited tonight bore the same unassuming flick of the head - although the curtains were gone - in much the same way as Julia Smith from my Maths class had continued to push an imaginary pair of glasses up her nose, long after she'd changed to contacts.

But this man was not a school boy. He was broad, with stubble, and showed no signs of the dismissive attitude Matt Scotts had presented me with throughout school.

He talked in the same quiet tones that make you have to really pay attention. He walked with the same enchanting glide. But this man, unlike Matt at school, looked at me when he spoke. This couldn't be the same boy who used to shrug me off, who, every break-time and lunchtime, was only interested in playing football, who never noticed me on the side-lines. This grown man, tonight, had done much more than just acknowledge me. I still feel the shivers in my chest, in my stomach, from when he took my hand.

At school, Matt was the cool, unreachable, older guy. His revelation on the bridge tonight showed me a side of him I've never seen before. He presented me with a new vulnerability. He opened a door that has always been locked. He has always been unreachable; unreadable. Now he's shown me this part of him I never knew was there. I never dreamed…

I don't know if it's always been there and he's denied it. I don't know if his… feelings… are newfound. I don't have any idea where they could have sprung from; what could have caused him, after three years, to come to my door.

Somebody up there is looking down on me… or playing games with me. I have imagined this moment for so long. I imagined it in the Orchard, in the classroom, at the beach. Sometimes in my head, he would quietly approach me and take my hand, and not say anything at all. And we would both just know. Other times, in my fantasies, he would break down and cry, and beg me to give him a chance. One time, he even climbed the trellis outside my bedroom window.

I genuinely don't believe it could be possible for anyone else in the world to feel about someone the way I used to feel about Matt. That was a one off. It was too big. If it exists for other people, why isn't there a bigger deal made about it? It's the biggest thing in the world. It eclipses everything. How could more people than me be going around feeling like that? I know there are love songs and there are soppy films. But none of them even get close to describing the enormity; the all-consuming, gut-wrenching, deep-down crippling emotions I felt towards Matt. How could that be what people mean by love? The world 'love' doesn't come close. I couldn't bear it sometimes.

After all this time, someone up there has answered my longings. I have been given everything I have ever wanted. Now that it's too late.

And now I'm terrified. Petrified I'm going to give up something I yearned for so long.

Lenny and me, we clicked from the off. We just work. He is my every day. We just fit. Lenny was a man when I met him - a

ALL THAT YOU WANT

man of twenty, but older than me- with a career already. Now Matt is a grown-up. A qualified mechanic. And I suppose, over the last three years, it's happened to me too. Without me noticing it, I've turned from a school-girl into an adult journalist. Is eighteen an age to make a decision about the rest of your life?

This living-room is unfamiliar in the dark. A room I've grown up in and should know well. But it dawns on me, I've never slept in here. I've never seen it at this hour. How much smaller it feels, with four bodies stretched out on the floor, the lights from the DVD player whiling away the witching hours. As I breathe in the sleeping-bag smell I realise the last time I slept in one was in the tent with Lenny. The metal zip is cold on my shoulder. As I twist, the body-bag follows my movements.

The rhythms of Beth's breathing and the ticking mantel-clock are out of sync. I can't tell if my sister needs to slow down or speed up to keep time.

The taste of jelly repeats in mouth and I am drawn to Sarah's earlier comment. But, as I think of the comfort and safety of Lenny's arms, compared with the awakening inside me with Matt's appearance, I'm led back to my question. Which is 'Jello' and which is crème Brule?

35

The airport is swarming the next morning. I struggle to move forward with my heavy luggage. The crowds are pressing in on me, bumping me. I turn to apologise to a woman behind me who has just barged me. As I turn, I see the floppy hair and the Roman nose, and the deep yellow-green eyes bearing into me.

Matt is standing behind the queue of people, looking, waiting.

I face forward and do not turn back again. Finally, my passport is checked and I am free of my heavy bag. Without looking behind me, I turn and almost skip now that I am not laden, dodging through families of American accents wearing Goofy hats and Mickey Mouse t-shirts, and avoiding old ladies on mobility scooters. I glide up the escalator three steps at a time, squeezing past other travellers. I remove my jacket and jewellery, throwing them into the little tray with my handbag. A security officer ushers me through. Still I don't turn back. As I step through the frame I wait for a beep. None comes. I am through.

Miami, June 2003

Miami is sticky and close. My grandmother greets me at the airport and takes me out into the overbearing heat. The sun is so blindingly bright I can hardly take in what the old woman is saying to me. It has been a few years since my last visit.

Her hair is still purple, her hugs still full of sharp fingers and elbows and her clothes are still loud. Her little house is still air conditioned and protected by mosquito nets, her sitting room still floral, and her cactus plants still dry and spiky.

ALL THAT YOU WANT

The evening brings slight relief from the relentless sun. I wear a loose white top, denim shorts and flip-flops as we make our way to the arranged venue. Grandma twangs at me all the way there, her purple curls bobbing with each word, and I nod and smile.

The beach bar is open air, with cool patios and low music.

Lenny, dressed in beach shorts and a loose t-shirt, is sitting at a table with three suited body-guards. Half of me wants to dive into his arms, while the other half wants to run away. He doesn't look up as Grandma and I walk in and order our pinna-coladas.

We seat ourselves a few tables away from him. Grandma hasn't spotted him and I wonder if she even knows who he is. Other diners are pointing and whispering at him.

'Well, Sweetie, I just can't believe you are doing so well with this journalism already. I am so proud of you,' my grandmother beams.

Behind her, I glimpse Lenny lean in to say something to one of his bodyguards. They are both looking our way now.

The bodyguard heads towards our table. 'Excuse me, ladies.'

Grandma and I look up.

'Mr Hunter would be honoured if you would join him at his table.'

Grandma looks over to the actor. 'That handsome fellow there?'

'That's Lenny Hunter, Grandma,' I whisper.

'The movie-star you met in Hollywood?'

'That's right.'

Grandma looks back up to the patient bodyguard. 'Tell Mr Hunter we'd be delighted.'

We pick up our drinks, our bags and our shawls and follow the bodyguard, who proceeds to pull up two extra chairs.

The sun is setting over the ocean creating a brilliant illusion on the water.

The whispering and pointing grows louder. People are barely trying to hide it now. Some even take photos.

Lenny smiles easily. 'Amy Minor, isn't it?' he asks me.

'Yes, and this is my grandmother, Joyce Bayer.'

'Pleased to meet you, Mrs Bayer.' He extends a hand and kisses hers and I am back at the staged photos in front of the private jet in California. He asks the bodyguard to bring us more drinks, then turns to me. 'I thought it was you, Amy, from the competition win. How long ago was that now? Two years ago? Three? It's great to see you again. Tell me, what brings you to Miami? What have you been doing with yourself?' And so the script continues.

His eyes send me a secret message that everything will be ok, but he lies so readily. And now all my living grandparents are victims of our scheming.

The nearby cameras continue to flash and the drinks remain flowing.

Suddenly, a new song begins. It is *If I Let You Go* by Westlife. 'My favourite song,' I utter aloud.

Lenny stands. 'Care to dance?'

I look around me and stand, on the spot.

He pulls me close to him and we move gently about the deck overlooking the beach. Our fingers are entwined but we can't we see other; we are too close. I lean into him and let the lyrics wash over me.

Finally, Lenny says, 'You must join me for lunch tomorrow, Amy, if you're free?'

The sun disappears completely now and it is cold.

The next couple of weeks are a blind bundle of crowded cafés, bustling beaches and swarming streets. Lenny advances confidently through the chaos, leading me; guiding me; forcing me through it. The bodyguards help us fight through teeming people, but even the burly blokes can't prevent the flashes of cameras, the glare of the sun or the claustrophobic heat. The sweet, intoxicating coconut drinks flow. Lenny tries to protect me but his touch is prickly to my sticky skin. I cannot hear anything clearly; there are too many people talking at once. And I cannot see past the piercing glares.

During this time I learn that Daniel and Beddingfield, the hamsters, didn't make it through it the year.

The aromas of grilled meat and fish waft from the barbeque. The sand is soft yet stony beneath my feet. A Reggae band plays on the stage and hordes of holiday-makers dance. My

ALL THAT YOU WANT

grandmother's purple mop bobs to the music and she tucks into a hotdog. It is my final night at her house.

Lenny holds my clammy hand. Still the cameras flash at us.

In a large pot a lobster boils, the lid bubbling, and I am sure it is about to burst. Lenny's hired people stand in a line, each holding a champagne bottle, ready to pop.

The music stops. Lenny raises his voice. 'Can I have your attention, please?'

The few eyes that weren't already on us now join the rest.

'I met this lovely girl two-and-a-half years ago,' Lenny beams, and his face is electric. 'And I haven't been able to stop thinking about her. She has since interviewed me for a London newspaper. And, this month, I have been lucky enough for our paths to cross once more. This time, I don't want to let her pass me by.'

Lenny is on one knee, staring at me earnestly, and the crowd gasps.

Sweat trickles down the back of my neck. The sun is harsh today. The barbeque sizzles. The lobster bubbles.

Lenny produces a small box from his pocket. 'Amy Minor.' He opens it. 'Would you do me the honour of becoming my wife?'

The ring is almost as dazzling as the sun. The people inhale. The cameras flash wildly. The lobster boils madly. Lenny smiles broadly up at me. The champagne corks are poised.

I close my eyes and answer. 'Yes.'

36

Southwest England, July 2003

We are in a hotel on the south coast of England, about twenty miles from Kiantown.

We are viewing the extravagant cliff-top Rock Point Hotel in consideration for a wedding venue. Lenny and I follow the smart woman in spiky heels and a pin-striped suit as she elaborately reveals the history of the ornate beams and intricate ceilings.

Lenny, walking beside me, is dressed in an expensive blue suit – he looks marvellous in a suit - while I wear a flowing summer dress and think how uncomfortably hot they both must be.

The marble floors clack under our shoes, and each step echoes. The windows stretch from floor to ceiling and beyond them lies the sea, shimmering in the sunshine.

The spiky woman opens a heavy set of doors and leads us into a vast hall. She lures us into the bright room, so open; innumerable chandeliers dangle above us, velvet curtains are swept aside from each giant window, and delicate lilies are placed around the table-tops.

'This is the reception-suite,' she informs us, and suddenly my mind's eye has filled the room with wedding guests, laughing, drinking and dancing, and I am in the middle, embodied by a huge meringue, bustled and twirled, with no control of my legs or my feet, or any of my body.

My chest is tight. I can't find my breath.

'Amy?' Lenny is instantly at my side. 'What's wrong?'

I gasp. 'I need some air.'

'Ok, I'll take you outside.' He holds my elbow.

ALL THAT YOU WANT

I pull away. 'I need some space. You stay here and... carry on... Just give me five minutes.'

He relents. 'Ok... We've only got to talk about the boring financial side of things anyway.'

I am gone. I almost run to the enormous front-doors and am out in the gardens, steadying myself on a statue. I find a bench and sit, staring out across the beach. My stomach is tight.

My family and I have visited this beach countless times over the years. I have endless memories of building sandcastles with Mum, eating ice-creams with Beth, and splashing in the sea with Dad.

But it is the one time I rode the bus here on my own that sticks in my throat the most.

I was eleven years old and I was one of the four musketeers. People think there were three, but they forget D'Artagnan. There were Athos, Porthos, Aramis and D'Artagnan.

In our gang, there was Jodie; there was Annie; there was me; and there was Nicole. Four girls thrown together in our year-seven tutor-group on the first day of secondary school. Jodie and Annie had gone to the same village primary school. Everyone else in the tutor-group had a buddy from their old school. Everyone except Nicole and me. My primary-school-buddy had moved away over the summer, and Nicole, for some reason, didn't have a buddy from her old school. The popular kids in the class soon grouped together in a pack. And Jodie wasn't about to let Nicole or me be left on our own, so she scooped us up, along with Annie, and bumbled us through our first few weeks of Kian Hill.

Jodie was a tornado, and the three of us followed in her wake. She led us on exploration expeditions and introduced us to the older kids from her school-bus. She chased boys while we watched shyly, and she had enough confidence and bravado for the three of us hangers-on put together.

One lunchtime, Jodie was playing chase with Thomas from the year above. His floppy hair bounced as he chased her round the sports-shed. Annie and I hung by Nicole's wheelchair, too scared to join in the game.

Nicole had to use her wheelchair at lunchtimes and break-times. She wasn't allowed to exert herself too much. Her bones were weak, and any knocks could cause a brake.

MICHELLE WOOLLACOTT

This lunchtime, she decided she was fed up of being careful. She didn't want to simply watch anymore. She rose from her chair and ran to the sports-shed to join in with Jodie and Thomas.

As Annie and I watched, standing with the empty chair, Nicole moved her frail little legs faster than she had ever before. She whooped and yelped with the freedom of running. And then came the crash. She fell on the corner, right into the side of the wooden wall. Her yells quickly turned from happiness to urgency. Blood covered her head. She lay in agony on the ground.

Then came the sirens, and an ambulance sped our friend away.

In English that afternoon, I unhooked from my schoolbag the clip-on key-ring that Nicole had given me for my birthday. I absentmindedly fiddled with the karabiner and stared out of the window.

When old Mr Banton asked me a question, of course I had no idea of the answer, so he swiftly confiscated what he thought was the object of my distraction; the key-ring.

I was determined to get the gift back so, after school, I hid in the girls' toilets for half an hour.

I immerged with the intention of creeping to Banton's classroom. I tiptoed down the empty corridors, passing cleaners' trolleys and bin-bags. I'd never smelt the school so full of woody polish and disinfectant. The sound of the vacuum gave away which rooms to pass with extra care.

Cautiously, I turned a corner –and bumped right into you. Your deep eyes and crooked Roman nose were closer to me than they'd ever been before.

I willed the redness to disappear from my face as we in turn asked each other what we were doing there. I explained to you about the key-ring, and you told me your mum was at a PTA meeting so you had to hang around to wait.

You wished me luck in finding Nicole's present and we both moved on.

As luck would have it, I found Banton's room unlocked and empty.

I dashed to the teacher's desk and tugged at the drawers. They were all locked.

Suddenly I heard footsteps running towards me. I froze. You appeared at the doorway. You darted into the room.

'Banton's coming!' you hissed. Before I knew it, you had grabbed my hand and pulled me under the desk.

We kept as still as we could and held our breaths as we heard the English teacher enter.

ALL THAT YOU WANT

I'd never been so close to you before. Our sides were pressed against each other as we squashed up under the desk. We could see the teacher's beige trouser legs as he rifled through his paper work. Then, apparently having retrieved what he had been looking for, the shiny black lace-ups strode away and we heard the door close behind him.

Each letting out our breath, you and I scrabbled up from under the table.

'Did you find it?' you whispered.

I shook my head. 'The drawers are locked.' I pulled at them to show you for good measure.

'You'd better go. That was close.'

I nodded and scuttled off.

At home, I thought of nothing but you; of the feel of your arm pressing against mine; of how you had gone out of your way to help me. I saw nothing but your face as I lay in bed that night.

I awoke, buzzing, and was ready for school half an hour early. I played with my cereal. My stomach was dancing.

In the hall, the phone rang. Mum answered it while six-year-old Beth babbled to me. I lifted the loops on my spoon and let them plop, plop, back into my bowl.

Mum returned to the kitchen with a serious face and sent Bethany away to brush her hair.

It was about Nicole, Mum said.

Pangs of guilt rushed through me. She had been in hospital all night and all I could think of was a boy.

'Can we go and see her after school?' I asked.

Mum sat beside me and held my hand. We couldn't go and see her. Because, with her fragile skull, Nicole had suffered severe head injuries and the doctors hadn't been able to save her. My friend had passed away in the night.

I spent all day at home, not knowing how to process this. I phoned Jodie's house in the afternoon, but neither of us knew what to say. It was the same when I phoned Annie.

The next day, not knowing if it was the right thing to do, I returned to school. Jodie and Annie weren't there so I sat at our table of four alone. I could have found Sarah at lunchtime but I preferred to be by myself. I wandered to the Secret Garden; the overgrown lawn of an abandoned house that the four of us had discovered, through a hole in the hedge at the bottom of the field, while exploring during our first weeks of school.

I sat under the old cherry tree, gazing blankly at nettles and fallen leaves.

It wasn't long before I heard a scramble from the hedge, and I looked to see you appear through the gap.

You emerged fully and brushed yourself off. 'I saw you come in here,' you said.

I shrunk into myself.

You sat beside me and reached into your pocket. 'I got it for you.' You handed me the clippy key-ring.

I took it. 'Thank you,' I murmured.

You shuffled beside me. 'Sorry about your friend.'

Neither of us spoke for some time. The wind picked up and we hugged our knees and our coats to our bodies, our black school trousers revealing our socks —mine white and yours grey.

Eventually, the bell rang.

You stood to go.

'Matt...' I called, more urgently than I had intended. 'Thanks.'

You turned to me. 'You should go the beach. Rock Point. It's nice... peaceful. I'll go with you if you want. Tomorrow's Saturday.'

My mouth hung open.

You shrugged. 'If you want.'

I nodded. 'What time?'

You shrugged again. 'Ten-ish?'

I nodded again. 'See you there.'

So after another night of broken sleep, I was on the bus to the beach. It was October so I wore jeans, trainers and jumper and a coat.

The bus was bumpy; the ride so rickety I felt sick.

I stepped off at the cliff-top hotel and made my way down the path. The wind was so harsh I wished I'd tied my hair back. The footing was uneven and sand and hair flew into my mouth.

Eventually I reached the bottom of the winding path and padded along the sand. I looked left and right but could only make out a lone dog walker with a Frisbee.

I decided to sit on the closest dune so I could see the path.

I climbed up between the spikey grass and chose a spot near the top, stuffing my hands into my pockets and clipping and unclipping the karabiner on the key-ring.

I could taste the salty air, as well as hairs that I kept pushing out of my mouth.

Every now and then, someone would descend the path and my stomach would crunch. But every time, as they would come into view as they neared the bottom, it wouldn't be you.

The sea crashed against the rocks and clouds covered the autumn sun. My feet and my neck were cold and my bottom quickly became uncomfortable.

The shadows became shorter, and then longer again.

Eventually I stopped blowing the hair from my face and let it stick to my running nose and my open mouth as I watched the dribs of dog walkers come and go.

The day grew colder by the minute and I needed a wee.

I sat in the dunes, with my hands stuffed into my pockets, and cried until my face couldn't get any wetter and I could hold my bladder no longer.

Then I stood, shaking my legs to make the blood flow back into them. I ascended the long windy path to catch the last bumpy bus home.

Now, I sit at the top of the cliff, in the grounds of Rock Point Hotel. The English summer, as usual, promises sunshine and warmth, but as soon as I take off my cardigan, the sun retreats behind a cloud. My little summer dress flaps in the breeze.

I look down over at the sand dunes and at the calm sparkling sea.

On my shoulder, I feel a hand. I turn, expecting to see Lenny.

But it is Matt.

Frantically, I look around. 'Did you follow me here?'

'I had to.'

I stand. And he sees I am looking towards the huge doorway of the hotel.

'Come with me.' He takes my arm and leads me to the path. He jumps down and I follow. The ridge concaves about six feet below the cliff-top and we back into the cove.

A sudden wild gust yanks my hair. 'Why didn't you come to the beach that day?' I demand urgently.

He frowns at me, confused.

'When you'd helped me find Nicole's key-ring, and you told me to meet you here?'

He gulps. And then he tells me his story.

Thirteen-year-old Matt came down to breakfast that Saturday morning wearing the biggest pair of jeans he could find. But they still swung at his ankles, revealing his holey socks. He stuffed his feet into his tattered trainers and sat at the table in the dingy kitchen. His mum was perched on her chair in her greying dressing-gown sipping tea, her dirty hair almost falling into her cup.

His dad stood at the window in his patched cardigan with a roll-up hanging from his mouth.

The boy scoffed down half a slice of cold toast and darted for the door, wiping crumbs from his mouth and t-shirt.

'Where do you think you're going, my lad?' his father called after him.

Matt held the door half open and replied, 'Out.'

'Not today, you're not. You need to help me in the garage.'

His dad's business was failing miserably and he couldn't afford staff. So Matt's weekends were mostly spent pottering with dirty cars. 'I'm meeting someone...' he shrugged.

'Oh, are you now? And when your mother and I can't pay the lecky, will your mates still be around then?' His dad had lost a lot of weight and was starting to show his age. His battered hands were as rough as ever. 'Come next term, when you need a new school uniform, are your mates gonna pay for that, are they?'

Matt shuffled his toes inside his too-small trainers and pulled his t-shirt down to cover his belly.

'If you want to go to school in clothes that are too small and come home to a freezing house, then you run along and meet your mates.'

So Matt spent that Saturday in the garage, handling dirty metal and trying to keep up with his dad's barking orders. The cold got under the boy's t-shirt and fumes got up his nose, but his father kept them going with Rock FM and continual demands of, 'stick the kettle on, Boy.' But the tea was always cold when they got to it.

'On Monday at school, I spotted you in the canteen sitting with Sarah Chine and Kay Summers and I half thought about going up to you to say, sorry about Saturday, I had to help my dad.

ALL THAT YOU WANT

But you were talking with them; you had friends to help you through this.' Matt shuffles. 'You probably hadn't even turned up at the beach anyway. So... I grabbed a cheese roll and went to the terrace to find the lads.'

In the crevice, below the cliff-top and above the beach, I shiver and look into his shrunken yellow-green eyes, and I see something new and open.

'My mum wasn't at a PTA meeting that night. I didn't want to tell you she was a cleaner at school.' He shuffles.

'I waited all day,' I whisper.

He looks at me and swallows. Then; 'Do you... do you want to go to the beach with me now?'

I fold my arms against the cold. 'You're eight years too late.'

The golden beach stretches out below us before an endless sea. Above us are the topiaried gardens and intricate sculptures of Rock Point Hotel. Although we can't see them, we know they are there.

I feel a lump in my throat and tears sting behind my eyes. 'Have you ever spent all night sleeplessly thinking of one face? Have you spent your days dying to catch a glimpse of one person?'

His face is crumpled. 'I didn't then. But I do now. Back then I was a kid; I wanted to play football and... potter with cars. I've grown up a lot in the last few years.'

My body tenses against the wind.

'And you finally feel it, in every bit of you,' he tells me, 'and it flows out of you and fills every space around you. And you can't think of anything else, so you travel three hundred and eighty-four miles to see that face, and find yourself following it, because you just need to see that one person. Nothing else means anything more.'

Above us we hear the distant cry of Lenny's voice. 'Amy?'

Instinctively, I push my back against the wall in the little cave. Matt does the same.

The voice calls again, closer this time, as though it is right above us, looking down over the beach, scouring the path with its eyes. 'Amy?'

I'm back under the desk in Mr Banton's English room, my side pressing against Matt's, hiding.

Matt grabs my hand. My chest thuds. His hand is rough and cracked.

We hear the footsteps above us move away, the voice still calling my name, but trailing back towards the hotel.

We step out of the little cove onto the windy path. For a moment I stand in limbo, and by Matt's face, I know he thinks I am going to go back up.

He pleads once more. 'Come down to the beach with me?'

I hesitate. Then I nod.

He smiles and we make our way down the bumpy path, the smell of salty air becoming stronger as we grow nearer.

As we reach the sand, there is less wind than at the top of the cliff. We remove our shoes and find a spot between the dunes. We sit, side by side, looking out over the calm sea, sheltered from the wind down here. The sun warms our faces. Seagulls call above our heads.

I pick up a handful of sand from between the spiky grass. I eye it closely as the cold particles run through my fingers, feeling smooth yet sharp at once. 'This has been around for billions of years and covers most of the world. It has probably travelled all over the planet and retuned this same spot.'

He picks up two large stones and grinds them together. Small particles fall from the friction. 'New grains of sand are being formed every day. But just because they're new, that doesn't mean they won't still be here in billions of years.'

The tension in my muscles is still there. 'What do you want me to do, Matt?'

He looks down. 'I want you to be with me. This feeling has to be... once in a life-time. I couldn't ever feel this way about anyone else. If you marry him, Amy, I don't know what I would do. If you could be with me, Amy, I'll love you more than... more than....' He extends his arms but finds no words. 'And for as long as.....' He cannot explain the vastness but I see it in him.

My eyes are hot but I push the feeling back down. I close my eyes and lie back on the sand. When I open them, he is lying beside me. I think of all the times I've fantasised about this moment. Just us two, lying here, nothing else in the world. In my mind I've reached out and touched him, but here, in reality, I couldn't dare.

ALL THAT YOU WANT

We both look up at the blueness, broken with gentle wisps. The sound of the waves seeps steadily in and out. We allow our breathing to become deep and our muscles to relax.

Matt pulls out his Walkman and hands me a headphone. We lie without speaking, without touching, and listen to the haunting sounds of *Iris* by the Goo Goo Dolls.

He sits up and looks toward the cliff-path.
I take the headphone from my ear.
'I think you're being looked for,' he tells me.
I sit up and hand him back the wire. I follow his gaze and see a suited man begin to descend the path.

Matt turns to me. 'I'd better go.' He stands, picking up his shoes, and I watch him make his way between the dunes in the opposite direction, towards the smooth, wide entrance to the beach at the farthest end.

Once more, I am left alone in the sand-dunes with tears streaming downing my face.

I turn my head and watch the smart figure grow nearer to the foot of the cliff-path. When he reaches the bottom, he removes his shoes and socks and rolls up his blue trousers a little way. Then he looks left and right. His eyes fall on me. He makes his way towards me.

As he reaches me, he doesn't seem to notice my tear-stained face. His own face is solemn. 'My agent called. My dad's has been trying to get in touch.'

I stand and gather my shoes, unable to speak. I want to hug hum but I can't. His façade has dropped. It is just him and me and I see the agony in his face. He has confided in me about his father and all the time I've been hiding from him down here.

'I don't like it here; it's too cold. Let's get married in Miami?'
I nod, speechless.
He nods back and turns. I follow him and we scramble up the steep, long path to the top.

37

Kiantown, July 2003

I borrow next door's dog and retreat into the woods.

I've walked Sandy endless times over the years, as one of my more favoured chores. But today, I need it. The woods are really a muddy track at the back of our road, leading to the farmer's field on the edge of town. To the left of the path, the bank descends to the stream at the bottom of the valley. Sandy revels in tearing down the slope.

Somewhere below me, a flock of ducks squawk away. The lab has invaded their peace.

The morning is foggy and I can hear Sandy yapping at the water, but I can barely see what's in front of me.

I scramble a few paces down the hill and sit in the crook of a protruding tree. Sandy splashes beneath me and I sprawl my legs either side of the narrow trunk. I lean forward and close my eyes.

It hits me anew, washes over me, and if I wasn't sitting already it would knock me down. I can sit here, in the woods, and let it engulf me; here on my own, in this bubble of mist.

I pull out my notepad and open it to a blank page. I stare into the fog and think. Then, I click my pen, and don't.

You are really deep down buried in me. I need to get you out. I have no control over it. Life would be simple if only one of you loved me. I wouldn't have a choice then. But, if I could flick a switch and turn off these feelings, make my decision for me, I wouldn't do it. I wouldn't do it to make my life more straightforward. Because this aching agony is the biggest thing I could experience.

ALL THAT YOU WANT

I'm right back on that beach, waiting for you. Wanting to be hiding under that desk with you forever, your school-trousers pressed against mine, your smell scarily close.

I should not be indulging this.

Lenny loves me and wants to marry me – in a couple of short months. Lenny, who has looked after me these past few years; who I have sworn to myself I love. Nothing's changed about him. He's still the same Lenny. The same man who held me up after the rollercoaster. The same man I fell for and wanted to be with for all time. What is wrong with me?

I'm not a big enough person to cope with the enormity of this. I'm not strong. Although I tried, I tried to be a confident, well rounded individual, going into that London office to chase my career; taking a big chance in telling Lenny how I felt... it's not me, not really; I'm not a decision-maker. I'm a follower. I've always followed Jodie; let her tell me what's cool to wear, what to say to boys, what we're going to do at the weekend. Well, she can't make this decision for me.

I can't either. I can't do anything about it. I'm too small and unimportant. I don't have it in me to do this.

I close the notebook and take out my phone to write a text.

Matt, can we meet?

Sandy bounds into me and knocks me off my perch. I am off balance, with wet fur in my face. I can taste it and it curls the hairs in my nose. Cold padded-paws press into my chest and I heave him off. 'Sandy!'

As I scrabble around for my phone, beside me on the ground, I see the prize he has pulled from the river –the item he is so excited to present me with. A chewed-up, stinky tennis ball. The green-and-red matted ball is split and distorted. An unnatural invasion in this otherwise tranquil location.

I jump to my feet, brushing the twigs and foliage from my hands but indents remain in my palms. My bum is wet from where I sat. My socks are damp in my shoes.

The hairs on my arm prickle as the sun begins to creep into my cocoon. The dew is evaporating.

I stare at the screen on my phone and hover my thumb over the button.

'Come on, dog. Better get you back.'
Deleted.

38

London, July 2003

I'm hiding in the toilets at the wrap party of Lenny's latest film. *Trying* to hide. I can't be long as there is a woman at the sinks offering little towels for tips. I thought they only did that in the men's.

I make my way back through the crowded party-room. Food is served on huge platters in tiny portions. I have no appetite.

On our arrival, each chair was donned with a little gift big – I couldn't believe we were presented with what were essentially party bags at a celebrity party.

I'm wearing a hideous purple maxi-dress and high-heels that have taken weeks of practice to totter about in. The biggest challenge is not to hoik up the dress. I have a perfectly good LBD, which I am finally comfortable in. Lenny said, if it were up to him, I look amazing in the black number, but, he's learned over the years, we should wait for the stylists' input. He thought his suit from last time was just fine, but the professionals would probably tell him it was soooo last year.

He was right; the artistes disregarded our existing wardrobes in favour of thick-materialed new outfits. Lenny's original attire is, wait for it… a suit. The same as all his other suits, as far as I can see.

My marvellous incarnation is some designer number of this detestable colour and style. It does not flatter my figure; it weighs me down and trips me up.

I have just about learned to tread carefully in it by tonight, but it takes much concentration as I make my way through the dazzling ballroom. Lenny, of course, strides effortless about the floor, owning the room without realising it. He does look good in his suit. He tries to reassure me and include me, but he is show-Lenny tonight.

The stylist pulled a face of horror at the state of my nails, which sadly I have begun biting again, but she managed to have falsies attached, with what I'm sure was superglue. They dig into my cuticles, stinging. 'Be sure to let them fall off in their own time, Amy.'

These nails, unlike the cheap stick-on ones I've used before, have held fast all day. I've been assured they'll last at least month, but I'd never seen nails like this before.

Big stars look past me, while smaller parts and the behind-the-scenes people corner me for gossip. It's seagulls in the school playground all over again.

'So, tell us again, how did the two of you meet?' beams the movie's costume designer, I think.

'Oh, well, we met a couple of years ago, when I won a date through a competition. And our paths crossed again at the beginning of the summer...' I choke on the lie.

'And then you got engaged after just two weeks?' declares one of the minor character actors.

'Well, yes, I guess we couldn't stop thinking about each other for all this time...'

'Lenny wanted to seize the day.' Clive, Lenny's loyal agent, is at my side. 'After so much wasted time, he didn't want to let this diamond pass him by again.'

'Diamond?' I hear the costume designer cough under her breath.

'What is it you *do* again, Amy?' asks the minor actor

I bow my head. 'I'm just... just a student.'

'Amy is a journalist for a London newspaper, don't you know?' Clive boasts. Clive is big and fatherly, with a strong Chicago accent and a Dumbo-ringmaster suit.

'What a lucky break,' sneers the bit-part, through a sweet smile.

'Let's go and find that fiancé of yours.' The agent steers me away from the hungry pack.

'They hate me,' I hiss.

'No, Honey! They're jealous of you. They wanna be you.'

'They think I've had an easy way in to all this.' I gesture my hand around the glamour.

'Who cares what anyone thinks. You know you genuinely love Lenny. That's all that matters, kid.'

My body stiffens. 'I've gotta get some air.' I pull away from him and bump right into Lenny.

'Hey, Sweetheart.' He embraces me.

'Hi, I was just… going to get some fresh air.'

'No, no, stay. It's so good to be able to finally show you off as my girl,' he smiles. 'You look beautiful tonight.'

'I'll get you both a drink.' Clive disappears.

I look at Lenny. 'They all think I'm a gold-digger.'

'Who does?'

'Your costume designer, and the guy who plays the father.'

'Well, we'll show them. They only have to look at us together and they'll see we're genuine.' He holds my hand, and his eyes smile into me. He is proud to have me with him tonight, and all I want to do is hide.

Lenny's co-star approaches, Craig Doug, a house-hold name; a Hollywood actor who's been in more movies than even he can probably count. This major celebrity has not acknowledged me so far this evening. Now he is giving Lenny a half hand-shake, half hug and calling him *Buddy*. 'So, this is the whirlwind fiancée. Let me see the ring then, Doll.'

I gulp and hold up my left hand.

'Look at that thing. You must be something special, Girl. I've known Lenny here nearly a year, and never known him date a girl. You must be real smart to catch this one. How'd ya trap him, eh?'

'I didn't trap him -'

Lenny laughs nervously. 'Craig's kidding, Amy. It's a joke.' He strokes my arm. 'Amy's the one. That's what I know for sure.'

'Hey, I'm happy for you guys.' The star eyes me. 'She certainly is impressive.' He pats Lenny's shoulder and walks on.

'I have to get out of here.' I make for the exit.

Lenny is hot on my heels as I burst through into the night air. 'Amy,' he grabs me and I'm forced to stop. 'They're just hungry for gossip; don't listen to them. They're itching for a

ALL THAT YOU WANT

scandal, where there's none. But you know what they say; any publicity is good publicity.'

'What? For them to think *that* of me... is a good thing? For people to have a low opinion of me, is great publicity?' I'm screeching through hysterics.

'No – it's just a turn of phrase. It's just what they say. I don't know why I said that, I was just trying to make you feel better, I guess. I don't know. I don't have all the answers. I'm fumbling my way through all this as much as you are... I'll never get used to what's the right thing to do, or say-'

'I'm just a big fraud being here, Lenny. They're right to be suspicious of me...'

'This is why I wanted to hide you for so long; to protect you. I knew you wouldn't be able to cope with this -not just you; it's not easy for anyone to be... scrutinised and judged.'

We are at the back exit, away from the throng of journalists at the front door, but we are still surrounded by dotted security guards and a few smokers from the party.

Lenny keeps his voice low. 'I thought I was doing the right thing, but maybe it was stupid. This whole elaborate hoax was a dumb idea.' He looks lost. 'We should just go in there right now and tell them all the truth;' He whispers: 'that we've been in love for years. Then they'll see we're genuine. I don't know what I was thinking, making up this whirlwind romance, this quick engagement.' He looks from side to side.

He desperate, torn, trying to do the right this. He looks like a little boy.

He pulls me close to him. 'I just... we waited so long, and I want you to be my wife. I didn't want to put it off any longer with the charade of a long courtship. Come on, it's no good if it's making you feel this bad.' He turns and pulls me back towards the door. 'Let's put them all straight and end this right now.'

'No,' I cry.

A few heads turn.

I try to whisper but my voice spills up. 'I can't go back in there. I need to get away. I can't.'

'Ok, ok. We don't have to decide right now. We'll think it over; whether to come clean. We'll get out of here - we'll go to the beach. We can talk about it and work out the best thing to do. I don't know, maybe it would make it worse to confess we've been lying. I don't know. Let's go and get some headspace.' He tries to reach me.

'No. I need to go by myself. I need to get out.' I jump into a standing cab.

'Amy?'

'Please? Just give me some room. I can't... do this right now.'

He looks around him, shuffling. 'Ok, ok. We'll talk about it later.' He gives the taxi driver the address of our hotel. 'Take care of her for me, Buddy.' And I've escaped. For now.

In the hotel-room, I bury myself in the plush bed and curl into the foetal position.

When I've run out of tears, I still don't have any answers.

I lie still and exhausted until I hear the door open. He's back from the party. I squeeze my eyes together as he whispers my name. I don't move.

Eventually he gives up and lies down beside me to give in to sleep.

My body tenses as I feel his weight on the mattress. I want to be at home.

39

Miami, August 2003

The hotel lobby is beautiful. The walls are painted a brilliant white and the floors are marble. Elegant chandeliers hang from the high ceilings. On the table-tops sit delicate china and crystal. The sun fights its way in, uninvited, through the large windows, bouncing off the white walls. The air conditioning is unable to keep it out.

I sit at a table with Enrique, the wedding planner. We are waiting for Lenny to arrive so we can look through invitation design ideas.

A waiter approaches. 'Would you like to order drinks, Madam?'

I look at Enrique, who takes my cue. 'Coffee, black please.'

The waiter nods and turns to me.

'Erm, tea please. White. One sugar.'

'The British way,' the waiter almost smirks and turns to leave.

'Oh,' Enrique calls the waiter back and turns to me. 'Would you like to order for Lenny?'

I freeze. Tea or coffee? What does the love of my life drink, the man I am about to marry? I gulp. 'Urm, just a pot for two please...'

The waiter smiles. 'A pot of English tea with two teacups, and one American mug of coffee. Coming up.'

Enrique frowns at me. 'You've turned Lenny on to English tea? How long has been drinking that?'

'Well... I, well...' A long time? Or am I getting him to try something new? Whichever I say will be wrong.

'Has he always drunk it?'

'Well... sometimes he likes the same thing... sometimes he likes something different...'

'What does he usually drink?'

I gulp again. 'You were saying about desserts... I do think a cheese board is a good option... not everyone will like a sweet dessert. Some people like cheese. Maybe we could give them a choice; a sweet chocolate option and a cheese option...' I falter.

Enrique frowns again. 'Right, right. Chocolate and cheese.' He makes a quick note. 'Ah, here is the man himself!'

Lenny approaches through the main doors. He removes his sunglasses and greets me with a peck on the cheek.

'What did I miss?' he asks as he takes his seat.

'Oh, erm, we had briefly mentioned dessert options, but what I really wanted to talk to you about was the invitation designs.' Enrique presents the options. 'The roses are quaint and English, don't you think, while the champagne glasses bring a touch of elegance.' Enrique's sleek ponytail dances while he talks.

At the next table to us, a couple sits eating easily. She wears a light blue shift dress that falls off her beautifully tanned body, and laughs, relaxed, with her similarly lightly dressed male companion.

I am wearing a heavy dark-purple suit, made with thick, expensive material. It was chosen for me by Lenny's people. I never wear purple.

'Which do you prefer, Ames?' Lenny asks.

I sigh. 'The champagne bottles.'

Enrique frowns. 'Don't you want to bring some of your English heritage?'

I shrug. 'The roses then.'

Lenny shifts in his chair. 'Amy, don't you care?'

I shuffle in my uncomfortable suit.

The waiter approaches with our drinks. I thank him.

Lenny raises his eyebrows. 'You not going for the ginger beer today?'

'I'm just... craving the taste of home,' and begin to pour milk into our teacups.

'Wait,' stops Lenny. 'I can't drink milk.'

I freeze with the jug in mid-air and stare at him.

ALL THAT YOU WANT

'I just, I'm dairy intolerant, is all.'

'Dairy intolerant?' Spits Enrique. He scribbles harshly on his notes. 'You won't be wanting chocolate and cheese then, will you?'

Suddenly my dress feels even tighter and the sun feels even hotter. 'Do you know what… it's too hot. I need to change. Sorry, Enrique, I can't do this right now.' I stand and make for the stairs.

Once in our dramatically over-the-top suite with its elegantly detailed bedposts and heavy velvet curtains, I strip down to my underwear.

Lenny enters behind me. I spin round. His suit is heavy and his shoes are shined.

'What's going on with you, Amy? You're completely disinterested. Don't you want our wedding day to be perfect?'

I sigh. 'I'm sorry, ok? In the past month I've been back and forth across the Atlantic, and back and forth again. It's all happening so fast. I just… need a break from, from all this organisation. It's getting to me. Cakes and venues and, invitations. Too much choice. I can't make these choices. It's all too… too…'

'…much?' he offers.

He is being too understanding and I don't deserve it. I want him to shout at me. I nod. 'I'm sorry, Lenny. I just feel… railroaded and I didn't even know you're allergic to milk. What else don't I know about you? I don't know what you do first thing in the mornings, what your routines are – I've never seen where you grew up. I've never met your mum. I don't know how you wind down after work. I don't know any of your friends. I feel like I'm marrying a stranger.'

He stares at me. 'I thought you loved me? Why does it matter about all that little stuff? I thought you knew me inside out? All the important stuff. How can you say you don't know me?'

'I just need a break,' I say again.

He sighs and nods. 'Then a break is what we'll have.'

The day is flawless.

The sand, white as snow, burns my naked feet as they hang off the towel. The sun strokes me, blankets me, sticks to my skin. I have no choice but to surrender to the heat.

He has brought me here because he loves me.

I try to ignore the sand scratching under my horrendous false nails. The world is enclosed in endless blue. The horizon is barely distinguishable.

But I know it's there.

The palm-trees and the coconuts make this paradise complete. Around me, holiday-makers laugh, swim and sunbathe. The smells of sun-cream, ice-cream and sea-salt fill the air. My mouth is dry.

The ebbing sea and gentle sounds of laugher are all that can be heard.

A single yacht bobs beyond the swimmers. If I were on that yacht, with only the breeze for company, I'd sail straight for that horizon. I'd plunge into the ocean; I'd feel the water wash every inch of sun from me. Make me shiver with the cool.

There's a hand on my shoulder, and I'm back on the beautiful beach.

'I want you to know all the little things,' he whispers. 'They matter. I'll take you to visit my mom; you can see where I grew up. You can get to know my mundane morning routines and my annoying habits. I want us to know everything about each other. I want to spend a lifetime with you.'

He pulls me close and I have no choice but to give in to him. I am hideous.

'Now, come on; let's get back to the hotel. With any luck, Enrique will still be waiting for us.' He enwraps me in his arms, and takes me with him, away from the ocean, and the yacht, and the invisible horizon, to the hotel, to talk about seating plans, guest lists, colour schemes, and flowers.

40

Chicago, August 2003

'Hey, Sweetie! It's so great to finally meet you! Lenny's told me so much about you!'

'Hello, Ms. Hunter. Nice to meet you. You have a lovely house.'

'Well you know, Lenny looks after me.' Her sunken eyes try to focus on me, but she has the shakes. 'We haven't always lived in a house like this.'

'I know… Lenny… told me…'

'I'm sure he's told you how he grew up. He's done well for himself.' Her coarse hair is contrived into an up-do. 'Well, now, I would toast champagne for the happy couple, but, y'know, I don't keep alcohol in the house.'

'No, well, it's not needed…'

Her face is encrusted in make-up, failing to hide her sagging, damaged skin. 'So, so, let's sit on the terrace, and Cheryl can bring us some iced-tea. Lenny insists on all of this.' She motions to the house. 'I've never asked for any of it, you understand. Do you drink iced-tea? I don't suppose you do in England.'

'No, well, I'd like to try it… I've introduced Lenny to English tea, with milk and sugar… well no milk, of course.'

'Oh, how quaint. You know I tell him not to worry about me, but he doesn't listen. He doesn't have to let his old mother live in this house. Anyway. So, Honey, tell me a little more about yourself. Lenny tells me you're studying to be a reporter?'

'Amy's a *journalist*, Mom,' Lenny boasts.

'Well, I've… just finished my English A- levels, and I've been working for a local paper. I've been very lucky…'

'And what d'ya parents think about you living in the States after you're married? It's pretty far...'

'Well... we... haven't really decided where we'll settle... Lenny's making British films at the moment. So... we... could live in London, for the time being, at least.'

'What? You want Lenny to move to England?'

'Well...'

'He's the only family I have. Jeff excepted, of course.' She quickly smiles at her partner.

'Well...'

'What about the wedding? You're getting married in the States aren't you?'

'Er... probably... we've been... looking at lots of venues, on both sides of the Atlantic... we're keeping our options open.'

'I thought we'd decided on...' Lenny stops and throws me a quick smile. 'We'll talk about it later....'

'I just don't think it's fair for my grandkids to live overseas.'

'Grandkids?' I whisper.

'Your parents have your sister. Lenny is my only son. I need him. I'm a sick woman, Amy. You can't take a sick woman's son away from her. I didn't want to be like this,' she apologises again.

'Well... Lenny's job could take him anywhere in the world... I don't expect we'll settle in one place... I expect we'll travel a lot. And I can write anywhere.'

'But you can't move kids around. It's so unsettling. I used to travel with a theatre company but I stopped as soon as I had Lenny.'

'Well... children will probably be a while away yet...'

'Mom, Mom, slow down... let Amy sit down,' Lenny protects me. 'Let's sit down and have that tea.'

'Excuse me. I need to use the loo.'

'Sure, Honey. End of the hall, last door on the right.'

I make my exit and retreat to the bathroom.

I walk through hallways filled with canvases of amateur paintings.

The room is crisp white with down-lights above the mirror. I lock the door and sit.

ALL THAT YOU WANT

I cannot think about having children with Lenny. I do not want to be in this country, ripped away from where I should be, deceiving the man who has loved and protected me for all these years. I should not be invading his family home, deceiving his mother that he is my one and only.

I can't hide in here all day. I return to the garden and find Lenny and his mother on the terrace, where the round garden table has been set for a quaint tea.

'Ahh,' Sylvia beams. 'A light refreshment from the sun.'

The house-keeper, Cheryl, pours us some iced tea and I experience the new taste for the first time. The sweet, foreign flavour trickles over my tongue and I don't know what to make of it.

'Thank you,' we chorus, and try not to notice Sylvia's ice rattling as she steadies her glass towards her mouth.

'Did you see Mom's paintings?' Lenny enthuses.

'Oh yes… lots of lovely paintings,'

'Well, I like to paint a lot. I'm not very good. But I want to do something… I paint pictures for Lenny to take with him when he's away for months at a time. You must have seen them in his caravan?'

Lenny gives me a pleading nod, although I've never seen him display one of Sylvia's pieces.

'Oh yes – that's where I've seen them before…' I stumble.

Sylvia produces a board-game. 'I thought we could play a little "Mr and Mrs",' she grins. 'I thought it would be quite appropriate as you two will soon be, "Mr and Mrs".'

'Mom, I think Amy might like to relax. She's had a long flight,' Lenny protests.

'Nonsense,' his mother proclaims. 'This will help us get to know each other. We need to get close. I want Amy to feel part of the family. You're game, aren't you, Amy?'

'Um… yes, of course, Sylvia,' I force a smile. 'I'd love to.'

So Sylvia asks her son to sit on a bench further down the garden. Giggling, she dons him in a blindfold and a pair of head-phones. He patiently ignores her jittering hands, grinning, until he is deaf and blind. He looks so giddily happy and vulnerable. I feel a pang in my chest.

Sylvia skips back to us on the terrace.

She plucks a sheet of paper from the box and clutches a pen between yellow fingers. Shakily, she writes the numbers one to ten. 'Ok, so I take question cards to ask you ten questions about yourself. I write down your answers. Then we bring Lenny back and ask him the same questions. We add up how many matches you get and that's your score. After that, it will be your turn to be blind-folded and we repeat the process. Then, when you and Lenny are done, it will be Jeff and my turn. Ok, Dear?' She doesn't give me time to reply before diving in with the first question. 'Where did you go to school?'

'Kian Hill.' Lenny will know that. I talk about school enough.

'What's your favourite movie?'

'My Best Friend's Wedding.' Will he know that?

With an unsteady hand, she scribbles it down. 'And your favourite music?'

'My favourite song is *If I Let You Go* by Westlife.'

She jots it on her paper. 'What are your parents' names?

'Ellen and Karl Minor.'

'How tall are you?'

'Five foot six.'

'What do you drink in the mornings?'

'Tea.'

'What kind of tea?'

'White... milky.'

'With sugar?'

'Yes. One.'

She makes detailed notes. 'What is your favourite book?'

'Wuthering Heights.'

'What colour is your toothbrush?'

'Green. I always have a green toothbrush.'

'If you could go on vacation anywhere in the world, where would you go?'

'Miami. To see my Grandma.'

'And finally, what was your greatest ambition as a child?'

'To be a journalist.'

Sylvia notes my last answer and places her pen down. 'Ok, now to go get your fiancé. Get your game face on, Honey. Don't give anything away.' She beams and descends the terrace steps. Jeff pours us more iced-tea as we watch my fiancé jump at

ALL THAT YOU WANT

her touch, and the two of them laugh. His mother removes Lenny's headphones and blindfold. He thinks he is in the light again. She places the items on the bench and they return to us.

Lenny grins at me. 'It's a little unnerving, not being able to see or hear. I half-expected you all to run away and leave me there.'

Sylvia chitters, and holds the answer sheet to her chest. 'Ok. Lenny, where did Amy go to school?'

He looks at me.

I take a sip of tea.

'Kian...town... college? Kiantown college?'

'Kian Hill,' his mother corrects him smugly. 'What is Amy's favourite movie?'

He gulps.

I sip more lemony-sweet iced-tea.

'*When Harry Met Sally?*'

'Uh-uh. *My Best Friend's Wedding*. Ok, ok, you must know this. What is Amy's favourite music?'

'Westlife; I know that.'

'But what song?'

'Oh no. Do I have to get the song? *Flying Without Wings?*'

'*If I Let You Go!*' Sylvia almost cackles. 'A half-point. What are Amy's parents' names?'

'Oh, God. I haven't met her parents yet. Apart from your mom, briefly, three years ago. I can't believe I haven't met your parents yet. Mr and Mrs Minor? I should know because we had to put them on the invitations. Why haven't I met them yet? How could we miss that out?'

'Do you have an answer?' his mother presses.

Lenny gulps. 'I'm so sorry, Amy. I don't know.'

'Ellen and Karl Minor,' his mother reveals triumphantly. 'So what is Amy's favourite book?'

'Oh, gosh, what were you reading that time in London? *High Fidelity.*' Lenny grins, sure of himself. I lower my head and stare at the lemon flecks in my cold tea.

Sylvia can barely contain her excitement as she corrects him.

'What colour is Amy's toothbrush?'

He squirms. 'Purple?'

'Green!' Sylvia squeals.

'Well, her last one was purple…' he clutches.

'I hate purple,' I whisper.

Lenny answers the final two questions correctly, giving us a measly score of two-an-a-half points.

Sylvia delights in leading me down the garden path. I sit passively and allow her to blind and deafen me, unable to muster up the grins and giggles to reflect hers and Lenny's.

And now I am in darkness. The silence is more prominent than the light breeze it covers; a breeze that, until now it's gone, I hadn't noticed was there. Now there are no distractions. I can smell sweet flowers I hadn't noticed before, although I don't know what they are. No light; no images. No sound. The world is blocked out.

I know Sylvia has returned to the terrace and I will only have a few minutes of this tranquillity, returning to the real world at their demand. I am briefly escaped, yet vulnerable. I have no control.

Lenny didn't know where I went to school. Kian Hill is in me. It's part of me. It's where I grew up.

Where would I go on holiday if I could go anywhere in the world? I would always have said Miami. That's always been my dream destination. But a few months ago, when I was on that plane, and Matt had followed me to the airport, I would have given anything to stay where he was. Where do I want to be in the world? Miami, Chicago, Kiantown, Newcastle… it wouldn't matter.

Any normal girl would give anything to be where I am right now; travelling back and forth to the USA; experiencing all these exotic places with a Hollywood star – a Hollywood star who adores her. Lenny is flawless.

I might not know Matt's favourite food either. I might not know his favourite film, music or book. I might not know his biggest ambition, or his favourite place in the world. But I know, stronger than I know anything, that wherever he is, is where I want to be.

A baby with Lenny… They might as well tie me up as well as blind and deafen me.

ALL THAT YOU WANT

I jump at the feel of sharp fingernails at my ears. I hear the gentle breeze again. The blindfold is loosened and I see Sylvia's beaming lipstick-stained teeth.

'You can come back to us now, Honey!'

I follow her to the terrace to endure the humiliation once more.

I say Lenny went to; 'Chicago… College,' when he went to The Debbie Rutland Acting Agency.

I say his favourite movie is, 'The Sixth Sense', when it is in fact, 'Lethal Weapon'.

I seem to sink further into my seat as Sylvia appears to rise higher with each triumph, her pink-tinted teeth almost jumping out of her mouth as her grin grows wider.

I answer Lenny's parents are Sylvia and Jeff. Then I freeze and the grins fall from all of their faces.

'Jeff's not..' stutter Sylvia and Lenny together.

'I'm not… Lenny's dad.'

Of course I know that. I squeeze my fist in my lap.

'How do you not know this about Lenny? What have you two talked about all these years during your secret meetings?' Sylvia exclaims.

'Amy, I told you all about…' Lenny utters.

'I know, I know.' I gulp. 'Michael. Lenny's dad is called Michael.'

Sylvia sits back in her chair and folds her arms. 'Michael what?'

I look frantically at Lenny. 'Hunter?' I whisper.

'Stoneham,' Sylvia declares. '*I* am Ms Sylvia Hunter.'

'I'm sorry. I know. I just… said it… on the spot.'

'Look, maybe we could take a break from this game,' Lenny reasons, for me. 'Maybe we should take a walk - show Amy around.'

'No, Jeff and I haven't our turn yet.'

Sylvia and Jeff score twenty out of twenty, compared to our pitiful score of five. Jeff knows all about her rags-to-riches story. She knows he likes black coffee in the morning. They finish each other's sentences, giggling and lolloping over each other,

213

while Lenny and I sit rigid. Lenny tries to relax his body and smile but it turns into fidgeting.

He leans into me. 'Don't worry,' he whispers. 'We've got a life-time to find out all these little things about each other.' He puts his arm around me and I feign a smile. We share this moment as outsiders together, united in our awkwardness.

It is clear Jeff has saved her. But lines from years of alcoholism are etched into her face. This woman lived in a slummy apartment in her own dirt for most of her life, neglecting to care for her son. Lenny has made it despite her. Now he is supporting her lifestyle. She has this beautiful, grand home thanks to him, and now she plays the doting, protecting mother - when throughout his school-life, she couldn't even get off her drunken seat to feed him. I look at my fiancé and am overcome with admiration.

Yet, in spite of all that, this paranoid, recovering alcoholic can see me clearly through her shakes. It is *I* who am the fraud in this garden.

41

Kiantown, September 2003

Tidy rails of white dresses line the walls. Mum, Beth and Jodie, in their light summer clothes, watch on eagerly as the prim shop-assistants usher me in and out of the changing room, with me emerging each time in different meringue. This should be one of the happiest occasions of my life.

A stuffy, musty smell hangs in the air, of clothes that have not been disturbed for some time.

A bodyguard stands at the door and crowds of onlookers peer in through the large window, flash-flashing their cameras and phones.

'It's so good to have you back home, Ames!' Mum coos.

'You look gorgeous, Ames!' Jodie beams.

Beth scowls at the audience. 'Did you get this all the time in America, too?'

Mum, ever trying to see the positive, tells her, 'It's like being famous, isn't it?'

The bodyguard's phone rings and he turns away from the door to answer.

Seizing her chance, one on-looking girl darts into the shop. Like sheep, the others surge in after her. Suddenly we're surrounded by a mob of hysteria, with inaudible shouts flying around the room. The only word I can make out is, 'gold-digger!' We are pushed and pulled about the tiny shop. I can barely see. I struggle to stay on my feet. I feel tugging at my dress.

'Get off her!' I can hear my sister's voice but cannot see her.

I feel a rip at my alien dress. Then the culprit is pulled back away from me. I look for Jodie behind her. But it is my little sister who has ripped the savage off of me. Her sea-blue eyes call to me. I'm shoved sideways and lose sight of my ally.

I hear a loud whack and Beth's cry; 'Ow!'

Then Jodie; 'You bust her nose! She's bleeding! Get out or I'll call the police.'

The mood has changed to that of retreat. The throng begins to swarm out of the shop. As they push and shove, I am head-butted in the chin and I bite my tongue. Pain surges through me. A metallic taste fills my mouth. I bring my hand to my mouth and remove it to see red.

The last of the stragglers leaves the shop. We survey the room. Dresses have been ripped from their hangers and lie torn and crumpled on the carpet. I take in Beth's blooded nose and she eyes my crimson mouth. Mum, Jodie and the shop assistants are a little dishevelled in their clothes and hair but are otherwise unharmed.

Jodie darts her eyes to the bodyguard at the door. 'Fat lot of good you were.'

At home, Mum, Dad, Jodie, Beth, and even Sarah fuss around me. I have convinced them not to call Lenny.

'Are you ok, darling? Are you alright? Do you think we have to take her casualty?'

'I'm fine, I'm fine. I need to go. I need some space. I'm going for a walk. I'm going... Can I take the dog, Sarah?'

So I head, alone, into the woods with Sandy. We crunch through the leaves, me in wellies, the Labrador skipping ahead. Finally we are away from the houses and the noise, hidden in the trees and muffled by the sound of the river. The dog quickly gives up begging me to throw sticks and runs on, leaving me with the lead and the empty doggy bags in my coat pocket.

Lenny was right. I've always been in Jodie's shadow. I've always let her step forward first. I was never good enough to even be noticed by Matt at school. I've allowed myself to be bullied by Kay Summers for years. I'm pathetic. I've always longed to be noticed but been too scared to do anything about it.

But then Lenny Hunter was interested in me; little unremarkable me. He gave me the confidence to go for the

ALL THAT YOU WANT

journalism in London that I would never have dreamed of before. Still, I was the tea-girl – the skivvy. Even with Suzie, although she acts like I matter, I still feel like a fraud; like I don't belong.

I close my eyes I can taste Lenny's lips on mine. I feel his chest pressed against me. The man saved me. I want to surrender to him. When I try to think of Matt... there's nothing. Nothing tangible. I try to grasp on to the touch of his leg pressed against mine under the table... but it's gone. It's too abstract.

I've got all I could ever want. And I have no clue what to do. So I'm stalling. There's only so long I can hold out.

I stupidly believed I had matured, with my London job and great boyfriend; that I was finally a confident woman with her life planned out. Now it's come to the crunch, I find I'm still the frightened little mouse, retreating to the shadows, waiting for someone else to make my decisions for me.

I haven't grown at all. I'm still a little girl.

I've wandered to the end of the woods and have reached the gate to the farmer's field. I realise can't hear Sandy's bark. The quiet is deathly. I spin back, my ponytail flicking me in the face, and call to him. I try to whistle. There is nothing.

'Sandy!' The woods have begun to grow dark. I wander ahead through the woods, calling and yelling. I can't hear him. No rustle in the leaves, no distant bark.

I can't even look after a simple dog. 'Sandy! Sandy'

After I don't know how many more minutes of mindless searching and shouting, I stand in silence in the middle of the trees. There is a sick taste in my mouth. I am helpless. Hopeless. Useless.

Defeated, I head back for help.

I knock on Sarah's door. Her mum answers. 'Alright, Love? Where's the dog?' She reads my face and hers drops. 'Where is he? What's happened?' Sarah and Ryan are behind her. 'What's happened?'

So we all head back into the woods; Sarah, her brother, Mrs Chine, my mum, my dad, Beth and me, all in our wellies, hunting and squelching.

After a while, Beth calls us all over excitedly. But it's just a hedgehog. 'Don't worry,' her eyes smile. 'We'll find him.' The beady-eyed squirt has turned into my best ally since my big reveal.

The darkness is too much. Mrs Chine is bumping into trees and Dad twists his ankle in a ditch. We surrender to the night and begin our traipse back to the houses. Ryan suggests we dig out torches. Beth proposes we all make posters. Dad says we'll call the dog warden and report him missing.

We emerge from the woods into the street-lights and follow the path along the river. I've never appreciated the glowing pillars so much. Even the stifling damp smell of the trees clears into the fresh scent of the river.

As we near our adjoining back doors, Ryan, who has been trailing behind, suddenly bursts into a sprint. The rest of our sorry group, who have been dawdling with our heads bowed, look up as he races forward.

I hear him before I see him. The impatient bark that says, 'There you are. I've been waiting.'

There, sitting at the back gate, his tail wagging and his tongue panting, is Sandy.

The dog has brought himself home. He didn't need me.

Mrs Chine says maybe I shouldn't walk him for the time being, while I've got a lot on my mind.

I mumble that I'm sorry. I shuffle back to our house while Mum offers to make her potato, spinach and carrot soup to warm everyone up. I can't even make amends for myself; my mum has to do it for me. I am that useless.

In that moment, I suddenly want Lenny, to hold me in his arms and tell me everything will be alright. But I don't deserve him.

The English summer is warm but nowhere as unbearable as the Florida heat. It is a few days after the dress fiasco and Jodie and I are returning with milk from the corner shop. I have persuaded Mum I can't hide inside forever. The breeze whistles gently through the trees and the front garden is in full colour.

As we walk up the path, we hear the latch on a gate behind us. We turn. Over the low wall separating our garden and Sarah's, Kay approaches. Her hair has gown enough to be tied back harshly into a pathetically short ponytail, making her features look even more pointed than usual.

'Well,' she jabs. 'If it isn't Lady Muck.' She stomps up the path and leers over the wall. 'If it isn't enough you're planning a wedding to outshine mine, you're putting Matt through hell as well.'

Jodie stands tall. 'She's not doing anything to Matt.'

'Little Miss I've-been-in-love-with-him-for-years. Do you know what he's going through right now?'

'Probably what she went through for all those years,' Jodie hisses.

'I wish those girls had done a better job on you in that dress shop.' She spins round and raps sharply on Sarah's front door.

'Come on, Jo.' I lead her inside.

42

Southwest England, September 2003

I've lost track of the amount of times I've seen this swarming airport over the last few months; the familiar excitement in passengers' eyes; families on their first holiday this year; families lucky to get away.

Until this year, flying, for me, had been a rare and special occurrence. Now I am sick of it. I do not want to fly to Chicago. The next twelve hours, stretching ahead of me, in a confined seat with nowhere to go but further and further from home, to an alien world, make me feel like spots will erupt any moment. The stale air circulating the aircraft; the plastic unhealthy food. No matter how much water I will drink or the amount of times I'll wash my hands, I will not be able to free myself from the grime.

I lug my suitcase toward the queue and blow my heavy hair from my eyes. I stand at the back, glad the line is long to postpone my fate. My eyes dart around the hubbub of the gigantic place and I think back to the first of these cross-Atlantic trips at the beginning of the summer, when this boulder began rolling. I had run from him that day, darting through the people and bounding up the escalator. Each time since I'd wished he would follow me here. 'Please,' I say inside, to someone out there. I look frantically around this porthole and my heart skips each time I see a floppy-haired man from the back, or a black coat – any black coat, or a Roman-nose in profile. But of course, none of them is him.

The queue shortens and I lug my baggage a few reluctant paces forward. I lay the bag down again, glad to be free of the load, if only for a few minutes. My eyes are still darting and my lips continue silently praying.

A few dawdlers look and point at me. 'Is that...? Is it..?'

I push my dark glasses up my nose and pull my headscarf down over my forehead. I feel ridiculous in my pretentious disguise. After the incident in the dress-shop Lenny insisted on a round-the-clock bodyguard. I'd refused. I am not a glamorous Hollywood star.

A pre-teen in a Justin Timberlake t-shirt pulls at her mother's arm, staring at me.

I turn away.

The couple in front of me are at the check-in desk now. I take my time hauling my case up onto its wheels. I use the weight as an excuse to delay the inevitable.

It backfires, though, because some busy-body is instantly at my side, chivalrously taking my bag.

'It's alright thanks. I can manage.' I turn. And it is him.

I have to look again, as I have seen him here so many times. I take in those deep eyes. I have seen them so many times but never so open to me. I feel my cheeks redden and my chest thud. For a moment I can't breathe.

'Next please,' calls the plain girl behind the desk.

I know I should do the right thing, and get in that flight to Chicago to visit my fiancé and his family, to talk about seating plans and flowers and all those nice things that make me feel so sick.

'Can I help you with your bag..?' he is asking me. He is so close I can feel his arm pressed against mine. Our fingers touch on the bag's handle and I pull away.

'Can I help, Miss?' calls the check-in girl again.

I feel a large man behind me pressing forward impatiently.

I have no time to hesitate. No time to think rationally. I'm being forced into this journey from in front and behind. So all I can do is dart out sideways. To Matt. 'No,' I tell him, 'but you can take me out of here.'

The impatient man wastes no time in jumping in front of me. I pull

Matt's hand from the heavy burden and run.

221

We are out of the doors before the security guards can catch up to us for leaving an unattended bag.

'Go!' I yell.

Matt's car is parked in the short-stay car park. We are out of there fast and onto the motorway. We speed through the traffic. I blare up the music, drowning out the nagging in my head. I will him to drive faster.

Lenny will be waiting on the other side. I won't be on the flight. My stuff is abandoned at the airport. A handful of Lenny's fans saw me. I may have been papped. I don't give a toss.

I turn the music up louder and louder and wind the window right down. Half an hour ago I thought I would be on a dull flight to another world to roll ahead into a planned life. And now I am home. Free. Driving fast with Matt. Stuffy, stale air swapped for fresh, wild wind.

Motorway gives way to town, and then quickly to country roads.

My heart is still racing but the car has slowed and I turn the music down. We pass fields of cows and sheep and pylons and woodland.

Matt turns the music down further. 'Where are we going?' he asks.

I inhale. 'Anywhere. Take me anywhere.'

He drives in silence for a while longer, then turns onto a woodland track.

Our pace is much slower now. The sun speckles through the trees. Not a soul is around. Matt winds down the window. The breeze is gentle on the leaves and I cannot believe the ease of peace and tranquillity in this place.

He stops at a clearing. I feel him look at me. I get out of the car and lean back against the door. I can hear nothing but the gentlest breeze and my own unsteady breath.

Matt has emerged from the driver's door and is at my side. He is looking to me to find out what happens next. He is looking to me.

I risk looking at him and I can't move.

'Why did you come with me?'

My throat is dry and I can't answer him.

ALL THAT YOU WANT

'What happens now?' he ventures.

'Shall we... walk a bit?' I manage to utter.

He nods and we stroll, our hands that were, a short while ago at the airport, entwined, now clasp reservedly in front of each of us and I can't believe I really grabbed his hand back there.

The ground is uneven and we tread carefully.

'You came with me. I thought... well, hoped... I might see you, maybe even talk to you. But I never thought you would... abandon your flight...'

We walk on and I still can't speak.

'Shall we... sit?' he suggests.

I nod.

He places his jacket at the foot of a large tree and we sit together. The first leaves of autumn have begun to fall. 'What does it mean, Amy? You chose to come with me?'

His face is so close, his eyes so deep, I have to look away.

'Will you come away with me? Call it off? I don't know where we'll live, but we'll live. I know I won't have anything to give you; we'll both have to work hard to make ends meet. There might not be flights back and forth to the States, or fancy cars or hotels, or bodyguards, but, Amy, I'll love you so hard. I promise you, forever. I'll look after you as best as I can. We'll have somewhere... cosy, and small, and unglamorous. But it'll be ours. I never knew it was possible to feel like this... It's agony. I need you. Please, tell me what's going on?'

I'm shaking. 'Matt, Lenny has been so good to me. He's done nothing wrong and I... I care about him so much. But, I just know that, when I'm with him, the only place I want to be is where you are.' Without realising they had started, tears are streaming down my face. My body is heaving. Somehow my legs are entwined with his as we sit under this tree. He holds my arm.

I give in to his touch.

He takes a nearby leaf and runs it over my wrist. I tingle. My breath slows. I calm. 'Close your eyes,' he tells me.

I'm scared but I give in. I close my eyes, sitting rigidly, yet relaxing slightly at the tickle of the leaf on the inside of my lower arm. He runs it over my fingers, which stretch, responding all on their own. My eyes remain closed as he runs the leaf over my palm and back up the length of my arm.

'Lie down,' he whispers.

I gradually lie back. My head touches the bumpy ground and I feel a soft cushion placed under it. I open my eyes involuntarily to see he has removed his t-shirt to use as my pillow. His skin pimples at the early autumn breeze, naked and vulnerable as a baby. My eyes close again as the leaf tickles my cheek, my lips, my neck. I inhale as the leaf trails down my collar bone. My chest rises and falls. The breeze strokes my hair. I reach up to touch his naked chest. I feel him pull up my t-shirt. I shudder as he kisses my stomach. I feel the leaf tingling on my ankle now, then up the length of my shin. Little hairs stand on end as he tickles the leaf over my knee. Now it tingles on my thigh, moving slowly up and inwards. My legs part to allow the crisp leaf to make its journey up my leg, under my skirt.

But I jump up. 'I can't do this.'

I race back along unsteady ground as fast as I can.

Matt has replaced his t-shirt and catches me up.

I don't recognise this part of the woods and I can't see the car. I stop, disorientated.

'Are you ok? It's this way.' He leads me. 'I'm sorry, Amy, I thought you... wanted me...'

'I don't know what I want. I'm the one who's sorry.' We reach the car and stop. The day is drawing in. 'I don't know what to do. I'm sorry, Matt. I need to go. Please. Drop me at the train station and I'll make my own way home.' I climb into the car. We are silent for the return journey.

'What the hell happened?' Lenny demands.

'I got held up in traffic,' I lie down the phone. 'I missed the flight. I was in such a rush I left the suitcase in the boot of the cab.'

'Amy, that case was found at the airport. Someone was trying to impersonate you, but it seems they got cold feet and ran off at the check-in desk.'

I stagger up my road. The twisted ache won't be ignored.

'Amy, you're an easy target because you're my fiancée, and you have no experience of dealing with this sudden attention. The wrong kind of people will take advantage of you. You're vulnerable. And I can't always be there to protect you. I'm a world away. No arguing this time, Amy. We are getting you a round-the-clock bodyguard.'

I hold the mobile under my chin and turn the key to my parents' house. It's late. The train was delayed and I don't have the strength to argue.

He was expecting me, waiting at the airport, for I can't bear to think how long. Worrying about what might have happened to me, feeling helpless and wanting to protect me. And all the time I was in the woods. Behaving like a tramp.

He is right about one thing. He is a world away.

43

I was twelve years old. I edged into school, clinging my bag to me as though it held a ticking bomb.

Two year-ten girls tittered past me, one smelling a paper rose. I turned to 7b's lockers and Val Chambers pulled a red heart from her metal door, giggling giddily to her flock. I squeezed by to my own locker to retrieve my boot-bag. No red envelope greeted me, just the smell of unwashed trainers.

'How many did you get, Amy?' Val snickered and I pushed past to the classroom, my rucksack strapped tightly to my back.

I placed it on the table and checked the zip was closed for the seventh time that morning.

Jodie was at my side. 'Did you do it?'

I pictured the late-night cutting and sticking operation as I'd managed to attach the red heart to pink card with military precision, without Mum or Dad, or - worse- Beth, bursting in to my room. I'd agonised over the words. 'Be my Valentine,'…. 'Happy Valentine's Day, love your secret admirer'… 'Meet me in the orchard at lunch time'… 'I think about you all the time. Give me a chance. Let's hang out and get to know each other better. What have you got to lose?'…

I'd resolved to write no words. I simply drew a big question mark inside.

Then, I'd disposed of the evidence and hidden the card inside my maths textbook.

'When shall we do it?' I whispered to Jodie now, in the classroom.

'Break-time.'

So, after P.E, we told the prefects we needed the loo and crept to tutor-room 8c. No teachers were around. The coast was clear. We ran into the empty classroom and I unzipped my bag. I threw open my textbook and pulled out the hand-made card.

'How do we know which one's his table?' I hissed.

ALL THAT YOU WANT

'Just put it on the teacher's desk.'

No sooner had I set the hot thing down than a presence appeared at the door.

'Can I help you, girls?'

Jodie screamed. She ran towards the door and I scrambled after her, Maths book in hand, school-bag agape. Jodie ducked under the teacher's elbow in the doorway and I copied her, certain he'd be prepared to grab me. Thank goodness the tutor of 8c held a coffee mug in one hand and a pile of exercise books in the other. Although somewhat bemused, he didn't pursue us. I followed Jodie as she raced down the corridor. I turned to see the back of Mr Crop as he ambled in through his doorway.

Thud. I bumped right into Mrs Vex, the stern-faced German teacher.

'Walk girls, don't run!'

Jodie slowed to a fast walk and I followed her lead. My best friend barged out through the double doors to the playground. The deed was done. Mr Crop couldn't miss the red envelope on his beige desk.

He would read the addressee.

My heart had barely slowed down by lunch time. I couldn't stomach anything and my cheeks burned each time a group of year-eight boys entered the hall.

'You gonna eat that, Ames?' Jodie spluttered through a mouthful of tuna-pasta. I grudgingly put my straw to my mouth in the pretence of dinking juice. My eyes did not leave the door. He did not join the lunch line.

Jodie and Annie were laughing about Mr Kelly's card. Who had sent the good-looking student teacher a Valentine?

Matt still did not join the line.

After lunch, we wandered out into the February drizzle, looking for something to do.

And there he was, among a group of year-eight boys, drudging back from the football pitch, caked to the knee in mud. The front boy, Dougie Williams, held a sodden brown ball under his arm.

'Matt!' teased Jodie

I hit her in the arm.

She ploughed ahead. 'Did you get any cards?'

Matt looked down at the floor and continued to walk.

'I bet you didn't get any!' Jodie giggled.

'Jo, don't,' I hissed.

227

Dougie Williams turned to us. 'We knew it was you.' He eyed Jodie.
'What? What was me?' She held out her hands dramatically.
'The card. You sent Scottsy the card.'
'I didn't send him anything, I was just winding him up, saying, I bet he didn't get any.'
'Yeah right. It was definitely you. You're always hanging around him.'
'I am not! I don't fancy him! I have better taste than that!'
Annie stood, hands in pockets, staring at the ground. She and I reluctantly followed Jodie, who was swaggering towards the football boys as they sauntered in the direction of the changing room. Matt kept his head down and I felt my chest burning. My ears burned. My cheeks burned. I was on fire and no-one noticed.
I was just the big-boobed Jodie Parker's mousey tagalong. I had no personality in my own right. I was not pretty; I had mousey-brown, in-between hair; I had mousey undefined eyes. I stood awkwardly. I had nothing to say. I let Jodie do all the talking.
'It was me,' I yelled involuntarily.
Dougie and Matt couldn't help but look at me, and then at each other. Dougie smirked. 'I knew it was one of you annoying year-sevens.' He laughed and smarted off, Matt following suit.
Was Matt's laugh a nervous laugh? An involuntary laugh? Or a laugh at me? I cling to the former two. Was he embarrassed? Flattered? Shy? Did he care?
I couldn't believe I let her talk me into making the stupid card.
The rain was sticking my stupid mousey hair to my forehead.
Now he knew. And he didn't care.

Kiantown, September 2003

It's my birthday. Nineteen today. Lenny has organised an intimate meal for the two of us tonight, and tomorrow, a lavish party with all my family and friends.

So this evening I am sinking at my dressing table, applying a sweet mask of eye-liner and lipstick.

From downstairs, I hear a knock at the front-door. Beth pokes her head into my room. 'Your lover's here,' she sings.

Taking a deep breath, I close my make-up bag.

ALL THAT YOU WANT

I sling my evening-bag over my shoulder and force my feet downstairs. The front door is closed. I peer into the living room, where Mum and Dad sit in the sofa. 'Where's Lenny?'

Mum turns from the TV. 'I opened the door and no-one was there. He must have had to move the car; I saw the lights just on the road.'

I lean in to kiss her and Dad on the cheek in turn.

'Have a great night, Love. Happy birthday.'

'Night.' I force a smile and leave the house.

I make my way towards the headlights behind the front hedge. But as I approach, I realise it is not Lenny's BMW. I stop, the dress-shop incident flashing back. But fear is overcome by curiosity, or perhaps a morbid desire, and I peer closer. I move through the blinding headlights and see him. Matt.

His window is down and I move to it. 'What are you doing here?'

'I wanted to wish you a happy birthday,' he utters.

I shake my head. 'Lenny will be here any minute.'

'I've got a card for you...' He nods to the passenger seat and I spot the red envelope.

I'm dizzy. I can't take this in. Still I cannot fathom that he could care about me. This can't be the same Matt Scotts from school. I only ever dreamed. All those Valentine's Days, birthdays, Christmases, I yearned for a card from this boy... any little bit of acknowledgement that I was, in his eyes, a worthwhile human being. It was too much to ever ask. My wish could never come true. And now... it sits on that empty seat. For me. From him.

I step back. 'You need to go. Lenny's taking me out for dinner.'

'Come to dinner with me instead..?' he dares.

I stop. I see him retreat into himself. I think of him driving away, and of me sitting in a stuffy restaurant wrestling with shellfish, the spotlights staring. Then I imagine jumping into this car with Matt, to speed off to I don't know where. I shudder as I remember the leaf tickling my skin.

A new set of headlights pull into the cul-de-sac and my heart races.

Before I know what I'm doing, I dive into Matt's passenger seat and duck my head. Blood pumps in my ears.

Matt spins around and is away, racing past Lenny's BMW and out into the night.

My heart battles in its cage. I clutch the envelope, daring to raise my head. I clear my throat. 'Where are we going?'

'Erm… I thought we could… go to Kay's?'

'Kay's?' I catch the rise in my tone, then try again, more calmly. 'Are you still staying there?'

'Yeah. She's out with Thomas and her parents. They've gone to Rock Point Hotel. To sample the menu.'

'Oh, yeah. Their wedding plans must be getting underway too,' I murmur.

We travel out of town and along the windy country lanes through the dark. Neither of us can speak. My heart is fighting so loudly.

We enter the small village and pass a pub and post-office shop. Matt pulls into a small road and parks in what must be Kay's drive.

'So, you used to live next door?'

'Yeah.' He nods to the adjoining semi. 'An old couple live there now.' He fumbles with his key and we are inside Kay's house. He switches on the light and takes my coat. 'Thank you…' I clumsily allow him to remove it, my heart pounding at his closeness.

'Come through…' he leads me into the dining room; the table is laid for two.

My chest thuds.

'I hope you don't think I was being presumptuous…' He shifts from foot to foot. 'Hopeful, though…'

I risk a look at him, the first time I have properly dared to peek, and he is dressed in a white shirt and smart shoes; he has gel in his hair. His sleeves are rolled up to his elbows and he is wearing a skinny black tie.

Smells of garlic waft from the kitchen.

'You've… gone to a lot of trouble…' I'm glad I'm dressed up, but at the same time my heels feel too tight and I pull my dress down around my legs.

ALL THAT YOU WANT

'Take a seat...' he gestures, then moves through the archway into the kitchen.

The room is crowded with heavy furniture. I look around at the family portraits adorning the walls. Kay's mum and dad, I presume, and a girl in a wheelchair. Carla.

Suddenly, we hear the front door open. I freeze.

Matt is instantly at my side and pulls me through the kitchen. Before I know it, he has bustled me out of the back door and I am in the garden, alone.

I stand as still as possible and listen to the voices inside.

'You're back early,' utters Matt.

'Miss Fussy didn't like it,' says a man's voice, presumably Kay's dad.

'It was an absolute shambles,' declares the pixie. 'We both want oysters, don't we, Thomas?'

'Do we..?'

'They had no oysters – can you believe it? A girl simply must have oysters on her wedding day!'

'Well, it had limited wheelchair access, so it's out anyway,' Kay's dad tells Matt.

'Whose wedding is it?' Kay demands. 'Oh, as long as Carla comes first. Even on *my* wedding day-'

'Oh –are you having someone over, Matthew?' asks a woman, probably Kay's mum.

'Erm, no.'

'What's all this, then?' teases Kay.

'She... can't come now.'

'Who?' demands Kay. 'Oh, you haven't been stood up, Matt?!'

'Well... I suppose so.'

Kay squeals with laughter. 'Well, it smells good anyway. Good, cos I'm starving. I don't know; you go out for dinner and come home even hungrier. That place is out of the running!'

'Help yourselves. I need to pop out and fill up the car. Early start tomorrow... it will save me time in the morning if... I do it now.'

'Never mind, Matt.' This is from Kay's mum. 'Whoever this girl is, it's her loss.'

231

'Oooh, garlic mushrooms,' exclaims Kay. 'You weren't doing a three course meal?'

'It doesn't matter now. See you all in a bit.'

I wait, unsure what to do.

'Poor lad,' remarks Kay's dad form inside. 'Gone to all this trouble for a girl and she doesn't even show up. Newcastle's made him soppy.'

I deduce that Matt must have gone out the front door. I peer behind me farther into the garden and can just make out a pond, long covered-over, hidden in the dark.

Matt appears from the side passageway. 'Come on,' he whispers. 'I'll take you home.'

I follow him along the side of the house and we creep into the car.

We drive in silence. As he changes gear his hand brushes my leg and I jump.

We pull into my road. He finally speaks. 'Sorry, Amy.'

'I'd... better go.'

We stare at each other for a moment. His deep yellow-green eyes bear into me. His lips are slightly parted.

I tear away, out of the car. I utter, 'Bye...' and rush home, not daring to look back.

44

'Jodie was having boy troubles?' Lenny demands. 'Why didn't you just call me?'

'Sorry, Lenny... she just turned up, completely upset and, I just couldn't leave her.'

'I get that, I totally get that you went with your friend. But, we had plans to go for dinner; I came to pick you up and you weren't here. No message, nothing.'

'I'm sorry, it just, she seemed so distressed; I couldn't say, "hold on, hold your tears while I ring Lenny."'

We are standing in my parents' living room. I returned home a few moments ago to be greeted by my fiancé, sitting with my parents and sister, his mobile in his hand. Mum, Dad and Beth have scuttled out of the room but I can feel them behind the door.

I am hideous for lying like this. How can I keep doing this to him? I want to be anywhere but here. 'I'm so sorry, Lenny.'

'No, no, it's alright. You're here now. How's Jodie now?'

'Alright. She'll be fine.'

'She'll bounce back. It's always the end of the world at the time, but she'll have a new date by next week. Anyway, if we hurry, we can still make the restaurant.' He offers me his arm and I force a smile and take it.

In the back of the car I stare at the zig-zag pattern on the leather passenger seat. The engine hums, humdrum.

'Amy, what is it? You worried about Jodie?'

'No, I'm not. Where are we going?'

I feel him grinning. 'It's a surprise.' He touches my leg.

I grimace involuntarily.

'Amy?' he lowers his voice. 'What is it? You hardly let me touch you these days.'

I shake my head. 'There's just so much... going on.'

'Do you love me, Amy? Do you want to marry me?'

I force myself look at him.

'You've been so distant. If you're having second thoughts... please, talk to me. We used to be so open with each other. We can tell each other everything. Or we could. It's since we came out publicly. I knew it would be hard but I didn't know it would affect you this much. What can I do?'

'I don't know. I don't know, Lenny.' I can't say anything.

He waits, then, 'Amy, what am I doing wrong? Tell me and I'll put it right. I'll do whatever it takes, Amy, tell me. I'll stop taking Hollywood jobs; we'll get a house in the UK. You name it, Amy. What will make you happy? Do you need more space? Less protection? Tell me, Amy, what can I do?'

I take a deep breath. 'Lenny, you're not doing anything wrong. I don't deserve you, the way I'm treating you. You've... you've done nothing but try to make me happy. I'm an ungrateful brat. I'm sorry, Lenny, I'm sorry. I just... I just..... don't know what will make me happy...I'm an idiot. I don't appreciate what I have. I'm sorry... I don't know what to do.'

We step onto the sand, bare footed, shoes in hand. Lenny holds the pizza box and I wear his heavy jacket around my shoulders, weighing me down, making every step an effort. The sand is cold beneath my toes. I hop to avoid sharp stones and debris digging into my feet. The clouds hide the stars and moon tonight.

Lenny decided to cancel the restaurant; the restaurant that would have borne clams and oysters causing chaos under the spotlights like a thousand eyes. Ever trying to please me, he said we would go back to our first date, only this time we are on a cold British beach instead of the exotic Californian sands of three years ago. We are an ocean away.

We find a flat rock to sit on. It is hard and cold and Lenny places the pizza between us, as we did when we escaped the stuffy restaurant the first day we met. I take a slice of peperoni

ALL THAT YOU WANT

pizza, and the cheese — dairy-free cheese, I now know - burns my tongue. I try in vain to catch the yellow string but it smears Lenny's expensive jacket.

'Don't worry; it can be dry-cleaned.' He smiles, and I can't believe there is already sand tarnishing the fresh pizza. 'Do you remember we saw that hermit crab, that night we had pizza on the beach on our first date?'

I nod. 'The whole ocean stretched out in front of us.'

'Now we're practically the other side of the world', he remarks absently. 'Your school was about to end, my career was just beginning… Would you have guessed, that night, we would be getting married?'

I don't know what to say.

'And now…. are you happy in your new shell?' he half smiles, mocking the metaphor.

I smile back at him, laughing at the ridiculousness of our philosophical words. The tarnished coat is heavy on my shoulders. I think about removing the weight, but fear of the cold night prevents me from leaving my arms bare, so I endure the burden.

Lenny sleeps heavily beside me and I stare at the ceiling in darkness. A dull light hovers at the window and I can't figure out its origin. It can't be the moon.

Part of me wants to throw my arms around him and protect him so tightly. But I roll onto my side, taking care not to disturb his warm body. Silently, I open the bedside drawer and pull out the photo from the disco. Dark faces stare back at me and although I can't see them clearly I know by heart where the two stand. These figures stand in a time when I was insignificant; passed by.

I run my fingers over the picture and feel Lenny's hot breath on my back.

I place the dark faces back in the drawer because the glimmer through the window is not enough for me to see clearly.

45

Kiantown, September 2003

I drive the brand new Mercedes, my birthday present from Lenny, into the garage.

I switch off the engine and step out. The spotless soft-top looks out of place in the workshop. Oil stains dot the concrete floor, grubby tools hang from the walls and engine odours pollute the air.

At the back of the room is a small boxed office. An overalled mechanic emerges from the box and his deep yellow-green eyes meet me. I wonder if he can see what he does to me.

We face each other, and we appear to be alone in the garage. He steps towards me, his face and clothes black and oily. He extends a hand to me. I take it, immediately embarrassed by my freshly manicured nails. His hands are a worker's hands.

Quickly, he pulls away and wipes them on a dirty rag that hangs from the wall.

'You look very nice,' he utters, his head down. A tear-shaped oil-mark stains his temple just above his eye-line.

'Thank you,' I shuffle. 'Lenny had his people take me on a shopping spree… Do me up.' I have too much make-up on and my hair is freshly set.

He steps towards me, not meeting my gaze. 'Lenny. Not long 'til the wedding now, then.'

'Next month…' The wedding is a few short weeks away and I know this could be the last time I will see Matt before the looming day.

'Well… congratulations.' The words are forced. 'Good luck.'

Now it's my turn to look at the floor. 'You're doing well for yourself,' I manage.

'Not as well as a Hollywood actor.' He speaks so quietly, I have to lean towards him to check I heard him right.

'Lenny worked hard to get where he is now.' *He's made me feel like I matter*, I add silently.

'Smart motor,' Matt remarks, slightly louder this time.

'Well I...' I try to pull myself together. 'I wondered if you could look at it.'

He raises his eyebrows and looks at the '03 plates. 'You know, a car like that, you should take it back to the Mercedes garage. Anything I do to it will void the warranty.'

'But I want you.'

He blinks. 'Well... what seems to be the problem?' he attempts to sound professional.

'It's... I... I think it's got sand in it,' I stutter.

He folds his arms. 'Sand? Where?'

'Everywhere. It gets in and it... fills it. It overflows... it grinds and stutters.'

He nods slowly. 'The thing with sand,' he tells me, 'is...you can't... it's very difficult to get it all out. You may think you've got it all out of the system... but there will still be some... lurking. No matter how much you think you've got rid of it. It will resurface weeks... even months later...'

'But... you can try for me?'

'I'll do what I can.'

'I just want it gone,' I utter.

'Well... I'll just get the book.' He heads back towards the little office. 'Would you like... tea?'

I exhale. 'Yes. Please.'

As he potters in the office, I look at my crisp white suit and stupid stilettos picked out by Lenny's people and I just want to rub that dirty rag all over me. I want to grab one of those big spanner things hanging on the wall and dent the sickly shiny car. I want to contaminate myself with filth.

Muffled sounds of the radio flow from the office. Matt emerges with a square tray carrying two mugs of builders' tea and a biscuit tin. His navy overalls make him look like a little boy in dungarees.

'Custard cream or chocolate digestive? I love them both.'

I stop for a moment. 'What if you could only have one, for the rest of your life? Which would you choose?'

He sets the tray down on a rickety shelf. The skin on his hands is as thick and cracked as a man who's been working thirty years rather than someone fresh out of an apprenticeship. 'It wouldn't matter, because I love them both.'

I shuffle awkwardly. Lenny's hands are smooth and flawless with netball players' fingernails. 'But, say, whichever one you choose, you'd sacrifice the other for ever. How do you know... which one you could live without?'

He steps towards me. 'I suppose you... listen to your heart. Really, deep down, you know which one you love most. Because really, you can only have one... one favourite biscuit...'

'But what if... you can't bear to lose either..?' My mouth is dry. I sip the too-hot tea and it scalds my tongue, making it fuzzy, sharp and numb at the same time. I splutter.

Matt takes the chipped mug from me and places it back on the tray. 'We were running low on milk...' he murmurs. 'Sorry. I should have warned you.'

'Don't worry,' I rasp. My face is hot as I cough and I try not to shoot hot tea from my mouth.

He pats my back.

Soon though, I have recovered.

Silence fills the garage, apart from the muffled radio, trying to sing through the poor reception. I think he's saying something about the car but all I can do is stare at the tiny area of his chest visible above his overalls.

I know I should go but I lean on the bonnet.

Matt rests on the car too, facing me. His eyes are so close I see the distinction between the yellow and green like individual pixels. I realise he's stopped talking.

His oily smell fills me and his filthy blue overalls are close enough to grab.

His nose almost touches mine. I could lean against him and dirty my crisp suit.

Our faces lean closer.

Suddenly, his hands are on my back, grabbing my clothes.

A shiver runs right through me. I am pressed against his chest. He grips me into him and presses his forehead against mine. I close my eyes and wait for his lips.

Instead, he whispers. 'Don't marry him, Amy. Be with me instead.'

I'm shaking.

'We'll just go somewhere. Away from everything. We should be together. You and me.' His hold is more urgent but still he doesn't kiss me.

I rip away.

I make for the door, as quickly as my ridiculous heels will allow me. I am out of there and stumbling down the street. Peering down at myself, I see grubby marks on my suit. I reach for my forehead and pull my hand away to see dirt on my palm.

I scramble for my phone and make a desperate call.

'Hello?'

'Sarah? Can you come and pick me up?'

When I return to collect the car a week later, an overalled man steps out of the little box office and my heart skips. But this mechanic is in his fifties, round and greying. The garage is cold, dirty and lifeless. The oil has lost its freshness. Matt is on his lunch-break. His colleague deals with my custom.

46

Miami, October 2003

My mother fusses around my elaborate meringue. Jodie, Bethany, Sarah and Annie all bounce beside me in blancmange dresses I don't remember choosing.

This morning, I was vaguely aware of faceless women surrounding me, pulling at my hair and painting my face in a large dressing-room, while music and champagne flowed and my bridesmaids fastened each other's lilac costumes. All of them couldn't do enough for me – even Bethany brought me croissants and fizz. I have to admit, the dress brings out her pale eyes.

Now, we are gathered in the shade outside the titanic Miami church of Lenny's choosing. The day has arrived.

Security guards patrol the churchyard. Inside, the building will be full and Lenny will be standing at the altar already.

As we mill on the steps, waiting to be fashionably late, some commotion bubbles from the gate. Alarmed murmurs drift from the bodyguards that an uninvited man is hovering.

I lift my ridiculous skirts and head into the sweltering heat to see the would-be intruder.

'Ma'am, this gentleman doesn't have an invitation,' a guard informs me.

As they move aside, I see him, through the bars of the gates.

It has taken me so long to totter over here in my outlandish shoes and designer dress, that word has reached my groom and he is quickly behind me.

'Who is it? My father? He was *not* invited.' Lenny reaches my side and takes in the gate-crasher.

ALL THAT YOU WANT

'No,' I manage. 'It's, it's Matt; a... school-friend of mind. He *does* have an invitation...' The harsh sun smacks me in the face.

'Oh. Well,' Lenny smiles, 'apologies for the mix-up. Come through.' The actor signals for the body-guards to open the gate.

'No, no, I won't. I just wanted to... give you this.' Matt hands me a small gift-wrapped package. 'I'll, erm...' He signals to leave. 'I... hope you'll be happy.'

'We'll see you at the evening party, then?' Lenny asks. He looks at me.

I take in my fiance, in his gorgeous suit. This beautiful man, who wants to be mine forever.

He stares back at me, taking in my dress, my face, the day. I see it in his eyes. 'You look beautiful...'

So does he.

'Right...' he catches himself. 'Well, I'd better go back in. It's bad luck, I guess.' He shoots me a quick smile and strides to the church, mounting the steps three at a time.

On the other side of the bars, Matt turns away, the bodyguards closing the gate on him. I'm stuck. I want to stay here, but he is moving away. His face looks like it breaking. My heart lurches and I want to reach out to him.

The bodyguards and my entourage eye me expectantly. I have no choice. Slowly, I turn from Matt. Clutching the parcel, I teeter back to the steps, into the shadows.

As I reach the purple ladies, my mother makes to take the gift from me. 'We'll put it with the others.'

'No.' I pull back. 'I want to open this one now.'

My mother and bridesmaids hover as I unwrap the gift. Peeling the delicate tissue-paper aside, I find myself holding a jar of sand. The hand-written label reads; *From Rock Point Beach.*

'Come on,' Mum breezes, adjusting her hat. 'I'll take care of that for you.' She whips the jar from me and the girls begin to take their places. 'We've kept your gorgeous young man waiting long enough!'

And before I know it, I am bustled into the high-ceilinged church and faced with hundreds of faces, most of them grinning beneath hats, and all turned to me. Walking towards my beautiful fiancé, I grip my father's arm as my train is lifted by my purple ducklings. I am swimming, kicking for the surface.

MICHELLE WOOLLACOTT

The dazzling star beams at me as I reach him. The music draws to a halt. And we begin.

I am the fancy car, shiny and white and perfect outside. All the while, inside I am plagued with sand. It fills every crack and crevice; it grinds against my engine; it slows down my movements, impossible to be rid of and lasting billions of years.

And all too soon; Do I take him as my...?

I turn to the door, desperate to see a figure standing there, as if from a dream, leaning against the frame, watching me, pleading with me with those yellow-green eyes. But all who stand there are two black-suited security guards.

The surface of the church is too high and my plumage is too heavy to kick for it.

And the words tumble out of my mouth and I can't do anything about them. And I find myself saying, I do take him.

*

By the bar, Suzie Strite's blonde curls bounce as she flirts with Clive.

Jodie laughs conspicuously with Barry, the flight attendant, by the fountain. I *thought* those two might get on.

Grandma Joyce's purple mop glistens beneath the spotlights as she and Harry Sanderson help themselves to champagne. Harry has unnecessarily brought us cratefuls of the bubbly stuff. I think back to something Leanne once said about her editor – how did she described him..? Oh yes. Responsible yet frivolous.

Lenny's mother and step-father, Jim, sit at a table with my own parents and grandparents, sharing stories of our youth over canapés. Leanne and James, the reporter and the blonde cameraman, have a secret tiff by the loos while the runner (the very same who Lenny was snapped embracing – her script has still not landed on the right desk -) dances with Kay and Thomas. Lenny has flown them all out here.

Scents of perfumed flowers mix sickeningly with the aromas of hot pastries and meats.

My stunning husband and I slow dance on the floor. As I turn, my eyes flit about the room. I see so many guests. But one is missing.

I look up into the mirrored ceiling and we dance far away in an upside-down world.

ALL THAT YOU WANT

The evening draws on and he has not arrived.

I drink too much perfumey wine and I dance with Annie and Thomas, laughing forcedly and exaggerating the moves.

Then the tone slows.

The next song is *If I Let You Go* by Westlife. I stop in my tracks. It is the long version; the B-side on the single.

Lenny is at my side. 'May I cut in?' he asked my friends.

They nod vigorously and this smooth operator whisks me across the dance floor as the introduction is still playing. Does he know he has the room in his hands? He pulls me in and I give in, resting my head on his shoulder, forgetting for a blissful moment.

There is a tap on my shoulder.

I turn from Lenny.

Before me stands a short blonde police woman.

'May I have a word please, Mrs Hunter?' *Mrs Hunter*, I repeat in my head.

I frown and look at Lenny.

He falters too, but urges to me to go with her.

In the hotel lobby, two police officers have gathered my friends; Jodie, Annie, Sarah, Kay, Thomas and I.

They advise us all to take a seat.

We squeeze into chairs that appear soft, but feel hard.

Then the blonde officer removes her hat and speaks in her Florida twang. 'I'm afraid I have some bad news for you all,' she begins. The chairs become harder as she continues. 'Something has happened to a friend of yours, Matthew Scotts.'

We are all still.

'I'm sorry to tell you, he has taken an overdose. He was discovered in his hotel-room and has been rushed to hospital. I'm afraid to tell you, the doctors don't think it looks good.'

The music stops - I think.

'His parents, in England, have been called and are making arrangements to fly out here as soon as possible. Unfortunately, the doctors say, by the time they get here… it could be too late. So… his parents have asked that his friends might be with him in his final moments…' Slowly, she turns to face me. 'This was found beside him, with a note; *for Amy Minor.*' The foreign woman hands me the silver locket. She turns back to address us all. 'I am sorry. I know this is difficult news…'

I don't hear anymore. All I can smell is the perfumed food as sickness rises in my stomach.

I spring from the awful prickly seat and make for the stairs. I tear up, kicking off the hindering shoes, and finally find myself alone in the dark of the honeymoon suite. I press my back against the door without switching on the light.

I open the locket with a sick taste in my mouth. Two faces smile at me from the three-year-old photo. I touch his face.

My legs give way and I crumple on the floor. A harsh, piercing wail explodes from somewhere inside me. The tears erupt from my throat and I am wailing uncontrollably. It will never stop.

The sand is corrosive, grinding inside me at my cogs; my engine. I feel it in every part of me. I cannot move.

I howl like I've never howled before, pushing everything out of me. But the tide washing over me is relentless, forcing me deeper into the sand and I can't escape it. I can hear nothing but the crashing of waves. My eyes are full, my ears are full; my mouth is full of sand. It's in my throat; in my chest; it's deep in my stomach. It's under my acrylic nails that were filled in earlier today – I try to rip them off, but they are glued. The mineral sounds like fingernails on a chalkboard as it grinds against my ribs.

At last, after what seems like hours, the sea is calm and tide has retreated. For a moment I can breathe. I listen to my breath slip in and out with the far-off ebbing of the waves. The tears fall silently now.

My mouth is of full of salt water. I look up from the floor and see the stars out of the window. I am drawn to the fresh air.

I pull up the sash window and lean my head into the night. My eyes fall on Miami Bridge.

I see his face, but I can't force myself to conjure up any life in the image.

I sit at the desk I am leaning over and watch the bridge against the black sky. On the table beneath the window, my eyes rest on a small postcard of the same bridge. I turn it over in my

ALL THAT YOU WANT

fingers and I find the other side to be blank as the silent night floats into the room.

I reach for the hotel's logoed pen and scribble a word on the reverse side. I place the postcard in the middle of the desk and stand.

I leave the room silently, closing the door behind me.

I stumble down the stairs, through the now empty lobby and I'm out in the night.

I begin to run, past the dozy security guards who are playing with their phones, through the streets, across a road and down an alleyway. I run as fast as I can in my ornate wedding dress.

I tear through alleys and burst around street corners. I dart between streetlights and charge over desolate crossings. I hoik up my skirt but the perfect white is ruined by dirt as the hem scrapes the ground. The occasional glance shoots my way from a clubber or homeless person, who takes in my tearstained face and theatrical appearance. But I let the tears burst out of me, knowing they won't wash away the sand. My chest heaves with the weight of the waves as they crush me. I turn a corner and I see the bridge.

'Amy!'

I spin around.

Lenny's Mustang has pulled up behind a Ferrari at a red light.

'Stop,' the groom shouts.

I run past the traffic light. It remains red.

I reach the middle of the bridge and peer down at the water.

I hold a lamppost and pull myself up. I wobble a little. It's only now I realise my bare feet are sore and bleeding. I steady myself.

I look down at the black water beneath me, then up at the endless sky.

I think of the sand, clinging on, through decades of my life. I see myself at eighty, sitting in an armchair, side-by-side with Lenny at a warm fire, and feeling cold.

I see Matt's face beside me at Rock Point beach and hear the steady rhythm of the waves; his heart beeping on a machine. Then comes a long beep, until the end of my days, never to play its rhythm again.

MICHELLE WOOLLACOTT

I look at my finger. The gold band cuts my circulation like a chain, binding me, imprisoning me, 'til death do us part.

Lenny's car races onto the bridge and screech to a halt.

They jump out of the Mustang and take in the figure in a white dress before them, teetering on the wall, gripping a lamppost.

They begin to run, screaming, 'Amy!'

The shouts are background noise. I lean forward.

I let go of the lamppost.

And I jump.

THE END

Acknowledgements

First and foremost, I have to thank Jade, without whom this book would not be what it is today. Thank you for listening to your eleven-year-old friend tell you a story. Thank you for your enthusiasm and your input; thank you for developing characters with me. Thank you for slumber-parties spent devising plot-lines and back-stories; thank you for acting out scenes in my poster-adorned bedroom to boyband theme-tunes (-of course, the original idea was for a screenplay, not a book!). And last but not least, thank you for helping me develop Kian Hill. Hopefully it will not take another seventeen years to realise that vision.

Thank you to my family, especially to my parents, for supporting my ambitions and for seeing me through university to help me develop my craft. Thank you for always being there steadfastly –even when I didn't make it easy!

Thank you to the friends who have listened to me over the years, in particular those of you who have proof-read and critiqued my efforts. I want to express my gratitude to the Barnstaple Library writers' group for your motivation and encouragement.

Thanks to my teachers and tutors at school, college and university for your guidance, your wisdom and your brutal honesty. Thank you for helping me craft my skills as a writer.

Lastly, I have infinite gratitude to Edward, whose love and support has made my dreams come true in so many ways. Thank you for pushing me to fulfil my ambitions. Thank you for encouraging me to take the leap to become a freelance writer in order to reach for my goal. Thank you for listening to my story, for proof-reading, for your enthusiasm, your belief and your whole-hearted support. You are my rock, my soulmate, the love of my life.

Book Club Questions

Beginning
1. What do you think would have happened if Amy had told Matt how she felt in Chapter One, at the party? Or if she had taken the train to Newcastle? How might the story have been different?

2. How do you think Amy sees herself at the beginning of the story? How does her self-opinion differ from how others perceive her? How does Amy's self-perception change throughout the book?

3. Does Amy's competition win bring back memories of teenage fantasies for you, the reader? What teenage fantasies did you have of a celebrity?

Friendship Dynamics
4. How do the friendship dynamics change between the group of girls throughout the book? What sort of friend do you think Sarah is to Amy? How does Amy perceive Sarah and does she have an accurate view of her friend?

5. Is the relationship between Amy and Jodie balanced? Or is it one-way? How would you depict their friendship?

6. How do you feel about Amy's relationship with Kay's boyfriend, Thomas?

7. Is the bullying situation realistic? Would the girls resolve their issues so peacefully in real life? Is it easier to keep the peace than to break away from a peer group?

Romantic Interests
8. How do you think Matt felt about Amy at school? How do his feelings change? Do you think he is fair to Amy?

9. Does Lenny treat Amy fairly in keeping their relationship secret for so long? Similarly, does Amy treat Lenny fairly following Matt's return?

Ending
10. How do you feel about the end of the book? Was it a surprise to you? Did Amy have any way out of the situation? What are the repercussions of her actions on her friends and family, and on Lenny?